A MILES DARIEN DETECTIVE THRILLER

JUSTIFIED MALICE

HARRY PINKUS

North Carolina

Justified Malice: A Miles Darien Detective Thriller
© 2023 Harry Pinkus. All rights reserved.

This is a work of fiction. All of the characters, names, incidents, organizations, and dialogue in this novel are either the product of the author's imagination or are used fictitiously.

Published in the United States by BQB Publishing
(an imprint of Boutique of Quality Books Publishing Company, Inc.)
www.bqbpublishing.com

Printed in the United States of America

ISBN 979-8-88633-016-8 (p)
ISBN 979-8-88633-017-5 (e)

Library of Congress Control Number: 2023943497

Book design by Robin Krauss, www.bookformatters.com
Cover design by Rebecca Lown, www.rebeccalowndesign.com

First editor: Caleb Guard
Second editor: Andrea Vande Vorde

PROLOGUE

As instructed, Mateo walked into the bustling café on Calle San Rafael, Havana. The salsa music and laughter emanating from the jam-packed clubs he passed did little to calm his nerves. His assignment was to wait until after dark, pick up a package at the café, and deliver it, undetected, to El Jefe. The thought of meeting the new, and often brutal, crime boss had Mateo's brow dripping with sweat.

Once he had the package in hand, Mateo drove along Havana Bay toward the residential Miramar neighborhood. The full moon's reflection in the calm sea added an eerie backdrop to his drive. He pulled into the Quinta Avenida Habana Hotel parking lot at 10:00 p.m., parked his car, and set off on foot down several dimly lit streets to his real destination, a modest casita across the road from Monte Barreto Ecological Park.

As he approached the casita, the thought of meeting El Jefe was so intimidating that his hands were trembling, loosening his grip just enough for him to drop the package. The possibility that he may have damaged the contents of the box absolutely terrified him. El Jefe was rumored to be ruthless and unforgiving. He would not take kindly to such a misstep, nor would his associates in Mexico who had sent the package. When he reached the casita, Mateo had to take a moment to calm himself down before he knocked on the door.

The door opened and a huge man with a pistol tucked into his belt appeared.

"Stay here!" the man demanded in Spanish and grabbed the box. Mateo watched with trepidation as the man delivered the box to a well-dressed man seated at the kitchen table. Mateo was sure that man was El Jefe. The man ripped open the box, revealing a cell phone; several stacks of what appeared to be American dollars; and some documents, one of which looked like a passport. After he reviewed the contents of the box, El Jefe smiled, which also made Mateo smile.

El Jefe rose and walked toward Mateo. "Do you speak English?" he asked.

"Sí, señor. A little," Mateo answered, still trembling a bit.

"You were not followed." El Jefe's glare showed it was more of a statement than a question.

"No. I'm sure of it." Mateo had taken great pains to ensure he had arrived undetected.

"Good. Here are 1,000 Cuban pesos for a job well done. Make sure no one sees you when you leave," El Jefe said, and motioned for Mateo to go.

"Sí, señor. Gracias," Mateo replied as he made a hasty retreat. He had literally dodged a bullet.

CHAPTER 1

Miles Darien was sure the pounding in his head was from the three vodka martinis he'd had the night before. Turns out it was actually someone knocking loudly at his front door. He crawled out of bed and tripped over the pile of clothes he'd dumped on the floor after returning from a birthday party for his assistant, Anne. Before answering the door, Miles looked out his second-story window and, much to his surprise, saw his friend George Willis's car out front. When Miles opened the door, there was George looking downright bewildered and disheveled, with his shirt half tucked in and his hair sticking out in all directions.

"George, what in the world are you doing here at 4:00 a.m. on a Monday morning?" Miles asked.

"I've been trying to get you for an hour, but you wouldn't answer your phone," George growled.

"Come in. It's cold outside. Strange I didn't hear the phone." Miles then saw the phone sitting on the coffee table in front of the TV. He'd forgotten it there when he dragged his martini-addled self up the stairs to bed. "It's January, so you're not picking me up to go fishing. Why are you here?"

George's voice quivered as he spoke. "There's been an explosion at the marina. Our boat blew up in dry dock."

"Let's go!" Without a moment's hesitation, Miles grabbed

a warm jacket and slipped his phone in the pocket. His golden retriever, Molly, was wagging her tail and squealing, clearly indicating she wanted to go out to pee but she'd have to wait.

"What the hell happened?" Miles asked before George had even started the car.

"I have no idea. There was nothing flammable in the boat once we took it out of the water. I can't believe this happened! I'm out of business." George's voice grew louder with each spoken word.

"I assume the police are already on the scene investigating," Miles said as calmly as he could in hopes of settling George down.

"Yes, they called me from there. No one on the police force has the investigative skills, or the personal interest, to get to the bottom of this—not like you." George obviously thought this was more than a mere accident.

Miles had a million questions, but he knew it was likely the answers lay at the marina dry dock.

When they arrived at the marina, the crew of Lakeville firefighters had just finished stowing their equipment on the three fire trucks that had been called to the scene. Much of the water they'd used to douse the fire had already begun turning to ice thanks to the brisk, wintry breeze off Lake Michigan. The dark and cold January night had already erased any of the warmth the burning boat had created, and there was barely a whiff of the smoke left from the fire the explosion had produced.

Miles introduced himself to the cops on the scene as one of the boat's owners. In actuality, he was; and it was prudent to leave it at that, as they'd likely not be happy with a private investigator nosing around a potentially fresh crime scene. As he perused the damage, Miles first noticed the giant, charred hole in the center of the deck. The few boards remaining were badly burned and pointing downward, strongly indicating the blast had originated on the deck, not from the cabin below. This was more than odd, as none of the equipment on the deck contained fuel, or operated on a combustible material. All possible culprits lay below the deck or in the engine compartment.

This was unlikely to have been an accident, Miles thought. It appeared to him as if someone deliberately set off an explosive device intending to destroy the boat, and they did so in the middle of the night, likely to avoid turning this incident into a homicide. Miles stood off to the side simply observing the gathering of evidence by the Lakeville PD. When Jim Rathburn of the Medical Examiner's office pulled up to the scene, Miles realized that theory was, at least, partially wrong.

Miles watched as Jim maneuvered his large six-foot-four frame though the mangled wreckage of the boat. About thirty minutes after he had arrived, Jim and his team emerged from the boat's wreckage with a bagged body on a gurney. He saw Miles and walked over to say hello.

"Your boat?" Jim asked, offering his hand.

"George's and mine. At least what's left of it, I guess. Learn anything about the identity of the body?"

"Nothing definitive at this point. I'll keep you up-to-date as our investigation proceeds." Jim turned to George and asked how his wife, Cora, and daughter, Olivia, were doing.

"Fine, other than this mess. Since you brought them up, I want to thank you again for all you did to help Olivia through that nasty business with the loan sharks. She could have died if it weren't for you." George's eyes teared up as he spoke.

As they parted company, Jim added, "I'm so glad every-thing worked out for her. I can't believe that bastard Reese's company forced her to surrender a kidney to pay off a loan.

Hope he gets his comeuppance one day, and soon. Miles, I'll call you later. I have a couple of other issues to chat with you about. Sorry about your boat, by the way."

Miles smiled and waved as Jim walked back to join his team. When Miles turned back to George, he saw bewilderment and fear in his friend's face.

"Someone tried to kill us!" George exclaimed.

"Actually, it was not a murder attempt at all," Miles assured him.

"I don't understand."

"Think about it. If someone wanted us dead, the last thing they would do is set off a bomb in a deserted storage facility in the middle of the night. This was intended for another purpose."

"What other purpose?" George was obviously confused.

"I'm not entirely sure at this point, but I intend to find out." Miles's voice was ripe with resolve.

"Well, you're the private investigator. Where do you begin?" George asked.

Miles winked. "With breakfast."

After breakfast, George dropped off Miles at home. The first order of business was to take Molly out. She barely made it out the door before letting loose, while flashing Miles her most appreciative golden-retriever smile. Once back inside, he headed upstairs to wash up and get ready for a day at the office.

After his shower, he checked his phone for messages. There was a text from Jim Rathburn asking Miles to call as soon as possible. Miles called him back immediately.

"Hi, Miles. I have some preliminary information for you about the man's body we discovered on your boat. There was enough forensic evidence left on the body to identify him as Todd Morton, a small-time criminal who has been arrested numerous times in numerous municipalities. Does his name sound familiar?"

"Sorry, Jim. Doesn't ring a bell." Miles had hoped the man's identity would have been an obvious clue to who perpetrated this attack.

"Well, just be careful," Jim warned. "It's entirely possible somebody out there wants to harm you and George, and it may not have been the man whose body we found."

"Believe me, I totally understand. We'll take all the necessary precautions. Why don't you think the guy you found was the guilty party?" Miles asked.

"Did you see the article in the *Examiner* a month or so ago where a dog dug up a man's hand?"

"Of course. A guy was out walking his dog near a construction site, and the dog literally dragged him to the spot where it was buried."

"Yep, that's it. Well, the hand was sent to us for analysis, but there was no identification possible due to the length of time it had been buried and how the chemicals in the ground had eliminated the possibility of a DNA match, so we cataloged our findings and closed the case."

"Sure. But what's changed?"

"Well, a guy showed up at police headquarters the other day claiming the missing hand was his, and he wanted it back."

Miles burst out laughing. "Sorry, Jim. I couldn't help myself. Did you give him his hand back?"

"Of course not. Actually, it no longer exists. Apparently he was in a gang way back when, and they caught him stealing from their stash. They cut off his hand in retribution. He went to jail for an unrelated crime shortly thereafter. Once he was released from jail, he saw the article in the paper about the dog finding the hand. He thought it was probably his and wanted it back so he could feel whole again."

"That's hilarious!" Miles exclaimed.

"That part is quite funny, but this part isn't. The guy who came looking for his hand was Todd Morton."

"I'd never heard of him before all this, so it's unlikely he had a beef with me, or George for that matter. It would appear he was either just seeking shelter, or he was hired by someone I do know who wanted to blow up the boat. If that's the case, the question is who?" Miles was thumbing through his mental Rolodex, searching for a likely suspect.

"That's the right question, but unfortunately not much to go on. By the way, the police forensics lab is trying to find out what material was used to cause the explosion. I'll keep you posted on anything they uncover."

"Guess I now have myself as my new client," Miles acknowledged.

Jim's face turned serious. "Changing subjects, I'd like your advice on a personal matter. My son, Danny, came out to us the other night at the dinner table. It wasn't really a shock. My wife and I were fairly certain he was gay. Now that he's sixteen, he's getting pressure from his teammates on the football team to date. They've even tried fixing him up with one of the girl cheerleaders. He doesn't want to pretend, but he's afraid to to explain to his friends why he's resisting for fear ostracization, or worse. I was hoping you could offer me some advice on what to say to him." Jim's voice cracked as he finished his explanation.

"Jim, I'd be happy to talk to him if you'd like. Insights from someone who's been through it all would likely be more helpful for him," Miles suggested.

"Truth be told, that's what I hoped you'd say. How about dinner at our place on Wednesday evening?"

"That works. Text me your address and what time you'd like me to be there. Oh, and please be sure your son knows and approves of my reason for coming over. An ambush would be a big mistake."

"I will. Thanks, Miles. We really appreciate your help."

Miles's thoughts returned to the body they'd discovered on the boat. His training told him he could not totally dismiss a possible connection between him and George, and the man with the missing hand. At least, not until another more likely motive was uncovered.

CHAPTER 2

A fter the early events at the marina, it had been an uneventful morning at the office since Miles arrived just after 9:00 a.m. Uneventful mornings were unusual, as Miles's caseload had recently increased dramatically. The high-profile cases he had recently solved made him the go-to PI in Lakeville, Wisconsin. Not that there were a lot of PIs in Lakeville, but he was definitely at the top of that short list. The phone finally rang just after 10:00 a.m. and Miles's assistant, Anne, immediately answered it.

"Miles Darien, Private Investigations. Anne speaking."

"Hi, Anne. It's Ken."

"Agent Caldwell, how are you?" she replied.

"I'm fine. Is the boss around?" Ken inquired.

"Yes. I'll buzz him and let him know you're on the line." She put him on hold and buzzed Miles.

"FBI holding for you." Anne loved using a dramatic-sounding voice when announcing Agent Caldwell of the FBI was on the line.

Miles picked up the phone. "Hi Ken, I was just about to call you." He filled in his beau on what had transpired with the boat.

"Wow. That sure is troubling," said Ken, before shifting into full FBI-agent mode. "I can immediately see three possible scenarios. First one is that the guy, Todd Morton, was sent to blow up the boat and ended up blowing up himself in the process. The second is that he was simply squatting there, and was in the wrong place at the wrong time."

"What's the third possibility?" Miles asked.

"He was murdered and your boat was merely the scene of the crime."

"All reasonable hypotheses. We'll likely be able to narrow things down quite a bit once we get the lab reports on Morton's cause and time of death, and then the explosion analysis."

"How soon do you expect to receive the results?" Ken was now fully engaged in the investigation.

"In a day or so, I'd assume. Any chance I can get you to look into Todd Morton's background? I may have trouble getting that information from Lakeville PD, particularly if they decide to open a criminal investigation." Miles knew it was a big ask.

"I think I can make that happen. There's another possibility I hate to even bring up, but do you think there's any chance that George needed money and blew up the boat to collect on the insurance?" It was in Ken's job description to look at a crime from every possible angle.

Miles thought for a moment and then dismissed the idea. George was an incredibly honest guy, and if he needed money he would have at least tried to sell the boat before blowing it up. It was a vintage Chris-Craft that would surely bring him more from a sale than an insurance claim. Wouldn't it?

"Any news on your vacation request?" Miles said, moving the conversation to a happier topic.

"I've secured the last two weeks of March for our vacation," Ken proudly announced. He and Miles had been trying to find time for a getaway ever since they had become a couple several months before. They were both eager to escape the brutal midwestern winter, and now they had two full months to plan their warm-weather getaway.

"I'll come up with some potential destinations, and we can discuss them when I get to Chicago this weekend," Miles proposed.

"Good. Let's decide on where we'll go while you're here, and then book it right away. I have a ton of travel rewards points sitting in my credit card account, ready for action. Promise me you'll finish up all your cases before we leave town. I want us both to concentrate on simply having fun."

Ken put particular emphasis on the word "fun." This would be their first time traveling together, and Ken had made it perfectly clear he wanted to take every precaution to head off any work distractions. Miles promised to do his best to tie up any cases he had before they left on vacation. It would be difficult turning down any new ones, as he had just become accustomed to taking on all the new cases his newfound notoriety had delivered.

Miles set his work aside for the moment and spent the next two hours combing the Internet travel sites for possible vacation destinations. The place had to have warm weather, no more than a half day's worth of travel, and a load of fun activities to choose from. The good news was there were numerous viable candidates. The bad news was also that there were numerous viable candidates. He decided to take a break for lunch before narrowing his list to three or four choices. It was an unseasonably pleasant Wisconsin-winter afternoon, so he took a two-block walk to the Blackhawk Diner for a bowl of chili.

When Miles arrived back at the office, Anne was on the phone. She waved him over and gave him a couple of phone messages without missing a beat in her phone conversation. The only important message was from Bobbie Martin, his friend and former landlord. Miles returned Bobbie's call before the others.

"Hey, Miles. How are you and Ken doing?" she asked.

"We're good. Looking to plan a warm-weather vacation this March."

"I'm envious. I'm buried in cases and don't see a break anytime soon. On to the reasons for my call. First, I have some good news for you, which may actually help to fund your vacation. I've finalized the Jefferson/Shaw settlement for the case we worked on. As further thanks for a job well done, they've authorized an additional $5,000 bonus for you."

"That is great news! You said 'reasons' before. What else is on your mind?" Miles asked.

"I'd like to get a few more of the boxes you've been kind enough to store for me. I also have a potential new client for you. Oddly enough it's quite possibly another corporate-larceny-type case. Can I talk you into bringing the boxes to Madison on Friday morning and then meeting with the client over lunch?"

Miles quickly accepted but added a caveat. "I need to be in Chicago Friday evening, so I guess that'll work."

They finished their call with Bobbie requesting he bring boxes marked two, three, and four with him on Friday. She was extremely organized, having individually numbered each of the fifteen boxes she'd left in his care. Miles decided not to mention the boat incident, knowing Bobbie was a worrier and would be disturbed by his account of what had happened. He would only bring it up if he solved the case by the time they were together on Friday.

Miles returned the other calls, and even though it was just

a little past two o'clock, he decided to call it a day. All that had transpired since his 4:00 a.m. wake-up call had worn him out.

CHAPTER 3

Miles stopped by the marina early Tuesday morning to see if he could uncover any leads from the boat wreckage. Yellow police tape surrounded the boat on three sides, connecting to the chain-link fence serving as the fourth side, thereby securing the perimeter of the crime scene. He also noticed his boat was the closest one to the marina's refueling station. It was extremely fortunate the blast hadn't ignited the fuel-storage tanks. The resulting explosion would likely have severely damaged the entire facility, including the several dozen boats stored there as well as the six adjacent public piers.

He slipped underneath the police tape and walked around the boat, looking for any evidence the police might have missed. Sticking out of a footprint frozen in the mud was a sliver of paper. The police had probably missed it because it was obscured by the water from the fire hose. Once the water in the footprint had frozen over, it exposed the piece of paper. Miles went back to the car and retrieved a bottle of water from the cup holder, and a pair of nitrile gloves to handle the evidence. Using a few drops of water and his pocketknife, he was able to free the piece of paper intact. The numbers 6-6-2-6 had been written there, which happened to be the last four digits of his boat's license number. Obviously, Morton had used it to identify which boat he intended to blow up. It also pretty much negated the theory that Morton was simply an unlucky squatter.

Miles climbed into the boat to have a look around the interior. The area below deck was in shambles. None of the boat's equipment currently rested in its original location, and bloodstains were splattered throughout. After a thirty-minute search for additional clues, he came up empty. Apparently the police had been quite thorough in their combing of the rest of the crime scene. If they'd found anything, he might need Jim's help to get his hands on it.

Miles headed from the marina to his office, arriving at the office a little after nine o'clock.

"Good morning," said Anne. "May I mark the Fremont case invoice as 'final'?"

"Yep," Miles replied as he stepped into his private office. His rather mild OCD tendencies were on full display, with all his office tools and files neatly tucked away in his desk drawers. His desktop was uncluttered except for the bare necessities which included his computer; office phone; a small, neatly stacked pile of papers; and a digital clock Ken had given him at their Hannukah/Christmas dinner in Chicago. He decided to check in with George, who was likely still traumatized by the boat bombing. George answered the call on the first ring.

"How are you doing, George?" he asked.

"Okay, but I'm beginning to rethink our friendship. Every time you and I get involved in something, it blows up in my face." George laughed at his own attempt at a joke.

"It's totally understandable," Miles replied, sharing a laugh.

"Actually, it could have been far worse," George added. "After we lifted the boat out of the water for the season, I had the maintenance guys drain and remove the gas tank so it could be repaired. It had started to rust through, and it was sorely in need of a fix. Normally the tank would be full of fuel and a stabilizer."

"So, if the bombing had gone as it was likely planned, the gas tank would have also exploded and done far more damage."

"No kidding. Given the boat's proximity to the refueling station at the marina, the whole place and all the boats, buildings, and equipment could have gone up with it." George confirmed Miles's theory about the bomb's potential for destroying the entire facility.

Miles's mind immediately shifted to another motive for the bombing. "Who might have benefited from such a catastrophe?"

"The entire operation is owned by Bill Cisco. I know he operates it on a shoestring. It's unlikely he has enough insurance to survive the financial impact on the property, let alone when the insurance companies for all the boat owners try to hang him with the liabilities. It's pretty clear to me he wasn't behind it."

George's analysis made sense.

"Any other ideas?" Miles asked.

"Developers. The property has a wonderful location at the harbor's edge with plenty of land to build condos or apartments complete with piers for boat-access to the lake. Bill told me they have been after him big time, and he had told them he wasn't interested in selling."

"So, one possible way to force an underfinanced and reluctant owner to sell his property would be to destroy it," Miles theorized.

"Yep. If they'd done it right, there likely wouldn't have been enough evidence left to pin it on anyone." George was tracking right along with Miles.

"Thanks, George. We now have a theory about what happened. If I'm right, the bombing might not have been directed at us, but rather at the location of our boat."

"I sure hope that's the case. Then there would be no one out to get us, and Bill Cisco would have dodged a bullet." There was a definite note of relief in George's voice as he chose to accept this latest hypothesis.

After hanging up, Miles decided rather than wait for Jim to find out what the police had uncovered, he would be proactive and share what he had with the police. After all, they not only had all the necessary resources to investigate, they could initiate charges if they found a crime had been committed. Let them put in all the legwork, he thought.

A quick call to a former colleague on the force, Detective Don Maxwell, did the trick.

"Maxwell," Detective Maxwell answered using his officious police voice.

"Hey, Don. I have a piece of evidence for you in our boat bombing case," Miles offered. He went on to describe what he had found at the scene of the bombing.

"Thanks, Miles. This gives us a viable new lead. Can I send an officer to your office to pick up the slip of paper?" he asked.

"Of course. It's safely inside an evidence bag. I'll leave it with my assistant, Anne, in case I'm not here. Please keep me up-to-date on how the investigation unfolds." Miles knew he had just earned an informal attachment to the investigation.

"Will do," Detective Maxwell promised in closing.

Miles mused about how, based on recent events, he had wrongly assumed the bombing was about someone out to do him harm. The fact that Jonathan Reese, the man who'd forced his victims to sacrifice transplantable body parts to pay their debts, was still at large continually fed that paranoia. Even though Miles and the FBI successfully brought Reese's criminal loan-sharking enterprise down, his disappearance and penchant for eliminating those who opposed him, still fueled Miles's nightmares.

It was just before 5:00 p.m. when Miles left for home. It was already pitch-dark as the winter-shortened afternoon had already turned to nighttime. Molly's walk that evening was abbreviated considerably by an afternoon shift in the weather. Now lake-effect snow driven by a bitter cold breeze had left the sidewalk slippery and the landscape barely visible. Once finally inside the house for the night, he retreated to the basement to bring up the three boxes Bobbie had requested, leaving them by the back door so he'd remember to put them in his car.

Just as he reached the top of the stairs with the last box, his phone rang. It was Ken.

"Hi. I have some information for you on Todd Morton. As you mentioned, he'd been in and out of trouble for decades. According to his most current parole officer, he'd been working doing odd jobs in the Waukegan area. Most recently at the site of a newly completed apartment complex."

"Well, that could explain how Morton got involved." Miles immediately saw the construction work fit with his suspicions about who might be behind the bombing. He filled Ken in on what he had learned, and how the ever-growing number of pieces fit together.

"What time do you expect to be in Chicago on Friday?" Ken asked, shifting subjects.

"I have a lunch meeting in Madison on Friday. Bobbie has another potential client for me."

"So you don't have to rush, I'll make a seven-thirty dinner reservation. Any preferences?" he asked.

"Not really. Surprise me." Miles didn't really care what they would be doing as long as they would be doing it together.

With that, they hung up and Miles turned his attention to a

light dinner and an evening of *Seinfeld* reruns, which he knew would provide the perfect distraction from the dramas of the day.

CHAPTER 4

A s promised, Miles showed up promptly at six o'clock on Wednesday night for dinner at Jim's house. He approached the front door full of mixed emotions. While he welcomed the opportunity to offer counsel to Danny, it came with a huge responsibility. Coming out is always a milestone event, but for a sixteen-year-old boy, it was monumental.

Jim opened the door and stepped aside, allowing Miles to enter. "Hi, Miles. This is my wife, Laura, and my son, Danny."

"Nice to meet you both. Thank you for having me over."

Laura greeted Miles with a hug, which took him by surprise since they hadn't met before. He assumed it was likely a show of appreciation for what he was there to discuss with Danny.

After seeing the three Rathburns standing next to one another, Miles was struck by the height difference between Jim and Laura. She was much shorter than Jim, perhaps five foot three or so. Danny's height fit him right in the middle.

Jim took Miles's coat and motioned for him to have a seat in the living room. A bottle of wine and a platter of cheese, meats, and crackers filled the glass-topped coffee table in front of the couch. After he selected his seat, Jim poured Miles a glass of wine, and then he and Laura excused themselves. Obviously, they felt it best to let Miles and Danny talk before sitting down to dinner.

"Danny, let me first say how pleased I am that you've

decided to talk with me about your coming out. That's a huge step. Really brave!"

"I guess the real first step was telling my parents," Danny pointed out.

"Seems to me it was actually the second step. The first step was you accepting yourself for who you really are. I'm sure your mind is swirling with what to do next. Maybe, to start, I can answer some questions for you?" Miles offered.

Danny asked the first basic question. "Okay. When did you tell your friends?"

"I was about your age. Maybe a little younger. I started by telling my friend Ryan Duffy. In fact, I confided in him before I revealed it to my family. Ryan and I have been friends since the third grade. He actually laughed when I told him. Turns out he knew possibly even before I was sure. Anyway, once I knew Ryan was cool with it, I realized that anyone who was truly my friend would accept it as well. Those who wouldn't, well they could just go fuck themselves." Miles emphasized the last phrase in particular.

Miles's rather frank proclamation momentarily stunned Danny. He paused for a moment before he replied. "I have a group of guy friends who I've been all through school with, but none of them would be what I'd call a best friend. Also, I have a number of buddies on the football team, but we're not close outside of practice and games."

"Do you have any female friends?" Miles inquired.

"Sure," Danny replied, somewhat quizzically.

"Any that you'd feel comfortable confiding in?"

"I guess so. Why do you ask?"

"Because with your guy friends, their Y chromosomes may cause them to look down on you or feel threatened. Women are much less likely to assign any of those negative feelings toward you," explained Miles.

"And they don't have to share a locker room with me either," Danny astutely pointed out.

Miles chuckled. "Precisely. Listen, Danny. Being gay is simply part of who you are. Just like the color of your skin, how tall you are, what talents you have, on and on. It's just another component and one you will carry with you always."

"But I want to continue playing football," Danny lamented.

"You should. Football players are at their best when they go all out on the field. Leave it all out there, as they say. Self-awareness gives you the freedom to really leave it all out there, both on and off the field."

"So, where do I begin?" Danny asked.

"Ultimately, you need to decide that for yourself. You needn't feel rushed to share your story." Miles thought for a moment, then continued. "When you're ready, there are a couple of possibilities to consider. Maybe you begin by confiding in one of your female friends with whom you feel most comfortable. A bolder option would be to open up to one of your football team's leaders. Show him the strength of your commitment to the team even in the face of possible backlash over your being gay. Whichever direction you choose to go, find an ally."

"Sounds good, but if it doesn't go well, the prospect of being alone, or bullied, scares me to death." A quiver in Danny's voice accompanied his declaration.

Miles placed his hand on Danny's shoulder to comfort him.

"You conquer the bullies by standing up for yourself no matter what the result might be. You may also find, as I did, that your real friends will stand with you against the bullies. As for being alone, that's a choice—not a consequence—of your decision. I did a little research online before coming over here, and found it is estimated that as high as 20 percent of the US population is LGBTQ. Add to that all the right-minded people who couldn't care less about your sexual orientation, and you'll have way more than half of the population on your side. Plenty of friends to choose from. I can see your mom is putting dinner on the table, so let me close for now with this. Coming out is your liberation from the anxiety of hiding who you really are. Look at it as an opportunity, not a drawback. I promise, once you do that, you'll unlock your potential for finding happiness."

Miles handed Danny his business card. "This discussion is just the beginning. Please call me with all the other questions you will come up with. I'll do my best to be your sounding board." Miles stood, and they joined Danny's parents at the dinner table. A smile highlighted the look of resolve on Danny's face.

CHAPTER 5

With the three boxes tucked safely in the trunk of his Camry, Miles dropped Molly off at George and Cora's, and then took off for Madison for his Friday-morning meeting with Bobbie. The snow-covered landscape along the highway turned his thoughts to the warm-weather getaway he and Ken would be planning when he finally made it to Chicago that evening.

Once he arrived at Bobbie's building, he pulled up to the loading dock and rang the bell at the door. When an attendant opened the door, he asked, "If it's okay, I'd like to leave these boxes here for a few minutes. I'll just go park the car and come back to fetch them."

"I'll run them up to Ms. Martin's office if you'd like," the attendant offered, seeing Bobbie's name written on the boxes.

"That would be great, thanks." Miles still marveled at the "Midwest nice" he so often encountered in his new home state. After finding a parking space just down the block, he walked back to Bobbie's building.

As Miles left the elevator on Bobbie's floor, he saw her talking to her assistant through the glass door. The window behind her faced the dome of the State Capitol building. Quite a real-life mural, he thought. She saw him as well, and smiled as he entered her office suite.

"Perfect timing. We have about half an hour before we meet

with my client. Let's go talk in my office for a couple of minutes before we go." She motioned for him to walk down the hall to her private office.

"Sounds good. The guy at the loading dock said he'd bring up your boxes," Miles mentioned while taking a seat across from her desk.

"We don't have a guy at the loading dock!" she exclaimed.

"Oh, shit. I just gave some guy your boxes." Miles's face showed genuine panic; that is, until he saw the boxes neatly stacked in the corner of her office.

"Sorry. I couldn't resist," Bobbie said apologetically.

"Okay. Now that you're done giving me a heart attack, what's the meeting about?"

"We're meeting with Peter Gonzales. His company has an affiliate in Mexico whose principals he believes are stealing from him. I'll let him fill you in on the details over lunch. In keeping with the theme of the meeting, he's asked us to meet him at Garibaldi over on Butler Street. We'll leave in a couple of minutes and walk over to the restaurant. How's it going with you and Ken?"

Miles smiled. "I mentioned when we talked the other day that I needed to be in Chicago this evening. It's to spend a couple of days with Ken enjoying the city and planning a vacation somewhere warm. So, I guess you could say everything is going quite well."

"I'm really happy for the two of you."

"Anything romantic on your end?" Miles asked hopefully.

"Well . . ." Bobbie replied with a sheepish grin.

"Out with it!" Miles demanded.

"Jack McKay and I have been spending a little time together lately," she confessed. "He brought Maya here to see the city for the day about a month ago. After that we've spent a couple of weekends together, one here and one there."

"I am happy for the two of you as well." Miles cared deeply about both of them, so this was wonderful news.

"So far everything's pretty casual. We'll see what happens. Now we need to go." Bobbie grabbed her purse and motioned for Miles to follow her out the door.

Miles could tell she was carefully controlling her own expectations. He decided to leave further interrogation for another time.

After a short three-block walk, they arrived at Garibaldi Mexican Restaurant. A fit-looking man with dark hair and a thin mustache stood up from a corner booth and waved them over. "Hi, Bobbie. You must be Miles Darien. I'm Peter Gonzales," he said, offering his hand.

Miles took his hand. "Nice to meet you."

Once they were all seated, a server came to the table with menus and three glasses of water. He and Peter exchanged friendly greetings in Spanish.

Peter then asked Bobbie and Miles if they would be okay with him ordering some dishes for the table, as he knew the chef. They nodded in agreement so when the server returned to their table to deliver a basket of tortilla chips and some salsa, Peter gave him their meal order in Spanish. The server's approving smile gave Miles the impression Peter had ordered them something special.

"So, you're a private investigator?" Peter asked.

"Yes. I used to be a forensic scientist for the Lakeville Police Department, but decided I needed to be my own boss," Miles answered.

"Bobbie told me you handle some corporate investigations.

Turns out I'm in need of someone to do some snooping in that realm on my behalf." When he saw Miles wince a little, he added, "Sorry about the snoop reference. I meant no disrespect."

"No need to apologize. What can I do for you?" Miles's wince was actually him worrying that this case might interfere with the vacation he and Ken were planning.

Peter went on to explain that he owned PG Parts, an electronic components manufacturing company which produced and distributed aftermarket electrical parts of all kinds, mostly private label items sold in big box stores like Home Depot. The company made some parts locally in its Sun Prairie plant, but most of their products were made in Asia and Mexico. The products manufactured overseas were all shipped into the Sun Prairie operation and fulfilled from there.

"So, how can I help?" Miles asked.

"The products we bring in from Asia are contract-manufactured by independent factories. The products made in Mexico are made in a plant we co-own with a firm there. That's where I could use your assistance. I have reason to believe my Mexican partners are taking advantage of me." Peter's voice grew louder as he explained his theory.

"How so, exactly?" Bobbie asked, continuing the line of questioning.

"It's the 'exactly' part that I'm not sure of. I believe they're likely selling some of our parts on their own and finding ways to hide it. It's easy to do, actually. They may be simply accounting for the cost of making the stolen parts by falsifying raw material costs and claiming excessive amounts of spoilage," he explained, laying out one possible scenario.

"Why a private investigator?" Miles asked.

"I could send accountants and auditors, but if I'm right, what my partners are doing will not be easy to uncover using conventional bookkeeping forensics. I need someone who can see beyond the books and operating procedures. Interested?"

"I am. Where in Mexico is your operation?" Miles asked.

"Guadalajara."

The wheels immediately started turning in Miles's head. A paid vacation to Mexico with his FBI-agent boyfriend along to help with the investigation. This sounded perfect, except possibly the timing.

"Peter, how soon would I need to get started? You see, I have a number of loose ends I'd need to tidy up before I could head to Mexico." This was only partially true. Miles did have a few things to attend to, but nothing that would cause a long delay. He just wanted the timing to coincide with Ken's time off.

"It would be helpful if you could spend some time at our plant here in Sun Prairie to learn about our products and best practices. That way you'd know what you're looking for, and then be able to reasonably pose as a potential buyer when visiting the plant in Guadalajara." Peter's proposal made perfect sense.

"How does this sound? We begin my education in a week or so, and I plan to head to Mexico around March fifteenth." Miles offered, hoping the timing he proposed would be acceptable.

"Actually, I'd like you to get there before that. Once the holidays begin, everything is pretty much shut down."

"You mean Easter, I assume."

"And Semana Santa, which is the week before. In Spanish cultures, we celebrate the last week of Christ's life, which includes Easter week. Work-wise, everything comes to a halt for those two weeks," Peter explained.

This was definitely news to Miles. Details about such Christian holiday traditions were not taught in Hebrew school.

"I suppose March 1 then?" Miles offered reluctantly.

Peter nodded, and then asked Miles to send him a written proposal for the cost of his services. Miles agreed to have it to him by the end of the week. Just then the food arrived. It was an assortment of sizzling meats, cheeses, and vegetables accompanied by guacamole, chips, tortillas, and an array of spicy sauces. It was all delicious.

Once they were finished, Bobbie insisted on buying lunch. After they parted company with Peter, Bobbie and Miles walked back to her office, stopping at the entrance.

"I'll copy you on my proposal to Peter and keep you in the loop as things progress. Thanks again, Bobbie, for recommending me. I really appreciate it." Miles gave her a big hug and said goodbye.

On the ride to Chicago he wondered how in the world he would sell Ken on rescheduling his time off, and then also talking him into making it a working vacation instead of the romantic getaway they had been planning on. By the time he got to Ken's place, he had the problem solved. He could go to Guadalajara around March 1 and hopefully wrap up the case before Ken arrived. That way they could still have their romantic vacation as planned, and Ken wouldn't have to try and change the date of his vacation. He was sure Ken would prefer this plan anyway, as it would allow him to have his vacation unencumbered by acting as Dr. Watson to Miles's Sherlock Holmes.

CHAPTER 6

T hanks to the lighter-than-normal afternoon traffic, Miles
was able to make his way from Madison to Chicago by five
thirty. Ken's apartment in Andersonville, a neighborhood
in Chicago, was in a long row of look-alike brownstone. As
good a detective as Miles was, in order to find the right place
he always had to look for the building number displayed on the
front stoop. Ken had a designated parking space in back, which
came with his unit. Since Ken had no car, the space was always
there for Miles to use, which was fortunate since street parking
was scarce and most blocks also required a parking permit.

Even though he had a key, Miles politely knocked on the
door. Ken answered the door, already dressed up for their night
on the town.

After a giant hug, Ken asked, "How was the ride from
Madison?"

"Surprisingly smooth. The meeting was over around two
thirty, and after a short review of the proceedings with Bobbie,
I was on my way." Miles walked into Ken's living room and sat
down on the couch.

"So, what type of opportunity did she have for you?" Ken
asked as he joined Miles on the couch.

"A good one, and one that could fit nicely into our vacation
plans."

Miles went on to explain how PG Parts needed his help uncovering possible skimming by their Mexican partners. He was most animated when he described how the job could easily morph into the perfect warm-weather vacation they were planning.

"I expect to uncover what's going on with the missing inventory in two weeks at the most. You could then plan to join me in Guadalajara on the fifteenth, or we could meet at another destination nearby," Miles offered.

Ken smiled as he got up and retrieved his iPad. After reviewing a map of the possible destinations near Guadalajara on the screen, Ken pointed to Mexico's Pacific coastline.

"I'd really like a place on the ocean. So, somewhere between Cabo and Acapulco," Ken declared.

Miles was delighted Ken was on board. "A beach vacation sounds perfect. Let's each do some additional research and then compare notes in a few days. Now, what's up for dinner?"

"I made a reservation at Siam Café," said Ken, brimming with excitement. "It's a cool, upscale Thai place in the neighborhood. Afterward, I thought we could go to Benny's. It's a real Chicago-style blues club where a bunch of my gay friends hang out."

"You have 'gay friends.' Shocking!" Miles teased.

"If I didn't, you wouldn't be here," Ken shot back.

After they had a good laugh, Miles picked up his bag and went to the bedroom to unpack. He swapped his dress shirt and slacks for a more casual polo shirt and jeans. When he returned to the living room, Ken poured a glass of Merlot for each of them.

They only had time for the one glass of wine before their reservation half an hour later. The short drive and search for a parking spot landed them at the restaurant right on time. The dinner at Siam Café was a real departure from the rather tame

Thai restaurants in Lakeville. The variety, presentation, and amount of exotic spices were at a whole different level. He and Ken shared a few small dishes and a couple of beers to counter the heat of the food. After the meal, they moved on to Benny's as planned. After about an hour of music and a couple more drinks, the day's travels, big meal, and alcoholic beverages took their toll on Miles, who was fading fast. Ken sensed it was time to go back to his place. Once there, Miles headed straight to bed.

"I bought you dinner and drinks and now no sex?" Ken teased.

"Morning sex is good too!" Miles offered as he pulled the covers up around his neck and went to sleep.

It was almost 9:00 a.m. when Miles finally awakened. He could hear some noise coming from the kitchen, which he rightly assumed was Ken rustling up some breakfast.

"I guess the allure of coffee was more enticing than my offer of morning sex," Miles said in the most disappointed voice he could muster. He noticed Ken seemed preoccupied with something more than toasting bagels.

"Actually, that's not the case. I received a text this morning from the boss. She needs me to meet her at the office at ten."

"How is Agent Audrey Drummond?" Even though Miles and Agent Drummond were on a first name basis, he liked to refer to her by title and full name out of respect.

"She's fine, but something must be up if she's calling an impromptu meeting like this," Ken surmised. "It shouldn't take long. We'll still have the rest of the day today and all of tomorrow to hang out together."

"Works for me. I can use the time to see if any progress has been made in the boat explosion investigation."

"See you around lunchtime then?" Ken proposed.

"Perfect."

While Ken was at his meeting, Miles placed a call to Detective Maxwell, hoping he was on duty given it was Saturday. He was.

"Hi Miles. I'm glad you called. Did you or Mr. Willis by any chance leave a cell phone on board your boat?"

"Not that I know of, Don. Did you find evidence of one in the wreckage?" Miles asked.

"Actually, we found evidence of at least two. One in Todd Morton's pants pocket, and fragments of another were found in several locations in the blast zone. If it didn't belong to either of you, it was likely part of the bomb mechanism. Such a mechanism would allow the bomb to be activated anytime simply by calling its number."

Miles hadn't considered this possibility. "An interesting bit of evidence, but it doesn't really get you any closer to the culprits, does it?" he pointed out.

"Not really, but it does indicate the potential of a much more sophisticated plan than we had originally suspected. It also speaks to the resources and experience of the perpetrator and any possible accomplices."

"Did Morton's phone reveal any clues?"

"No, it was a new cheapie burner phone from Walmart. No calls, in or out. One more thing. The explosive used was ammonium nitrate, the type commonly used for demolition by construction companies."

These revelations certainly supported the possibility that real estate developers were behind the bombing. They would definitely have had the resources to come up with a more sophisticated detonator than a simple timer, but there was another possibility as to who and why Todd Morton was hired to plant the bomb with cell phone activation. Maybe there was someone else who wanted to plant the bomb in the safety of a deserted marina, and intended to set it off at a more opportune time, maybe when their real targets were on board. Miles decided until he had more to go on, he would keep this newly formulated theory as to "who" and "why" to himself. At this point, there was no need to frighten George any further.

When Ken returned from his meeting, the look on his face indicated he had something unpleasant to share.

"What's up?" Miles asked as lightheartedly as he could muster.

"Quite a bit. Unfortunately, I'm only at liberty to share a small amount of information with you. I have to leave on Monday morning for an assignment of indeterminate length." There was regret in Ken's voice.

"So, you can't say where you're going or how long you'll be gone?"

"Regrettably, that's the case," Ken replied.

"I assume our vacation plans are also off, then."

"I'm really sorry. I was looking forward to it too." Ken walked over and gave Miles a huge, prolonged hug.

As much as he wanted to stay, Miles decided Ken needed time to prepare for his assignment, so he reluctantly packed his bag, kissed Ken goodbye, and drove back to Lakeville.

CHAPTER 7

Miles started feeling sorry for himself the moment he walked out of Ken's condo. As he started home, he couldn't stop thinking about how Ken's mysterious assignment had ruined their perfect vacation plans. Looking for sympathy, he called his most likely sympathizer: his best friend, Ryan.

"What a bummer!" Ryan said. "I've got a bummer of my own to report. Rebecca and I have decided to break it off." Ryan and Rebecca had dated for a couple of years and had finally decided to buy a place together less than a year ago.

Miles's self-pity turned into sympathy. "I'm so sorry, buddy boy. Must be complicated with you having combined your households."

"Rebecca has agreed to buy me out of the condo. Now that her TV show has been picked up for three more seasons, she will have no trouble securing the financing. I've moved into the second bedroom until I decide where I'm going." Ryan's voice was neither sad nor angry, but in shock.

Miles thought living in the same apartment with your ex, especially if your relationship had just collapsed, sounded like torture. Ryan had always been a strong, independent person, so surely he would adapt to his new circumstances as he plotted his next move.

"Somewhere in New York City, I assume." Miles knew his friend was a die-hard New Yorker.

"Actually, I'm not sure. By the way, thanks for not asking what happened."

"I assume you'll fill me in if, and when, you feel it's appropriate. So, you might actually consider relocating?" Miles couldn't conceive of Ryan actually moving into any place other than another New York apartment.

"I can write essays for the *Times* from anywhere. A change of venue might do me some good. I just know I need to move out sooner than later," Ryan mumbled sadly.

"If you can figure out what to do with your stuff, you're welcome to stay at my place until you figure everything out." While Miles was heartsick about the demise of Ryan's relationship, he would love to have his friend come to Lakeville, if only for a visit. It would help his own outlook, given the uncertainty of Ken's assignment.

Miles remembered he had some important news of his own to share, so the conversation then shifted to his upcoming assignment in Mexico, and then the big news: the unsolved boat bombing.

"Holy shit!" Ryan exclaimed. "I thought my news was explosive, but this . . .!"

"Very funny. I'm pulling into my driveway. Keep me posted on any new developments. Like I said, the guest room is all yours if you want it!"

"Thanks, I'll be in touch."

On Monday morning, George sent over a few ads for boat sales to solicit Miles's opinion. None of them had anywhere near the charm of the now-cratered Chris-Craft. The technical and fishing attributes were George's area of expertise, so Miles's comments went to aesthetics and amenities. However, he did really like the one with the automatic flushing toilet. Ultimately, it would be George's decision since the Chris-Craft was actually his. Miles's "ownership" stake was a gift from George, an unnecessary and over-the-top thank-you for saving his stepdaughter Olivia's life.

Miles replied to George's boat choices with a few comments, and then went online to make his flight arrangements for Guadalajara. His best option was a nonstop flight on AeroMéxico from O'Hare. Since the duration of the trip was yet to be determined, he booked a one-way ticket for March 1. His client, Peter Gonzales, had recommended he secure a room at the Hotel Riu Plaza. It was upscale, and befitted an American businessman on a buying trip. The room was expensive, but it was ultimately on Peter's dime. Assuming the role of a businessman would be an interesting departure from Miles's usual modus operandi.

The room Miles booked for his "education" in Sun Prairie was far more modest than his Guadalajara accommodations, but was certainly nice enough and conveniently located, less than a mile from PG Parts headquarters. He still had two weeks before he was due there, so he spent his days until then finishing off all of his current cases and, reluctantly, turning down a few. Anne's work schedule while he was gone was next on his to-do list. He settled on offering to pay her for twenty-five hours per week, which she could split as she saw fit between time in the office and working remotely. She accepted it and promised to take good care of things while he was gone. Miles had no doubt she would do just that.

Keeping occupied would be great medicine for the loneliness Miles was certain to feel with Ken gone until who knows when.

When his thoughts turned to Ryan's situation, he realized his relationship with Ken was simply on hold whereas Ryan's was over. His musings were interrupted by Anne standing in his office doorway.

"There's a young man named Danny Rathburn here to see you," she said with a puzzled look on her face.

"Please show him in."

Danny walked in carrying an envelope and sporting a big smile. "Hi, Mr. Darien. My dad said he had an envelope to deliver to you, and I asked if I could deliver it for him."

"Nice to see you, Danny. Thanks for the delivery. How's everything going?" Miles was pleased to see the dramatic change in Danny's body language since they last met.

"Well, that's why I wanted to make the delivery. I decided to take your advice and tell a couple of people about my coming out. It was strange. They had questions but didn't seem to judge me at all. I can't tell you how relieved I am. Thank you!" The smile on Danny's face was ear to ear.

"I'm so happy for you. Now you can shift your focus to being a better quarterback."

"Actually, I play linebacker, but I know what you mean." Danny held out his hand and Miles shook it. As Danny turned and walked out the door, Miles realized Danny's news had eased his sadness, at least for now. He was elated at what Danny had accomplished, and that he had played a small role in it. If only it could be the same for more young people in that situation.

Miles turned his attention to the envelope Danny had delivered. A review of its contents confirmed Miles's suspicions. It also prompted a call to Detective Maxwell asking to come to the station to share those suspicions with the Lakeville PD.

CHAPTER 8

M iles had been invited to George and Cora's for dinner
that night. It was a perfect time to tell them the news
about the culprit behind the boat bombing. He arrived
around seven, bottle of Cabernet in hand. Cora greeted him at
the door with a hug. George and Olivia were busy setting out
their meal on the dining room table.

Miles smiled at Olivia. "So nice to see you, Olivia. How are
you doing?"

Olivia smiled back. "Quite well, thanks. Although I'd be
even better if that horrible Jonathan Reese wasn't still on the
loose."

Miles wrapped his arm around her. "I understand, but he
no longer has a reason to harm you. Your story has already
been documented by the FBI, so his only concern at this point
is avoiding capture. I suspect he's a million miles from here by
now."

Olivia nodded and went back to helping George set the
table.

After they sat down, Miles filled them in on the latest
revelations about the boat bombing.

"Well, it appears we now know who and why our boat was
bombed," Miles announced.

"What? Who?" George shouted.

"As often happens, Occam's razor explains it perfectly."

Miles knew they probably didn't know what that meant, so he went on to explain. "Basically, Occam's razor is a scientific term that says when you have conflicting explanations for an experiment's outcome, the simplest explanation is likely to be the correct one. It applies here because it turns out the simplest explanation is that the only person behind the bombing was Todd Morton."

"I don't understand. Why would he bomb our boat?" George asked.

Miles took a sip of wine. "Actually, I don't believe it was aimed at us at all. Years ago, Todd Morton belonged to a gang. His hand was cut off by angry members of that gang as retribution for attempting to steal from their stash. You may have read in the paper a while back that a hand had been found. Well, it was Todd Morton's hand and, when he was released from prison, he came to claim it. Of course, it had badly decomposed over time and had been discarded. My hunch is that his anger over its removal still festered, so I looked for something to connect that anger to the bombing. I found a possible connection when I revisited the marina looking for additional clues. While nosing around, I peeked into the shop where our fuel tank was being repaired. On the side of the tank, there was a strip of masking tape. What do you think was on that strip of tape?"

"The license number of our boat?" George asked.

"Correct. The same set of numbers written on the slip of paper I'd found in the mud next to the boat. It got me thinking about revenge as a possible motive for the bombing, so I asked Jim Rathburn to send me a list of the names of suspected members in Morton's gang from back then. I compared that list of names to those of the marina employees listed on their website. Turns out one gang member, Chaz Ramsey, matched up with one Charles Ramsey, who works for the marina."

"I know him. He's the guy who's repairing our fuel tank." George was starting to get the picture.

"Precisely. Todd Morton was targeting his old gang buddy Chaz. Probably the one who actually severed Morton's hand. The slip of paper was how Morton found out on which boat Chaz would be installing the newly repaired fuel tank. Morton most likely stole the explosives from the construction company he worked for. It's not a stretch that he learned bomb-making somewhere during his illustrious criminal career. Once Morton planted the bomb, he'd simply keep an eye on our boat. When he saw Chaz on board working on the repairs, he'd drive off and call the cell phone attached to the bomb. Instant revenge with little or no chance the explosion would ever be connected to him."

"I guess you could say Morton's plan blew up in his face," George quipped.

Cora slapped George on the arm for his inappropriate joke. "Have you shared your theory with the Lakeville Police Department?" she asked Miles.

"Yes, I stopped by there a couple of hours ago and shared my findings with Detective Maxwell and a couple of his associates. They thought it was a plausible explanation and promised to pursue it." While Miles was confident he had solved the mystery, he would wait for confirmation from Lakeville PD before he considered the case closed.

When Miles returned home it was only eight thirty, so he grabbed a beer out of the refrigerator and took it into the living room. He wasn't much of a beer drinker before moving to Wisconsin, but his friendship with George included an education on the joys of smooth lagers and hearty ales. With a bottle of Riverwest Stein in hand, he sat down at his coffee table to review his mail. As usual, mostly junk mail and a couple of bills. An unread copy of Sunday's *New York Times* at the end of the table caught his eye. It reminded him to check in on Ryan and his unusual new living arrangement. He thought it would be wise to start the call with his latest news about the bombing, and hope Ryan would be forthcoming about how he was getting along.

Miles proceeded to lay out his findings in detail, both the scientific and the theoretical. He finished by repeating George's funny response.

Ryan offered another possibility. "Do you think the bomb went off because Morton was careless or, by some enormous stroke of bad luck, the phone attached to the bomb had been activated and then received a spam call?"

"Would have been the ultimate spam call, wouldn't it? But I'd rather think he was simply careless. Either way, the outcome was the same. Speaking of outcome, anything new there?" Miles had decided to probe.

"Not really. Just perpetual awkwardness."

"What about work?" Miles hoped Ryan had better news on that front.

"Frankly," confessed Ryan, "I've been so preoccupied with my personal life that my professional life has been in a holding pattern. Thankfully, the *Times* hasn't been pressuring me for another series. At least not yet. I suspect that'll change as soon as Ted runs out of other new essays, but for now I have abundant time to wallow in self-pity."

Suddenly an idea popped into Miles's head. "I have to go to Sun Prairie for a few days to work on my new project for the electronic components manufacturer who hired me. After that I'll be going to Mexico for a couple of weeks to investigate their suspicions that all is not well with their joint venture in

Guadalajara. Why don't you come here, hang out with me for a little while, and then look after Molly when I have to be away? It will be a nice escape from your 'perpetual awkwardness.'" Miles tried his best to sell the concept.

"When do you leave for Sun Prairie?" Ryan was obviously giving this serious consideration.

"In about two weeks. If you come soon, it would give us some time to pal around before I have to leave." Miles pitched the idea in the most convincing manner he could muster.

"I'll be there day after tomorrow." Ryan's quick response caught Miles a little off guard.

"Wow, great. Send me your flight information and I'll pick you up. I'm really happy you're taking me up on my offer. Molly will be happy too!" Miles was amazed Ryan had so readily accepted.

After hanging up, Miles made a mental list of possible activities for Ryan's visit. Maybe Anne could look into some upcoming happenings in the area for them to explore. Obviously Cora and George would be excited to see Ryan again, not to mention happy to be relieved of long-term dog sitting duty. Miles also wondered if Bobbie still had an interest in getting to know Ryan better. During the last conversation Miles had with her, she mentioned she had been seeing Jack McKay off and on, but it didn't appear to be a steady thing.

The sadness over Ken's assignment still lingered but had dissipated now that Ryan would be visiting. With all he needed to do to prepare for that visit, Miles decided to take Molly out for one more walk and then turn in early. Tuesday would certainly be a full day.

CHAPTER 9

A s Ryan returned to the condo he shared with Rebecca, he realized leaving New York would mean so many of the issues surrounding the end of their relationship would be left unresolved. At the very least, he would emphasize that their relationship was irrevocably broken.

"I'm leaving on Wednesday. Not sure when I'll be back. I'm sure you'll be glad to have the place to yourself." Ryan's tone insinuated that Rebecca would be able to "entertain" a guest without him in the next room. "Where are you going?" Rebecca asked.

"To see Miles," Ryan replied curtly.

"Listen, my suggestion that we have an open relationship never meant I didn't want us to be together. I just wanted you to know my position on monogamy."

Ryan paced as he spoke. "I know that. As I've said before, your view of our relationship no longer matches up with mine. This is an opportunity for both of us. I could be gone for several weeks, which will give me time to figure out where I'm heading both emotionally and geographically. Surely it will be a welcomed break for you as well." Ryan mustered a small smile. And as he returned to his room, he noticed Rebecca on the couch studying her script and wiping away the tears running down her cheeks.

Ryan pulled his suitcase from the closet and proceeded to

pack. He decided to add a second one so he could pack for a trip of indeterminate length and a number of potential destinations.

After dinner, Miles retired to his couch and fell asleep while studying the Home Depot catalog in an attempt to educate himself on the electronic components market. The ring of his cell phone awakened him from his unplanned nap.

"Hello," he said groggily.

"I didn't realize you went to bed so early," Bobbie remarked.

"Reading pages of descriptions of electronic components could put anyone to sleep." Miles looked at his watch; it was only eight o'clock. "I'm wide awake now, so what can I do for you?"

"Actually, it's what I can do for *you*. You're due in Sun Prairie a week from Monday morning. Correct?"

"That's the plan," Miles answered, wondering what she had in mind.

"Why not come in on the Sunday night before? I can offer a wonderful early dinner at my favorite restaurant, Bravado, followed by a concert at the Orpheum."

"Sounds interesting. What's the concert?"

"Alicia Keys."

"I'm in. She's terrific." Miles was genuinely excited. "One question. You obviously have two tickets. Did someone back out on you?"

"Ever the detective," she acknowledged. "Jack was originally planning to go with me, but he had to cancel. The organization he's been working for has opened an office in DC, and he's moving there to manage it."

"What about Maya?" Miles's thoughts had immediately turned to Jack's daughter.

"He's still working that out with Sandy. I guess he'll come home periodically, and Maya will come there when she's not in school. He's a devoted dad, so I'm sure they'll figure it out."

"And your relationship?" Miles asked, even though he had a pretty good idea of what the answer would be.

Miles heard the tinkling of ice cubes in a glass, which he assumed was Bobbie pouring herself three fingers of Scotch to help ease her disappointment over the lost relationship.

"I've resigned myself that it's over. At least, any romantic involvement." Her halting, whispered response echoed her sadness.

"I'm sorry it didn't work out." After a brief pause to decide whether he should divulge his news, he continued, "There's a lot of that going around these days. Ryan and Rebecca are ending their relationship as well."

"What happened?" Bobbie probed.

"She wants a polyamorous relationship, which he has no interest in. He's stuck sharing their condo with her until he finds his next place of residence. In fact, he's headed this way in a couple of days to escape their unusual living arrangement, at least for a little while. I think he might even be contemplating a move out of New York." He decided not to play Cupid, even though he would be thrilled if his two friends eventually got together.

If Bobbie entertained a Ryan-related possibility, she kept it to herself. She simply replied, "I hope he lands on his feet."

"He will. I have no doubt. Listen, Molly's scratching at the door to go out. I'll call you in a day or two to continue our chat."

"Looking forward to it," Bobbie said as they ended the call.

When Miles returned from walking Molly, he decided he'd had enough "switches and sockets" studying for the night. He turned his attention to Ryan's visit. Miles had a legal pad with a heading that said, "Activities for Ryan." The heading was all he could come up with, so he sent Anne a text to ask for ideas on anything he and Ryan might enjoy doing together before Miles was due in Sun Prairie.

Miles knew he'd have to alert George, Cora, and Olivia that Ryan was coming. He decided it would be on Ryan to bring them up-to-date on his current events when he arrived. Miles was confident George and Cora probably never had any other acquaintances with that dilemma, but they would most assuredly be understanding and sympathetic. Miles hoped the change of venue, hanging out with good friends, and Cora's cooking would brighten Ryan's outlook. Not to mention the possibility of an escalated relationship with Bobbie.

Before turning in, Miles realized he'd neglected his email inbox all day, so he moved to his desk and opened his laptop. He found the usual "Special Offers," which he quickly deleted, a couple of new case possibilities he'd have to decline, and finally an important one from the Lakeville Police Department. After they concluded their investigation, their findings corroborated Miles's theory on what went down with the boat bombing. This was great news, particularly for George, who could now collect the insurance money and also sell what remained of the Chris-Craft to a boat builder in Manitowoc, who wanted it for parts. He immediately forwarded the police department email to George.

The combination of his unplanned nap, his conversation with Bobbie, and the email from Lakeville PD would undoubtedly affect his ability to fall sleep. So, Miles checked the Internet for information on his trip to Guadalajara. What he discovered was far more exciting than switches and sockets. So many noteworthy historical sights, restaurants, art galleries, and markets to occupy his off-hours there. When he finally looked up and checked the time, it was twelve thirty in the morning. It was time to give sleep another try.

CHAPTER 10

As usual, the Wednesday-morning traffic on the way to O'Hare was slow-moving, particularly now that construction season was full-on. Ryan's flight was due in at ten thirty, and Miles was still a good forty minutes out at ten o'clock. Just as Miles exited the highway onto the O'Hare spur, his phone rang. Ryan was just outside the baggage claim. Miles's timing turned out to be perfect.

When Miles pulled up, he was surprised to see Ryan with two large suitcases and a backpack in tow.

"Planning to stay awhile, I see," Miles teased.

"Just prepared for all Wisconsin weather contingencies," Ryan shot back.

He's not planning to return to New York any time soon, Miles thought. They squeezed Ryan's luggage into the trunk of Miles's Camry, and then they were off to Lakeville. Thankfully, the northbound traffic was slightly less congested than what Miles had encountered on the way to O'Hare. Having grown up in New York without a car limited Miles's driving experience, particularly the kind he encountered on the Chicago freeway system. He kept his eyes glued to the road and let Ryan do most of the talking until they reached the Illinois-Wisconsin border, where the traffic traditionally thinned out.

"I suppose you're wondering why I really brought so much stuff with me."

"Crossed my mind," Miles admitted.

"Well, obviously I'll be in Lakeville for a while, with you off to Sun Prairie for your crash course in electronic components and then to Guadalajara for a couple of weeks," Ryan pointed out.

"Still a lot of stuff." Miles continued with his abbreviated answers as the car was once again surrounded by rumbling semis and speeding cars.

"Once my services here are no longer required, I'm thinking of doing some additional traveling," Ryan explained. "I'm not anxious to return to my uncomfortable situation in New York, so I have a couple of additional destinations in mind. Even brought my passport along just in case."

"For a vacation or something else?"

"Both. First, I could use some time to relax in a warm-weather locale, and then I'd like to scout for a possible new home base."

Miles was right about the possibility of Ryan looking to relocate. "Looks like you're fully prepared for both. Have you identified any potential landing spots?"

"Nothing specific, which is why I brought clothes to accommodate wherever I may go. I'll have plenty of downtime while I'm here to consider my next steps." Ryan sounded rather wistful, Miles thought. It was as if he hadn't totally thought out everything a major move like this would require. But as Ryan said, he'd have plenty of downtime to sort that out while in Lakeville.

Having now safely crossed the border into Wisconsin, Miles relaxed a little. "I hope you don't mind, but I accepted an invitation to George and Cora's tonight. Once they heard you were coming, they wouldn't take no for an answer."

"That's fine. I have the afternoon to relax and get settled before we go over there. Is Olivia still living with them?"

"Not any longer. She made some good friends at art school, and now she's rooming with two of them. She loves the school, and since Milwaukee's only a forty-five-minute drive away, she comes home frequently, or they drive up to see her."

Dinner was both wonderful and excruciating all at once. The food and friendly vibes were equally delightful. Telling George and Cora about his breakup with Rebecca was beyond difficult for Ryan.

Cora reached over and took Ryan's hand. "You will be fine. It may take a while until the pain subsides, but you will be fine." Cora emphasized the last phrase.

"I know," Ryan responded, giving Cora's hand a squeeze. "I've had relationships end before, but never one where I was left feeling like I wasn't enough."

"Seems to me no one guy can be enough for her," George added in a most disapproving tone.

"George!" Cora shouted.

"It's okay, Cora. He may be right. Anyway, it's over and time to move on. What's for dessert?" Ryan obviously wanted to change the subject back to something more pleasant.

Miles decided to comply. "I have Anne compiling a long list of fun activities for us to enjoy while you're here, buddy boy."

"I'm not much for outdoor winter sports," Ryan replied.

"We'll focus on the indoor ones then."

"Please take George with you!" Cora pleaded.

Their laughter lightened the mood, at least for the moment.

Not much was said on the ride back to Miles's house. Ryan's day had been long and tiring. As they rolled through Lakeville, Ryan was struck by how much of what they drove past was familiar and welcoming to him. His last visit was short, but the city had somehow become etched in his mind. He wondered if this, or some other location like it, would be the type of place he could actually be happy living in. It would definitely be the next addition to the list of possibilities he had in mind.

When they got to the house, Miles took Molly for a walk while Ryan sat down at the dining room table, pulled out his laptop, and began returning emails. One in particular caught his attention. It was from Ted, his editor at the *Times*.

Ryan, I'd like to get another series of essays booked with you to start next month. Are you working on anything? Ted.

Ryan responded, *Ted, nothing in the works at the moment, but I'm looking. Ryan.*

Ryan knew that would only hold Ted at bay for a short time. He'd either have to come up with something or find another, more creative way to hold Ted off. Even as a freelancer, Ryan felt the pressure to produce, both from this relentless editor at the *Times* and himself. He spent the rest of the evening scouring the numerous news websites he had stored on his laptop, looking for an interesting topic, one worthy of a series in the *Times*. There was no shortage of topics, but none that struck the necessary chord with him.

CHAPTER 11

T hanks to the list Anne had compiled, Miles and Ryan spent the next few days exploring a wide variety of sites in southeastern Wisconsin. They walked several miles of the historic Geneva Lake Shore Path, which circumnavigates Lake Geneva; took a tour of iconic Frank Lloyd Wright buildings in Racine and Milwaukee; browsed the Harley Davidson Museum, where they were dazzled by the sculpture-like machines on display; took a tour of Lakefront Brewery, which concluded with a fish fry and beer tasting; and they even climbed the 178 steps up to the top of the Holy Hill Basilica to view the snow-covered Wisconsin countryside with the skyline of downtown Milwaukee off in the distance.

Anne had done a great job finding interesting activities for them to do. She also saw to it that each place required a car ride of some length. Smart planning on her part kept the number of attractions to a minimum and assured she would have peace and quiet at the office.

Bright and early Sunday morning, Miles said goodbye to Ryan and Molly and made his way to Sun Prairie. Even on a mostly cloudy day, the snow-covered landscape was so monochromatic that he needed to wear his sunglasses to add some contrast. The ride only took a little over ninety minutes. Thankfully, his room at the Hampton Inn was ready even though he arrived several hours before check-in time. When

Miles made plans to spend Sunday evening with Bobbie, he also arranged to meet Peter Gonzales that afternoon at the PG Parts plant to begin his education. Miles's morning arrival allowed him some time to unpack and finalize a list of questions before their meeting.

The industrial park where PG Parts was located consisted of a number of large nondescript warehouse-type buildings, each fronted by a smaller office structure. Miles parked the Camry in a spot closest to the entrance, marked "Reserved for Visitors." He assumed correctly that the only other car in the lot was Peter's.

When he walked into the office lobby, he was surprised to see it was decorated with a collection of Ansel Adams photographs of the American West, not pictures of the company's electronic components. Peter greeted him and they adjourned to his office, which was decorated with even more Adams photographs. So much for the stereotypical factory decor, Miles thought.

"Peter, I see you're quite a fan of Ansel Adams. Your collection is wonderful."

"Thanks. I've been collecting these photographs for decades. There's a certain quiet majesty to them which I find to be quite calming." Peter then shifted the conversation to the job at hand. "Let's take a walk through the plant as a starting point for your education." Peter motioned Miles toward a door in the back of the large general office area.

As they walked through the surprisingly immaculate manufacturing section of the building, Peter pointed out each station's role in the manufacturing process. "This will come to life tomorrow, so you'll get to see exactly how each piece is made."

They then went through the warehouse/distribution center. There were neatly arranged crates of parts from Asia and

Mexico waiting to be unloaded and added into inventory, as well as PG Parts packages staged to be shipped to customers. It appeared all very straightforward to Miles.

"Questions?" Peter asked.

"Many, but for now just one. In my role as a potential customer, how much of what we just saw would I be expected to know?"

Peter smiled. "Good question. Actually, very little. I just wanted you to have it as a frame of reference in case they ask you whether or not you've had a tour of the plant. A customer who would travel to Mexico to see their operation would certainly have been here first."

"Makes sense."

"Good. We'll resume in the morning. By the way, my employees think you're here as a potential investor. That will explain the level of 'training' you're receiving."

"Works for me," Miles said as they walked back through the building to the front entrance, where they said goodbye.

Driving back to his hotel, Miles was struck by how on top of it Peter was, and how organized the whole place was. It must certainly be driving him crazy to think his partners in Mexico might be messing with his ultra organized operation.

Miles had agreed to meet Bobbie at a restaurant called A Pig In a Fur Coat, a hip and happening place near her home on Madison's East Side. When he arrived promptly at five thirty, Bobbie was waiting at the entrance.

"Glad you're on time," she said. "It'll be nice to have an unrushed dinner before we have to leave for the concert. How did your tour of PG Parts go?"

"Quite a neat and tidy operation. Definitely speaks volumes

about Peter's personality and management style. Oh, and I loved the collection of Ansel Adams photographs."

Their conversation was interrupted by the server, who stopped by to take their order. As a frequent customer, Bobbie knew the menu backward and forward, so Miles asked her to order for them. She ordered a Belgian endive salad, bucatini alla Bolognese, and the Arctic char for them to share along with a bottle of California Pinot Noir she liked.

"I suspect your education will shift into high gear tomorrow. By the way, I assume Molly is staying with Cora and George?" she asked.

"Actually . . ." Miles paused for effect before elaborating. It drew a quizzical look from Bobbie. "Ryan's at my place taking care of Molly. He's taken refuge away from his predicament in New York."

"His predicament, as you call it, is really sad. I don't fault her for what she wants in a relationship or relationships, but she should have had the decency to put it out there before they became so heavily invested in each other." Bobbie was obviously not taking any joy in Ryan's new availability.

"No shit! Heavily invested in more ways than one," Miles pointed out, alluding to their collection of financial and logistic entanglements.

A few minutes later the server showed up with their meal. Their conversation switched to small talk while they ate. Miles did detect a certain twinkle and wry smile from Bobbie while they spoke. He assumed it was the wheels in Bobbie's mind beginning to turn in Ryan's direction.

CHAPTER 12

T he ten-minute drive to PG Parts gave Miles an opportunity to phone Ryan. "How's Molly doing? Does she miss me?" Miles asked, only half kidding.

"She hasn't mentioned you at all since you left," Ryan replied, keeping in step.

Miles shifted the conversation to more realistic subject matter. "Bobbie and I had a great evening. A wonderful meal followed by a spectacular concert. Alicia Keys is the best!"

"Glad you had fun. Sounds like you're in the car. Heading off to electronic components school?" Ryan asked.

"Right on both counts. I'm hoping my couple of days in the factory and some material to take home to study will do the trick. What's on tap for your Monday morning?"

"I'll try and write something. No idea of what it will be, but that's the fun of it." Ryan's desire to write brightened Miles's spirits. It was certainly an indication that Ryan was returning to some form of normalcy.

"Hope you come up with a Pulitzer-Prize-winning opus. Time to sign off. Pulling into the parking lot. Bye."

Miles grabbed his briefcase and headed into the office. The briefcase, like his suit and tie, were not part of his normal investigative ensemble but necessary to give him credibility as a businessman and the means to carry out this particular aspect of his mission.

He was met at the door by Peter and another man he didn't know. The sharply dressed man was half a foot taller than Peter and appeared much younger than his boss.

"This is Miles Darien. He's the gentleman I told you about. Miles, say hello to Phil Conrad," Peter said, introducing his Executive Vice President.

"Hello, Miles. We hope you'll find our firm worthy of your consideration," Phil said.

Miles thought Phil's tone sounded less than enthusiastic, which was understandable. As second-in-command, it was in his DNA to look out for the best interests of the company. A new investor could pose a threat to their already-successful enterprise, particularly if he tried to move the company in some different direction. It was also an indication Phil was not in on the little charade Peter had initiated.

Peter asked Phil to take Miles through the facility and explain each of the manufacturing operations. The detailed tour took up the balance of the morning. Phil showed Miles how raw materials such as steel and copper wire were transformed into sophisticated electrical devices. At each station, the employees explained in detail what expertise their particular job function required. Miles was impressed by both the sophistication of the manufacturing process and the skill of the people doing the work.

After a brief lunch break, Peter showed Miles to an office down the hall from his. It was sparsely furnished with only a large steel desk and a couple of well-worn wooden chairs.

"There are a couple of file folders in the right-hand desk drawer with documents that should provide you with some background on our Mexican partnership. Feel free to study them, but they're originals so they need to remain here. I didn't make copies, as I don't want to take a chance that someone might notice you removing paperwork from the building. You may, however, take pictures of them with your phone if necessary. I've arranged for you to spend some time with Arlene Powell, the head of our finance department, at three o'clock. She'll take you through our balance sheet items, which is where we would naturally begin with a potential investor. Be sure to ask questions, particularly as it relates to Mexico." Peter's organizational skills and attention to detail were again on full display.

"I will. What's the plan for tomorrow?"

"That depends on how comfortable you feel about portraying yourself as a customer. I have an appointment in the morning, so let's reconvene in my office at ten to discuss the next steps." With that Peter gave Miles a nod and left him to study.

The information on the Mexican partnership was enlightening. It detailed Peter's extensive study on the pros and cons of opening a manufacturing facility in Mexico, which subsequently led him to conclude a joint-venture-type arrangement would be, by far, the best path forward. It also included how they narrowed down the potential partners and eventually settled on Fabricación de Eléctricas Ltd. in Guadalajara.

Most enlightening was the exclusivity of the arrangement. Their agreement required Fabricación de Eléctricas to manufacture products exclusively for PG Parts, and PG Parts guaranteed to provide 120 percent of their current year's output for the following year and at a 10 percent increase each year thereafter. Add to that the value of streamlining their operation by eliminating all their existing sales and marketing expenses, and you had a big win for the Mexican company. The lower cost of goods for PG Parts made it a sweet deal all around.

Unfortunately, the documents didn't shed any light on the key individuals at Fabricación de Eléctricas. That would be Miles's first line of questioning at his ten o'clock meeting the following day with Peter.

His meeting with Arlene Powell was more stressful than enlightening. His knowledge of corporate accounting was limited, so portraying a knowledgeable investor was extremely challenging. If he had failed to convince Ms. Powell of his legitimacy, she did not let on. Surely Miles would hear of any missteps from Peter.

Miles spent the entire evening going over his notes, reviewing PG's product information, and developing questions for his meeting with Peter. He also made a list of some parts samples he wanted to take with him to Mexico to show the items he was ostensibly planning to purchase.

Around eleven o'clock he noticed an email from Bobbie asking for Ryan's contact information.

Here we go, Miles thought.

Miles walked into the PG Parts office exactly at 10:00 a.m.

Once again, Peter met Miles at the door. "Miles, thanks for being on time. I have to be in a production meeting at eleven. Arlene thought your meeting with her was satisfactory. Did you?"

Relieved, Miles replied, "I did. She was informative. I do have a few questions and a couple of requests to go over with you, but they won't take long. We should have no problem getting through them in the hour we have before your next meeting." Miles handed Peter a list of the samples he wanted. "Tell me about your Mexican counterparts."

"Excuse me for a moment." Peter stood up and walked out

of his office with Miles's list in hand. He returned a couple of minutes later.

"I'll have your samples for you before you leave. By the way, why did you pick these specific parts?" Peter asked.

"They are not particularly complicated items," Miles explained. "I researched their applications and saw how they were made. It appeared to be straightforward, so I think I can pull off sounding knowledgeable enough about them to pass inspection from the folks in Guadalajara. I also think by narrowing my focus I can cut short my time here and leave today."

"Good plan. Moving on to my partners, the principals at Fabricación de Eléctricas are two brothers, Francisco and Carlos Alvarez. Francisco, who is called "Pancho," runs the business: finances, personnel, logistics, and so on. Carlos runs the manufacturing and distribution. Pancho is smart, well-educated, and personable. Carlos is a highly skilled technician, a more blue-collar type, but don't underestimate him. He has a shrewd side." Peter obviously had great respect for the expertise of these two men.

"I assume you thoroughly vetted them before entering into your business arrangement." Even though he was sure Peter had done so, Miles had to ask.

"Of course. But you of all people should know vetting is only as good as the information available," Peter pointed out.

"Very true. Anyone else I should be on the lookout for?"

"Yes, Adriana Ruiz. She's Pancho's assistant and oversees the office. Based on my experience with her, it appears she has her fingers on the pulse of all that's happening at the company." Peter appeared to have great respect for her as well.

"Last question. Specifically what will they be told about my visit? Who I am, what I'm looking for? What have you authorized them to say or not say to me, that kind of stuff?" Miles wanted to ensure his cover was as buttoned up as possible.

"I just sent them a long email describing you and the parameters of your visit. Here, read the email on my phone. Can't be too careful." Peter obviously wanted to do everything he could to keep Miles's real identity a secret from others in both organizations. He gave Miles a couple of minutes to read the email, then asked, "Anything else?"

"The email and the samples should give me all I need at the moment. I'll head to Guadalajara on March 1 as planned. Please keep me posted on any new developments."

Just then a box containing the samples was delivered to Peter's office. He handed it to Miles along with an envelope. Miles's eyes grew wide as he opened the envelope revealing a large wad of cash.

"What's all this?" Miles asked.

"Ten thousand pesos."

"Sounds like a lot of money. Why?"

"Actually, it's only about 500 bucks. Always a good idea to land with some local currency in your pocket. Also, make sure your debit card is approved for Mexico. Should you need more cash, using your card at a local bank ATM will get you the best rate." Once again, Peter demonstrated his penchant for organization.

Miles offered his hand. "Thanks, I'll be in touch."

"Be sure you do," Peter said emphatically as he completed the handshake.

CHAPTER 13

M iles's phone rang as he was getting ready to check out of his hotel. The number with the 312 area code looked somewhat familiar, so he accepted the call.

"Hello," Miles said.

"Hi, Miles. It's Audrey Drummond. How are you?"

"Fine. To what do I owe the pleasure?" Miles wasn't sure he wanted to know the answer.

"First, I want you to know that Ken is fine. Second, I have a favor to ask."

Miles gave a sigh of relief. "I've been really worried about Ken, so thanks for the good news. What can I do for you?"

"Before Ken went on his assignment, he told me about your upcoming investigation in Mexico and how it would facilitate a vacation there for the two of you. Sorry we messed that up." Agent Drummond sounded genuinely apologetic.

"Thanks. What he's doing is vitally important, I'm sure. Once he's finished with his assignment, we'll get that vacation," Miles conceded.

"Yes, you will. On to the purpose for my call. We have reason to believe our old friend Jonathan Reese may have resurfaced and is establishing a new criminal enterprise in Mexico, specifically somewhere along the Southern Pacific coast."

Miles could not believe his ears. The thought that the FBI

might finally bring Reese to justice made his heart pound and his palms sweat.

"Unfortunately, even if they could track him down, the Mexican authorities have nothing to arrest him for at the moment. Besides, they have all they can handle with their own criminal investigations. The FBI has no jurisdiction there, so our hands are tied, officially." Miles did not see the next part coming. "We can, however, support you unofficially looking into his activities. If you're willing, we'd appreciate for you to be on the lookout for him, and if you come across any concrete evidence of his involvement in any wrongdoing there, hopefully we can interest the Mexicans in arresting and extraditing him. And of course, we'll provide you with appropriate expense reimbursement and per diem."

Agent Drummond's offer was incredible. The fact that his assignment in Mexico might give him another chance to affect Reese's capture made Miles rise out of his chair and nervously pace the room.

"Count me in," he replied in a voice louder than it needed to be. "I'd have done it for free, but I'll gladly take the financial assistance. After what Reese's organization did to Olivia Sims and so many others, nothing would make me happier than to see him in handcuffs or worse."

"I know how much you despise Reese, but you must keep it professional," she demanded.

"I consider my hatred for Reese to be justified malice," Miles pointed out.

"Justified or not, you are not law enforcement, so no heroics. Do not take matters into your own hands. Remember, you're only there to uncover his whereabouts and observe possible criminal activity. Understand?" It always fascinated Miles how she could so easily switch back and forth from her "Agent Drummond" persona to her "Audrey" one.

"Of course I do." Understanding and complying are not the same thing, Miles thought.

"I'll send you an encrypted file with a rundown on what we know and information on the expense reimbursement we will provide. Once you've looked it over, please get back to me if you have any questions. When do you leave for Mexico?"

"March 1."

"I'll let you know if any new information becomes available before you leave. Be sure to keep me posted every step of the way. Safe travels."

After they hung up, memories of Reese's coercion of people in financial trouble came back in sharp detail. Reese and his former associates conned numerous clients into pledging their transplantable body parts as loan collateral. Their desperation caused those misguided souls to sacrifice their collateral when they failed to come up with the cash to pay back their loans. As a result, these victims had to endure enormous long-term suffering and tragically, in some cases, death. The fact that this despicable criminal had avoided punishment gnawed at Miles ever since Reese had evaded capture. He vowed to do whatever possible for it to never happen again.

Before he left the hotel, Miles opened his laptop to view the information Agent Drummond had sent. Fueled by his hatred for Reese along with the details Audrey provided, Miles spent the ride to Lakeville developing a plan for the hunt.

The ride from Sun Prairie had given Miles plenty of time to digest the information from the FBI files and develop a preliminary strategy. As soon as Miles walked through his front door and saw Ryan, he blurted out the details.

"Wow," Ryan exclaimed. "That's a big ask. Locating Reese by yourself will be problematic enough, but uncovering enough significant criminal activity for the Mexican police to arrest him will be a tall task."

"True," said Miles. "But if there is solid evidence of Reese's criminal activity, the FBI will apply significant pressure on the Mexican authorities for his arrest. My bigger concern is that, once exposed, he may run again. It's critical for our investigation to go undetected until he can be apprehended."

"You look like you could use a stiff drink," Ryan observed, and pulled out a bottle of bourbon and two glasses from the liquor cabinet.

"Thanks. You'll need one too after I ask you for a huge favor." Miles's comment drew a quizzical look from Ryan. "I'd like you to join me in Mexico and assist." Ryan's expertise as an investigative journalist would be a tremendous asset in the search for Reese.

Ryan's quizzical look turned from one of surprise to one of excitement, clearly indicating he wouldn't need any convincing.

After they clinked glasses and each took a long swig of bourbon, Miles elaborated on his newly conceived plan. He first shared some key points from the FBI file he had received. A large sum of money, from an account believed to be controlled by Reese, had been transferred from Republic Bank Limited in Anguilla to BBVA Bancomer in Mexico. Over the years, Reese had been known to frequently visit the small coastal town of Punta Mita, just north of Puerto Vallarta. Hence the assumption of his approximate location on Mexico's West Coast.

"My assignment in Guadalajara should only take a couple of days. I can handle that on my own, so I'd like you to get a head start looking for Reese. A good place to begin will be in Puerto Vallarta. It checks all the boxes. It was close in proximity to Punta Mita, and it was the one city in the region large enough for Reese to hide in plain sight. The area in and around Puerto Vallarta is thriving, so there's plenty of money floating around particularly from expats and tourists. Also, from what the FBI's information points out, its local law enforcement is focused primarily on cartel activity, which would quite possibly allow Reese to operate his schemes under their radar."

"That all makes sense. What are the travel plans?"

"I'll book a flight for you from O'Hare to Puerto Vallarta on the same day as my flight to Guadalajara, and as close as possible to my departure time. Go ahead and check out accommodations there, starting March 1. The FBI has authorized me to book a place for up to a two weeks, so check out condo rentals. One with two bedrooms and a kitchen should give us enough living and workspace. Hopefully, Agent Drummond will authorize your airfare as well."

"If she doesn't, I'll gladly pay for the ticket. Another chance to snag Reese and some quality time on the beach is just what I need about now," Ryan said without a moment's hesitation. "I'll have to break my date with Bobbie though."

Miles only smiled back in response. Obviously, Bobbie had wasted little time in using the contact information for Ryan that Miles had provided. Any possibility of a new relationship would now have to wait.

The two men spent the rest of the evening making travel plans. Ryan booked a nonstop flight to Puerto Vallarta that would depart a little over an hour after Miles's flight. He also found two potentially suitable condos available for rent in March and sent the rental agency an email expressing their interest.

Miles's first call was to George and Cora to ask them to look after Molly while he and Ryan were gone. Not wanting to get their hopes up regarding the Reese portion of the trip, he decided not to mention it. Instead he merely told them he needed to go to Mexico on an assignment and that he'd invited Ryan along for some badly needed R&R, which necessitated their recruitment as dog sitters.

Miles would need more assistance from Agent Drummond than just an authorization for Ryan's airfare. He sent her an encrypted email requesting special clearance to travel on a commercial flight with a sidearm.

CHAPTER 14

Miles spent the morning in the office going over his open cases with Anne. She had all five files ready to go when he arrived shortly after nine o'clock. He quickly reviewed each one.

"These four are complete except for the write-ups and invoices," Miles said as he handed them back to her for disposition.

He turned his attention to the file marked "Carl Rafferty—Current Cases." Carl was Miles's friend and a prominent local attorney. Carl often hired Miles to do investigations on behalf of his clients. The only case in the "Current" file concerned Carl's client, Bradley Richardson. Mr. Richardson had been arrested and charged with allegedly breaking into and ransacking the house owned by him and his soon-to-be ex-wife while she was at the grocery store. The couple had been at odds over the valuation of the property, and the disagreement had escalated into a public shouting match between the two at a court hearing. Unfortunately, Mr. Richardson had sworn he would "wreck the place" rather than let her have it for what he described as "peanuts." Further compounding his problem, Mr. Richardson did not have an alibi for the night in question. He claimed to be alone in his hotel room that night.

Miles spent the morning studying the evidence the police

had accumulated to charge Mr. Richardson. Suddenly a case for Mr. Richardson's innocence presented itself, so he called Carl.

"Hi, Carl. Got a minute?" Miles asked.

"Sure. What 'ya got?"

"Compelling evidence that it was Mrs. Richardson and not her husband who vandalized their home," Miles announced proudly.

"Explain. I'm all ears."

"I carefully examined the police photographs of the scene and compared it to the listing of the damaged items. One fact stood out. All the damaged items were either photographs of the two of them, or stuff with importance to Mr. Richardson alone, like his golfing trophies. This strongly suggests it was actually Mrs. Richardson who did the damage; both to erase memories of them as a couple and to destroy items of importance to her husband, and then to hurt him further by implicating him in the crime. As for her alibi, she could have easily done her dirty work and then gone to the store, promptly calling the cops on her return."

"How do we prove that?" Carl asked.

"As you know, fingerprints won't help as they've both handled all these items in the past. One other interesting clue that does point to Mrs. Richardson as the culprit is all the damaged items were in drawers, on tabletops, or on the lowest shelves of their bookcases. She is only five-foot-one and would have to climb on something to reach the items higher up. Since she had already destroyed what she likely considered a sufficient amount of property to implicate her husband, why bother?"

"This all makes sense but it's highly circumstantial." Carl apparently wasn't sure Miles had nailed down enough significant evidence to clear his client.

"So is the assumption that he did it," said Miles. "No one

saw him at the house that night. There was no incriminating evidence left at the scene. My interpretation of what happened is no less credible than the case the DA will be presenting. The ball's in your court now, Carl."

"Yes, it is. Nice work, Miles. Thanks."

Carl now had something to base a defense on.

By the time Miles returned home, Ryan had a condo booked for them in Puerto Vallarta pending receipt of payment. Miles was pleased with the selection, and since it was within the allowance the FBI had agreed to reimburse, he gave Ryan his credit card to pay for it.

"Well, that's done," said Ryan. "I went ahead and canceled my get-together with Bobbie. Now I'd like to contact Ted at the *Times* to tell him I'm going to Mexico to work on a story. I need to get moving on something for him."

"It's fine with me as long as you keep the actual mission—and particularly the FBI's involvement—out of it," Miles cautioned him.

"Of course. I plan to tell him I'm looking into the incredibly robust, gay-friendly environment in Puerto Vallarta. Oh, and I'm taking my gay friend along as my interpreter," Ryan deadpanned.

"Very funny. What will you really tell him?"

"As I was looking into activities to do while we're there, I came across a couple of articles about the rapidly growing expat population. One article that particularly intrigued me spoke about how the growth in the number of employees who are allowed to telecommute has fueled an enormous influx of people relocating to warmer climates, particularly the lower cost of living locales."

"Do you think he'll go for it?" Miles asked skeptically.

"Absolutely, because I'll tell him I'm going there for a vacation so he doesn't have to pay my expenses. If he doesn't end up liking the story, he's lost nothing. Besides, I will actually look into this trend." Ryan appeared genuinely pleased with his two-for-one plan. "Oh, by the way, can I borrow the Camry for a few hours tomorrow? Since I had to cancel my date with Bobbie for March 1, I'm going to Madison tomorrow to have lunch with her. I can rent a car if that's inconvenient for you."

Miles gave him a simple nod both as an endorsement for what he would tell Ted and his request to use the Camry. He adjourned to the kitchen to see what he could cobble together for a meal.

Ever since Reese had escaped capture, Miles had been haunted by guilt for his part in letting him get away. This assignment was a real opportunity to finally see Reese apprehended. Miles intended to make the most of it.

CHAPTER 15

R yan spent Thursday morning working on an outline for the expat article he would be pitching to the *Times*. He divided it into two sections: Why are expats moving to locations like Puerto Vallarta? And: What effect has that migration had on the infrastructure and local culture? He was able to add numerous questions to each section. With each question added, he became more excited about the trip, as if hunting for Jonathan Reese wasn't excitement enough.

His excitement was interrupted by the ringtone of his cell phone. He hesitated to answer it when he saw the caller ID read "Rebecca.". Deciding he would have to speak to her sooner or later, he reluctantly picked up.

"Hello," Ryan said unenthusiastically.

"Hi. I feel terrible about what's happened and I don't blame you for hating me," she admitted.

"I don't hate you. I'm mostly just sad and disappointed." The somber tone in his voice was palpable.

"You have every right to feel that way. Please know—"

Ryan interrupted her. "Stop. Spare me another it's-not-you-it's-me speech. I'm well aware it's not me."

"I would really like for us to try to make it work," she offered tearfully.

"If by *'make it work'* you mean go back to where we were

with you wanting to sleep with other guys, that's not happening." The anger in Ryan's voice accentuated his response.

"No, I mean going back to just you and me," she said, almost whimpering.

Ryan couldn't help but wonder if she was sincere or just utilizing her formidable acting skills to get him back. Regardless, he wasn't buying what she was selling.

"Don't you realize that our relationship is forever broken? I know your preferences, and even if you were able to successfully suppress them they'd always be there. I'm sorry, Rebecca, but I need to move on and so do you."

After a brief silence, she replied. "Okay then. Bye." Her voice trailed off in a way that indicated to Ryan that she may have finally accepted, as he had, their relationship was beyond repair.

The emotional exchange had a strangely therapeutic effect on Ryan. Any thoughts he had of a reconciliation were gone now, and his resolve to move on had been fortified. As long as he had his phone in hand, he decided to call Ted at the *Times* to fill him in on his essay idea about the migration of telecommuters to the beach communities in Mexico.

After a brief back-and-forth, Ted accepted his essay proposal mostly based on Ryan's exemplary track record. The acceptance came with a caveat. He must have the first installment no later than March 15. With that decided and coupled with the closure from his call with Rebecca, Ryan headed to Madison in an optimistic frame of mind.

As was common for a late-February day in Wisconsin, it was chilly and windy with a drizzly mix of snow and rain, which accompanied him all the way to Madison. The weather did not, however, dampen Ryan's enthusiasm for seeing Bobbie again. There had been some attraction when they'd met on his previous visit to see Miles, but nothing came of it as he was deeply involved with Rebecca at the time. Now unattached, he was ready to explore this new opportunity. In a rare moment of coherent self-counseling, he vowed to proceed cautiously. Moving headlong into a committed relationship with Rebecca had cost him dearly, so if the friendship with Bobbie appeared to be escalating, he would definitely proceed slowly and much more carefully this time around.

He had agreed to meet Bobbie at noon at the Coopers Tavern, a restaurant near her office. Ryan had a little trouble finding parking and was further challenged by the angular one-way streets leading to and from Capitol Square. He arrived at the restaurant a few minutes late. He found Bobbie already there, seated with an iced tea in hand.

"Sorry I'm late. I was a little parking challenged," he said as he gave Bobbie a brief hug.

"I totally understand," said Bobbie. "The area around the Capitol can be congested and really confusing for a first timer. My office is just across the Square, which was a distinct advantage for me to get here on time. How was your drive in?"

"Damp but uneventful. So nice to see you again. How have you been?"

"Mostly busy with work." After a brief pause she added, "I understand you've been going through a difficult time lately."

"I'm sure Miles has brought you up-to-date on my relationship issues." Ryan knew he had.

"He just told me your relationship had ended. I've been there myself recently and it really stinks."

"It does. But we each have to move on to the next challenge, don't we?" Ryan pointed out in the most optimistic way he could muster.

"Which is?"

"What to order for lunch." Ryan's answer made them both laugh and exchange a look acknowledging new possibilities.

When Ryan arrived back at Miles's house that evening, he dropped his backpack off in his room and went in search of Miles. He found his friend making piles of clothes on his bed.

"Let me guess," Ryan said. "One pile is business attire for Guadalajara, the other is casual items for Puerto Vallarta."

"You should be the detective," Miles acknowledged.

"Aren't you going to grill me about my lunch with Bobbie?" Ryan was quite surprised the interrogation hadn't started the minute he walked through the door.

"Not yet. We have a bigger issue to discuss at the moment," Miles declared.

"What could be more pressing than that?" Ryan asked.

"Amazing you should say 'pressing.' I'm facing a huge challenge finding things that are clean and pressed enough for my Mexican business charade. I hate ironing, but I will definitely need to touch up an item or two."

"My sympathies," Ryan teased without adding an offer to help.

"Speaking of clothing issues, you didn't come to Lakeville with a trip to Mexico in mind. What are you doing for warm-weather attire?"

"Thought of that. First I did bring a few things that will work. On top of that, Bobbie directed me to a department store I would pass on my way out of Madison. Three pairs of shorts, two swimsuits, four T-shirts, and a pair of sandals later I am now fully stocked. I'm sure they have plenty of additional items in Puerto Vallarta should my wardrobe need expanding."

Ryan was pleased he had handled this even before Miles

could bring it up. It hadn't always been the case. When they were young, Miles was always in charge of logistics. What they would do. How they needed to prepare. On and on.

"Good, so you have time to help me with the ironing," Miles suggested, only half kidding.

Ryan gave Miles the finger, then turned and walked away.

As organized as Miles typically was, deciding what to take on a trip was not evidence of his organizational skills. He rummaged through his drawers, throwing likely candidates on the bed. Shortly after Miles finished sorting his clothes into piles, he heard his phone ring. After hurriedly digging it out from under the pile of clothes on the bed, he saw it was Carl Rafferty.

"Hi, Carl."

"Just wanted you to know the police dropped the charges against Bradley Richardson. When I confronted the DA with your evidence, she realized she had no clear-cut case. In this sort of domestic dispute, without an obvious culprit she just couldn't see utilizing her limited resources on it. Good job!"

"Glad it worked out." It occurred to Miles that he and Carl were about the same size and Carl was always impeccably dressed. "Do you, by any chance, have a warm-weather business suit I could borrow? I'm off to Mexico and need to look like a well-dressed businessman. None of my stuff fits the bill."

"I have a couple of suits that might work. If you're going to be home around nine tomorrow morning, I can drop them by on my way downtown."

"I'll be here. Thanks a million, Carl."

Miles was so sure Carl's suits would be a far better option than his own, and likely wouldn't need pressing, that he hung his suits back in the closet. Relieved, he spent the next hour deciding which casual clothes he would take. Before turning in, he popped into Ryan's room and handed him an envelope.

"What's this?" Ryan asked.

He reprised Peter Gonzales's advice. "It's 2,000 pesos. You shouldn't land in Mexico without some local currency."

Ryan laughed and pulled the passport wallet from his carry-on bag. He opened it so Miles could see the stack of pesos it contained.

"It's not my first time venturing overseas," he proclaimed as he added the extra 2,000 pesos to the stack. It was apparent Ryan had made one other stop on his way out of Madison.

Miles laughed good-naturedly, knowing he'd been had.

CHAPTER 16

A s Miles lay in bed, the reality he would once again face off against Jonathan Reese kept him awake. So many, including himself, had fallen victim to Reese's brutality that he felt immense pressure to end this man's ability to hurt others once and for all. Slowly, his anger and anxiety turned to resolve. Hopefully, his assignment in Guadalajara would be completed quickly so he could begin the pursuit.

He got up out of bed early the next morning and went to the basement to fetch his sidearm and a box of ammunition. Thankfully, Agent Drummond had made arrangements for him to travel to Mexico with it in his carry-on. She approved the request on the condition that he promise to only use it in self-defense. He agreed, but deep down he hoped he would have the chance to use it to exact revenge on Jonathan Reese, whose loan-sharking scheme had taken so much from his victims, like Olivia Sims. Miles couldn't help but think back to that final encounter in Reese's penthouse apartment where he would have been another of Reese's victims had the FBI not arrived just in time. The fact that Reese avoided capture that day gnawed at Miles ever since, and recalling it made for a night of fitful tossing and turning.

Carl promptly showed up at nine carrying a suit bag containing two suits. Miles made his way to the door, still bleary-eyed from his mostly sleepless night.

"I won't be wearing either of these anytime soon, so just hold on to both of them until we see each other again." Carl handed Miles the bag.

"So very nice of you, Carl. I'll take good care of them," Miles said.

"I'm sure you will. Hope your Mexico trip is successful. I'm due in court in an hour, so I've got to go." Carl waved and walked to his car.

"Thanks again, Carl," Miles called after him.

After hanging the suit bag in his closet, Miles washed down a third cup of coffee, grabbed his car keys, and went to meet Anne at the office so they could tie up any loose ends before he left for Mexico.

"I turned down two more cases this morning," Anne announced, somewhat annoyed, as she walked through the door to his office.

"Good morning to you too," Miles teased.

"Sorry. Hi, Miles. How are you today? I turned down two more cases this morning," she responded in a cheerful but sarcastic voice.

"Much better. I'm fine, thanks," he said, approving the revised greeting. "Unfortunately, you will likely be doing quite a bit of turning down while I'm gone. That said, I expect to only be gone for a couple of weeks, so if they can wait, you can certainly sign 'em up."

"Not likely. Everyone who calls seems to have a case as urgent as a fire alarm. Do you have anything else you need handled while you're gone?" Anne asked, steno pad in hand.

"Just please check in with George Willis from time to time to see how Molly's doing and if he or Cora needs anything. Also, please send Carl Rafferty a no-charge invoice for the Richardson case. I'm trading my work on that one for use of a couple of his suits."

"I don't understand." The tilt of her head along with a squint showed her confusion.

"I need to look like a successful businessman when I go to Guadalajara and nothing in my wardrobe will convey that, so I asked Carl if I could borrow a couple of things for the trip. Simple as that."

Rather than delve any deeper, Anne merely shrugged and retreated to her desk in the outer office.

Miles finished off the few remaining items of his office work around twelve thirty and, after a brief stop to pick up a sandwich, returned home to pack. Ryan was busy with the research for his essay when Miles arrived back at the house. They both agreed to finish packing before going to George and Cora's for dinner. They also decided to take Molly along and have her stay there so in the morning they could leave without making an additional stop.

When they arrived at George and Cora's, they were elated to discover Olivia would be joining them at dinner. She was on break from art school in Milwaukee and had come home to pick up a few warm weather clothing items before leaving for Florida with a couple of her fellow students. Given Olivia's and her family's suffering at the hands of Reese, Miles so wanted to tell them all about his assignment, but he had promised the FBI and himself that he would not. No sense passing along any of his anxiety or creating any unreasonable expectations.

"How are you getting to O'Hare tomorrow?" George asked.

"Just planning to leave the car at one of the long-term lots on Mannheim Road," Miles explained.

"Let me take you. No sense paying for a couple weeks' parking when I can drive you both ways," offered George.

"Very kind of you, George, but that's not necessary," Miles replied.

"Yes, it is!" Cora demanded. "He needs to get the heck out of here for a few hours. Since the new boat still hasn't arrived he's been constantly underfoot and driving me crazy."

Everyone at the table laughed wholeheartedly. Molly chimed in with a big bark. It was settled. George would pick them up at seven thirty.

After dinner, Miles and Ryan said goodbye to Cora and Olivia, and then each gave Molly some love as they walked out the door.

Once they were in the car, Miles shared a private conversation between him and Olivia. "Olivia pulled me aside to thank me again for all we did during her unfortunate near-death experience at the hands of Reese and his cronies. She went on to say she'd been in counseling and that her head was now in a much better space."

Ryan smiled, punctuated with a sigh of relief. "That's really wonderful."

Once they arrived back at Miles's house, they each retreated to their rooms to finish some last-minute packing and get some sleep. Even though Miles hadn't slept much the night before, sleep did not come easily tonight either.

When George arrived on Sunday morning, the guys were ready to go. Once they loaded the luggage and were ready to depart, George handed each of them a paper bag.

"Cora didn't want you to be subjected to airplane food, so she packed lunches for you," he said proudly.

"You married well, George," Ryan declared.

"Thanks to you, Miles," George acknowledged.

"All I did was introduce you two, and then got you a bullet to the chest for dessert," Miles pointed out.

"Protecting her from those thugs was worth the pain," said George. "Have you heard anything about that asshole Reese?"

"Nothing to report, I'm afraid." Miles's response was the truth in the sense that he wasn't allowed to report anything.

Ryan's relationship issues had been thoroughly covered at dinner the previous night, so for the balance of the ride, they talked about the new boat George had ordered and other lighthearted topics.

George pulled up directly in front of the Aero Mexico sign at O'Hare's Terminal 5. After exchanging handshakes and thank-yous, Miles and Ryan grabbed their bags and went inside to check in. As expected, the terminal was teaming with passengers. Thankfully, the line at the Aero Mexico ticket counter was short. After Ryan had checked in, Miles stepped up to the counter and handed the ticket agent his travel documents. After she checked his passport, handed him his boarding pass, and tagged his luggage she called her supervisor over.

"Mr. Darien, I'll be escorting you through security. Mr. Duffy, please proceed to your gate through the security checkpoint around the corner to your left," the supervisor said.

Miles was not surprised. He had expected some sort of special procedure given his FBI weapon authorization. Rather than go through the standard metal detectors, he and the supervisor proceeded to the TSA office. After his documentation was approved and his carry-on was thoroughly examined, an agent escorted him directly to his gate through the bustling throngs of travelers. Ryan saw them pass while he was seated at a coffee stand near the Aero Mexico gates. He would give Miles a couple of minutes to get situated at his gate before joining him. Since Ryan's flight was to depart about an hour after Miles's, they could keep each other company until Miles needed to board.

"Well, buddy boy. Another in our long line of adventures," Miles said once Ryan arrived at the gate.

"Much more than just a simple adventure. This time it's a mission," Ryan reminded him.

Their conversation shifted focus specifically to their pursuit of Jonathan Reese. Ryan reassured Miles he had properly secured his copies of the information that the FBI had supplied and would devote the lion's share of his time in Puerto Vallarta looking for evidence of Reese's activities. There was no question his essay for the *Times* would be his secondary assignment. They reaffirmed their decision not to engage with the local authorities unless absolutely necessary. As for the FBI, Miles had arranged with Agent Drummond for him to send her any updates either by a secure phone app she had supplied or via encrypted email. Ryan was to verbally relay any information he had to Miles, who would then send it on to her.

"See you in Puerto Vallarta soon," Miles said as he got in line to board.

"Sí, señor," Ryan replied as he turned and started down the concourse to his gate.

CHAPTER 17

T he flight afforded Miles the opportunity to catch up on his sleep for a couple of hours. It was unusual for him to fall asleep on a plane, but the two previous nights of tossing and turning had worn him out. The jolt of the aircraft's wheels touching down woke him instantly. His senses had returned to full function by the time the plane parked at the jetway.

The walk to immigration from the plane seemed to last forever. Both the line for Mexican citizens and the one for foreign visitors were extremely long in the crowded hall. After about thirty minutes, Miles passed through the checkpoint and proceeded to baggage claim. He passed through the checkpoint without incident. Given the contents of his carry-on, Miles was elated that the Mexican customs agents had, in fact, received the proper authorization documentation from the FBI.

He exited the terminal through a doorway marked "Taxi" and quickly hailed one.

"Hotel Riu Palace, por favor," Miles instructed the driver, using some of his limited Spanish.

"*Muy bien, senõr. Cómó estás*?" the cabbie replied.

Miles figured he'd better switch back to English before the conversation went any further.

"I'm fine. And you?" he asked in return.

"*Excelente!*" The cabbie must have realized that even a gringo like Miles would understand that statement.

The driver then named and described each monument and square they passed in great detail. He stopped in mid-sentence to swear at a motorcycle that sped past, nearly cutting him off.

"¿Eres tonto o . . .?" he screamed.

Miles didn't know the actual translation for the words, but the delivery made the meaning perfectly clear.

"That was close," Miles said, stating the obvious.

"Those runners are going to kill somebody." The cabbie's voice sounded agitated.

"Runners?" Miles asked.

"For the cartel. Dropping off or picking up money, drugs, you name it."

"How did you know it was a 'runner'?" Miles asked.

"Easy. Motorcycle had a box strapped to fender and no license plates."

"Won't they get stopped for not having a license, or for driving like that?" Miles said, showing he still hadn't grasped the big picture.

"The *policía* knows what I know. You don't mess with the cartel or POP. You're *el muerto!*"

They spent the rest of the ride in silence. Miles concentrated on the unique mixture of traditional and modern buildings they passed during their twenty-minute ride. Both styles were beautiful in their own way.

As they pulled into the driveway, Miles was blown away by the size of this ultra-modern hotel, which rose up forty-five floors from ground level. His well-appointed room was ready when he arrived, so he deposited his bags and decided to take a walk around central Guadalajara to stretch his legs and enjoy the warm Mexican afternoon. He wandered somewhat aimlessly. These days, getting lost was not likely as long as he had his cell phone with its GPS in his pocket. The fact that his skyscraper of a hotel was visible from everywhere made it virtually impossible. As Miles walked the streets, he marveled at the colorfulness of the city, with its artistic murals, brightly painted storefronts, and tropical plants dotting the walkways. Guadalajara was a large city, but so unlike the big cities he was most familiar with like New York and Chicago. Those cities were beautiful in their own neon-light sort of way, but the charm and whimsy of Guadalajara was breathtaking. Needing to unpack and wash off the day's travel, he cut his walk short after an hour of exploring and returned to the hotel.

Around seven, he ventured down to the lobby bar for his first official Mexican margarita. While sitting at the bar, he sent an email to his contact at Fabricación de Eléctricas, Adriana Ruiz, to confirm his arrival. After a second strong drink, he decided it would be prudent not to venture out, so he chose to stay and have dinner at the hotel restaurant instead. It was a smart choice, as the food proved to be excellent. As good as it was, he decided to pass on both the dessert and an after-dinner drink, and returned to his room. Before plugging in his phone to recharge it, he noticed three important emails.

The first was from Adriana Ruiz, who welcomed him to Guadalajara and let him know she would pick him up at nine o'clock the next morning. Miles responded with a brief thank-you.

The second was from Ryan to let him know he'd arrived on time and that the condo they rented was beautiful. He suggested they plan to talk tomorrow evening. In his reply, Miles agreed to call once he had returned to his hotel room the next evening.

The third was from Peter Gonzales requesting twice daily email updates on his findings at Fabricación de Eléctricas.

Miles agreed to do so even though he believed it would make more sense to send updates when he actually had something of interest to report.

Oh well, Miles thought. *He's paying the bills.*

Miles awakened early, showered, dressed and went out in search of coffee and some breakfast. He found the perfect spot just down the street from the hotel. The quaint storefront bakery on the corner had quite an interesting array of pastries. Miles opted for a fruit-filled croissant and a cup of strong Mexican coffee *con leche*. The bakery had no inside place to eat but provided picnic-table seating outside. Miles took a seat and went about studying the passersby, deciding where each was heading and what their story was. Was the woman rushing past heading to work? Was the man with the satchel off to the market? Sitting outside was a real treat. It had been months since the Lakeville weather would have allowed such a thing. After he finished off a second cup of coffee and made up several more stories about the people walking by, he returned to the hotel to fetch his briefcase and await his ride to Fabricación de Eléctricas.

Promptly at nine, a bright-red pickup truck with the Fabricación de Eléctricas logo on the door pulled up to the front door of the hotel. The driver was, as expected, Adriana Ruiz. She was attractive, in an understated way, with jet-black hair pulled back into a ponytail and just a hint of makeup. He guessed she was around thirty-five.

"Hola, Mr. Darien. So glad you're here," she said, adding a smile.

"I'm glad to be here and equally glad you speak English. My Spanish is extremely limited and, I'm afraid, poorly pronounced," Miles admitted.

"Multilingualism in today's business world is a huge asset, particularly for a small Mexican company that's in partnership with one in the States." The way she said it, with such a confident smile, showed how proud she was of her company.

"And to communicate effectively with gringo clients like me," joked Miles.

The ride was short. After about fifteen minutes, they pulled into an industrial park not unlike the one in Sun Prairie. The building which housed Fabricación de Eléctricas was also quite similar in design, except for its Guadalajara-appropriate paint job of a terracotta exterior accented with bright-blue trim. Inside there were no Ansel Adams photographs. Too black-and-white for Mexico, Miles thought. Instead there were pictures of Mexican street scenes and landscapes. The decor oozed cultural pride.

As they entered the main office area they were greeted by a nice-looking man with a thick head of pitch-black hair and a muscular build. "Hello, Mr. Darien. I'm Francisco Alvarez. Please call me Pancho."

"*Mucho gusto*, Pancho. Please call me Miles."

"So, Miles, you speak Spanish?" Pancho asked.

"Not very much. Just a few phrases. As I told Adriana, I'm glad you speak English. Love the artwork, by the way," Miles added, pointing to one of the pictures.

Once the small talk subsided, Pancho gave Miles a tour of the facility, which was humming with activity. The first thing Miles noticed was how much they utilized hand labor. PG Parts's factory was far more automated than this factory was. Since labor costs were low here, this operation could remain competitive while employing many more people in lieu of additional machinery—not a dissimilar formula to what factories in Asia had long capitalized on. Pancho's brother,

Carlos, joined the tour and went into detail about how each part was made.

The pride of the owners and the efficiency of their operation impressed Miles. He struggled to understand how these dedicated professionals could possibly be guilty of cheating their US partner. But Peter was convinced they had stolen something from him, so Miles kept his eyes open to all the ways that might be accomplished. He wondered if whatever was going on was all in the bookkeeping or if there were some operational shortcuts he might detect. Since it was unlikely he'd have a chance to look at the books, he would focus on the operational aspects. After the tour of the manufacturing process, they adjourned to a large conference room.

"I took the liberty of ordering lunch," Pancho declared as one of the staff members walked in carrying several bags.

"We wanted you to feel at home, so we're having cheeseburgers," Carlos added.

"Kind of you, but I'm a vegetarian," Miles said with a straight face. After a moment he let his embarrassed hosts off the hook by taking a bite of his burger.

Miles's little joke accomplished just what he hoped it would. After the laughter died down, everyone appeared more at ease and less guarded. If Miles's investigation was to succeed, he had to be in their confidence. After lunch, they all took a few minutes to check emails and return any important calls.

Miles decided to send a quick email to Peter Gonzales.

Morning tour of manufacturing facility did not reveal any "smoking guns." More later.

The afternoon activities began with a tour of the fulfillment center. It appeared to be a typical pick, pack, and ship operation. Interestingly, he noticed there were two pallets of unassembled boxes: one with "Fabricación de Eléctricas" stenciled on them and the other unmarked. At first he thought the unmarked ones just hadn't been stenciled yet, but then realized both piles had come from the box company that way, as the flat boxes were all strapped in bundles of the same style. It was the first detail that made him pause. Certainly something worth further scrutiny.

Once the tour concluded they returned to the conference room.

"Any questions about what you've seen so far?" Pancho asked.

"Not at the moment. I must say how impressed I am with the efficiency of your operation. You have been gracious with the time you've given me here today. Hopefully, as our next step, we will take a look at the specific items my firm is looking to purchase. May we reconvene tomorrow morning?" Miles proposed.

"Sounds good." Pancho said, then instructed Adriana to return Miles to his hotel.

On the way back to the hotel, he asked Adriana for a restaurant recommendation. After confirming he liked seafood, she suggested La Panga del Impostor. He promised to give it a try and provide his review the next day.

"Pick you up again at nine?" Adriana suggested as she dropped him off.

"Perfect," Miles agreed.

CHAPTER 18

After a terrific meal at La Panga del Impostor, Miles returned to the hotel at eight o'clock. He hadn't noticed them before, but three cars were parked at the front of the hotel in spaces marked *Hotel Riu Plaza Vehículo de Renta Gratuita*. Miles figured, based on his limited Spanish skills, they were likely courtesy cars, so he asked the desk clerk about them.

"Sí, senõr. You can use them for two hours at a time."

"Just what the doctor ordered," Miles decided.

Believing Fabricación de Eléctricas operated a second shift, he would use one of the cars to check out the factory at night. It would be far easier to avoid detection under the cover of darkness. The GPS on his phone took him directly to the factory. He drove by once to see if any of the executives he'd met earlier were still at the office. Thankfully their reserved spaces in front of the building were unoccupied, greatly reducing the possibility he would be identified should someone see him. To be safe, he parked down the block and walked between two buildings so he could approach the property from the back without anyone seeing him.

The loading dock was clearly visible through the chain-link fence in front of him. A rather beat-up, unmarked delivery vehicle was loading up at the dock. The skids going onto the truck were carrying unmarked boxes, the same type he had seen on his tour of the firm's fulfillment center. During the meeting that afternoon, Carlos had made a point to tell Miles about the favorable contract they had negotiated with DHL to handle all their shipments. This truck was definitely not from DHL and this shipment was obviously not headed to PG Parts. His suspicion that the unmarked boxes might be connected to the disappearing assets he had been hired to find, grew into a likelihood.

The truck was soon fully loaded, so Miles hurried back to his car hoping to follow the truck. As Miles started the car, he saw the truck in his rearview mirror, pulling out of the parking lot and rushing away in the opposite direction. He did a U-turn and followed the truck at a safe distance. At one point he was close enough to see that the truck had no license plate. He wondered, could this unmarked truck be a 'runner' like the motorcyclist the cabbie had pointed out on the way in from the airport?

Miles continued following the truck for twenty minutes through the city to a neighborhood of run-down buildings and potholed streets. When the truck turned down a particularly dark alley, he decided it was time to abandon his surveillance and head back to the hotel. Just then a police car pulled him over.

"*Qué* haces aquí?" the officer asked.

Miles decided it was in his best interest to play ignorant tourist, so he responded, "Do you speak English?"

"Yes. Now what are you doing here?"

Miles tried his best to appear frazzled. "I'm here on a business trip and the hotel loaned me this car, so I decided to see a little of the city and now I'm lost."

"This is not a neighborhood you want to be lost in. Follow me!" The officer returned to his car and drove with his arm out the window, waving for Miles to follow.

In ten minutes he was back at the hotel, appreciative of the officer's help and now armed with some valuable clues. He decided to keep the information he had uncovered to himself until he had a more well-developed set of facts, so his email to Peter simply said, *Nothing new to report. More tomorrow.*

As promised, Adriana was waiting for Miles as he walked out of the hotel at nine o'clock.

"Sleep well?" she asked.

"Quite well, thank you. By the way, the clam birria at La Panga del Impostor was outstanding."

"So glad you enjoyed it. Any questions before we arrive at the factory?"

"Just one. Where should I eat tonight?" Miles decided not to tip his hand regarding the shipment of unmarked boxes.

"Sorry we couldn't be with you last night, as we all had prior commitments. Considering you're leaving tomorrow, Pancho, Carlos, and I would like you to join us this evening for a night out."

"I'd like that." Miles accepted even knowing it would be hard to actually enjoy himself, given his hosts were likely guilty of stealing from his client.

Once they arrived at the factory they went directly into the conference room. The large table had been covered with an array of electrical parts and various packaging configurations. Thanks to his crash course in electronic components, Miles recognized a good number of the items and he would be sure to confine his comments and questions to those.

"Do you offer your parts in bulk or individually packaged?" Carlos asked.

"Some of both. The ones sold in our retail stores are, for the most part, displayed in bulk bins. Items ordered online are most often individually blister packed." Miles was relieved Carlos asked a question he had been schooled to answer.

The question-and-answer session went on for the next three hours. Miles thought they were buying his portrayal of a customer.

"Thank you for all the time you've given me. Your operation is top-notch, as are your products." Miles was actually sincere in his admiration for the organization. He did not relish needing to expose their wrongdoing.

Pancho smiled enthusiastically. "Thank you, Miles. Adriana will return you to the hotel. We've made a reservation for seven o'clock at Saloon del Bosque. It's a local favorite serving traditional regional dishes and drinks. I think you'll really enjoy it."

Miles wasn't sure if his enthusiasm was for the restaurant or for having completed the two-day interrogation.

"Sounds great," he said. "I'll meet you there at seven."

"I have to go past your hotel on my way, so I'll pick you up. Six forty-five okay?" Carlos asked.

"Of course. Thank you," Miles responded affirmatively, realizing any other answer would be an insult.

After returning to his hotel room to relax before dinner, Miles realized he had been so caught up in his assignment that he hadn't spoken to Ryan since his arrival in Guadalajara. He immediately picked up the phone and called.

"Been so undercover you couldn't risk a call." Ryan always loved giving Miles the business.

"Actually, I've been so immersed in this project I simply

forgot. I'm sorry. Have you found any evidence of Reese's whereabouts or activities?"

"No one I've encountered has seen or even heard of him. Not the local police, the press, nobody. One potentially interesting thing I've uncovered is a real estate development company that has started acquiring property here. The company is called Hollins Properties, Ltd."

Miles was puzzled. "Why is that interesting?"

"Thought you'd never ask. Before heading down here, I researched everything I could find on Jonathan Reese. One of the items I uncovered listed his family tree. Turns out Hollins is the maiden name of Reese's mother."

Miles could sense the pride in his voice. "You're good! What else have you found?"

"Nothing yet. I plan to spend tomorrow seeing if I can locate an office or other contact information on the company. What time will you be here?"

"My flight is scheduled to arrive at 1:50. Since it's a domestic flight, I should be out of the airport quickly." Miles was hoping to find a much less busy airport scene than the one he had encountered when he arrived in Guadalajara.

"Text me when you're in the cab, and I'll be waiting for you in front of our condo building."

"Will do. See you tomorrow."

Before Miles could shift his attention to Jonathan Reese, he had unfinished business to take up with his dinner companions. There were a couple of different ways he could play the finale. He decided to wait and see how the discussion at dinner would go before deciding whether or not to confront the issue head on. How that played out would likely provide the substance of the email he would send to Peter.

As promised, Carlos picked up Miles at the appointed time.

"I think you'll find the evening interesting," Carlos promised. Miles thought it strange that Carlos said the evening, not the restaurant, would be interesting. He wrote it off as nothing more than a Spanish-to-English vocabulary thing.

When they arrived at the restaurant, Miles was surprised to see it was a traditional-looking cantina. Somehow he had expected a fancier place, the type meant to impress a prospective client. When he saw that the restaurant featured live entertainment with traditional Mexican music and dance, he understood why Carlos used the term "evening" instead of "dinner."

While they ate, the business-only conversations they'd had during Miles's factory visit turned to a more personal nature. Spouses, children, favorite activities. Just the sort of thing you'd expect once the business side of things had concluded. Miles really liked these people. Hardworking, down-to-earth, dedicated to their families and, on the surface, honest.

Miles knew he had to get to the bottom of the asset theft or he would have accomplished nothing but adding circumstantial fuel to Peter's ongoing suspicions about his partners. He downed the remainder of his margarita and dove in, wanting to ask his pointed questions before the entertainment began.

"There was one thing I noticed at the factory that I forgot to ask about. What do you use the unmarked boxes for?" Now Miles's voice turned serious.

"There are various uses, like shipping machinery parts back to the equipment company for refurbishing," Pancho replied without a hint of hesitation.

Miles decided to lay it all out there. "Or like late-night shipments of off-the-books parts?"

Carlos started to rise from his chair, anger taking over his facial expression. Pancho grabbed him by the arm and motioned for him to sit back down.

"What are you suggesting?" Pancho asked in a surprisingly calm voice.

Miles had seen a separate dining room when they arrived at the restaurant. It was unoccupied, so he said to Pancho, "Let's adjourn to that room over there so you and I can talk privately."

Pancho nodded and motioned for Carlos and Adriana to remain at the dinner table. Once the two of them were seated alone in the private room, Pancho asked, "Who are you really, and why are you here?"

Miles knew now was the time for full disclosure. "I'm a private investigator hired by Peter Gonzales to find out why there appears to be a siphoning of assets happening on your end of the partnership. I think I've done just that."

"What evidence of that do you have?" Pancho asked.

Miles told him about the truck without license plates, loaded with unmarked boxes, that he'd followed into town. Pancho thought for a moment before responding. He got up from his chair and circled the room before answering.

"So, what do you think is going on?"

"I don't think you are stealing from the firm in the traditional sense. It's my guess that you are using inventory to pay the cartel to keep out of your business," Miles said.

"What do you suppose the cartel would want with our electrical parts?" Pancho was testing to see exactly what Miles had figured out.

"Seems pretty straightforward. They get the goods at no cost, sell them to the typical outlets at a nice discount, and still make a huge profit."

Pancho's facial expression turned to one of despair. Miles's hypothesis was apparently spot on.

"Listen, we have no choice," Pancho confessed. "Either we pay them off or they shut us down. Paying with merchandise is much easier to hide than cash would be."

"Except you were only able to hide it for a while. I'm curious, what do you get in exchange?" Miles asked.

"There are some benefits. First, we get to stay in business with a level of security. Our employees are protected as well as the company. I guess you could say it becomes a fringe benefit." Pancho half laughed at his analogy.

"You could also say it's a cost of doing business," Miles suggested.

"I don't understand," Pancho said.

"I recommend you be upfront and call Peter, or better yet, go to see him. Explain this is what you have to do to keep the business functioning. Playing ball with the cartel allows you to operate the business free of concerns about the safety of the operation and the well-being of your employees. Peter understands Mexico and will certainly understand that what you're doing is for everyone's benefit and not to line your own pockets." Miles had made a strong case for the benefits of coming clean.

Suddenly, the usually buttoned-up Pancho started to weep. "Thank you, Miles. You could have simply exposed what we were doing, and then Peter would certainly have ended our arrangement and moved the business elsewhere, probably destroying our company in the process. I will take your advice and see Peter immediately."

A great weight had been lifted from Pancho's shoulders. He motioned to Carlos and Adriana to join them. Once they had been brought up to speed, they too became emotional. Miles was right. These were good people stuck in a no-win situation.

Neither Miles nor his hosts wanted to stay for the entertainment after the emotional scene they had just been through, so they parted with handshakes and hugs. Once back at the hotel, Miles had one more dilemma to deal with. What to report to Peter? He vowed to let Pancho explain the situation directly, so his obligatory email only said: *Still working out the situation here. More to follow tomorrow.* It was truthful but certainly not the whole truth.

CHAPTER 19

Miles got up very early the next morning to check his email before packing and leaving for the airport. There were the usual collection of special offers from places where he had purchased products, spam emails offering all forms of miracle remedies for ailments he didn't have, and finally a couple from Anne with billing questions. Shortly after he finished dealing with the emails and packing, his phone rang. The caller ID indicated it was from Peter. He let it go to voicemail, not wanting to get in the way of Pancho's pending confession. As soon as he heard the beep indicating a voicemail had been left, he played it back.

"Hello, Miles. It's Peter Gonzales. Pancho just called me and asked to come to Sun Prairie to discuss the results of your visit. I assume it's not simply about you as a customer but rather some sort of a mea culpa for whatever is going on there. Please call me back and fill me in."

Miles knew he had no choice but to call his client back.

"Hi, Peter. Sorry I missed your call," he said.

"Apology accepted. So, like my voicemail said, Pancho called asking to come to Sun Prairie to talk about your visit. I need you to fill me in on what you uncovered."

Miles couldn't decide if Peter was angry or just anxious. He knew he needed to convince Peter to hear what Pancho had to say. "I think it's in the best interests of everyone involved if I leave the explaining to Pancho. You should know that I find your partners to be the good, hardworking, and honest people you thought they were when you selected them for your joint venture. Also, I believe you will want to continue that relationship going forward."

"Pancho will be here tomorrow, so I'll go along with your evasiveness until I hear what he has to say. Expect a call from me after he leaves to make sure I'm getting the straight story."

Peter hung up before Miles could say another word.

―――――――

Before he boarded his flight from Guadalajara to Puerto Vallarta, Miles emailed Agent Drummond to fill her in on Ryan's theory about Hollins Properties being Reese's current front. She would undoubtedly uncover any confirming evidence of his ownership, and likely a whole lot more.

The flight took about an hour, and after arrival, he quickly made his way from the plane to baggage claim, and out the door to the taxi stand. After giving the cab driver the address of his condo building, he texted Ryan that he was on his way. The ride from the airport to Old Town took a route that hugged the Pacific shoreline. Frequent glimpses of beaches, and boats cruising on Banderas Bay, were often visible between the buildings they passed. The streets along the way were colorful and lined with shops, their beachwear and souvenirs visible through the open storefronts. With the cab's windows rolled down, the mouthwatering smell of grilled seafood and barbacoa filled the cab. Soon they crossed the bridge over the Río Cuale and were in the Old Town of the city.

Their condo building was located on Calle Basilio Badillo, one of Old Town's main thoroughfares. Ryan was waiting in front of the building when the cab pulled up. They each grabbed a bag, and headed into the building and up the elevator.

"How was your flight?" Ryan asked.

"Easy, thanks. Anything new here?"

"Not concerning Reese, unfortunately. In other news, since I have no intention of returning to the place I've shared with Rebecca, I asked a couple of friends in New York to pack up my things and move them into a storage facility," Ryan said proudly.

"So, you're homeless," Miles sarcastically pointed out.

"I'd hardly call this beautiful condo with a spectacular view of the Pacific Ocean a homeless shelter."

"So, in a month you'll be homeless."

"Still working on that. You hungry?"

Miles conceded he was, so after dropping off Miles's luggage in his room, they ventured out to explore the neighborhood and get something to eat. They ended up at Mariscos Cisneros, a family-run place a few blocks away. It featured a traditional indoor restaurant as well as an outdoor food stand with its own grill. Since they had come to Mexico to escape the winter weather, they sat outside. After seeing the guy next to them served the appropriately named Giant Shrimp Burrito, they decided to share one.

Their conversation then turned to the task at hand.

"You said there was nothing new on Reese," said Miles. "I assume that means you haven't tracked down anything on Hollins Properties."

"Just the corporate paperwork they filed," said Ryan. "Nothing on any properties they've acquired. The company was incorporated in Mexico City, but the address is nothing more than a post office box. From what I could gather, a few well-placed pesos can easily facilitate anonymity."

"Eventually they'll have to do something with their properties like put up a building, sell preconstruction units, or just flip them," Miles speculated.

"True, but that could take months or years."

A strategy took shape in Miles's head. "Then I suggest we take a much bolder approach to draw him out. Rather than simply waiting for him to surface, what if we go to the local real estate companies and tell them we represent a well-heeled investor from the States. One who is looking to acquire several pieces of property like the ones Reese's company just purchased and is willing to pay top dollar?"

They agreed if their plan had a chance of succeeding, they needed to show interest in all similar properties in order to establish a credible cover story. For the balance of the afternoon and evening, they assembled the tools they would need to pull off their subterfuge.

At the top of their list of tools were business cards for their fictitious front company, Get Real Properties. They also needed to use assumed names to avoid any possible detection by Reese or his associates. Miles decided he would rename himself Michael Martin. Ryan chose Richard Daniels. For practice, the two referred to one another by their new names for the rest of dinner.

CHAPTER 20

After an early-morning walk on the Malecón, Miles's first order of business on Thursday was to find a printer. Ryan supplied Miles with a flash drive containing a digital layout he had created for the business card, and a logo for their fake business. The security guard at the front desk of the condo building directed Miles to a small shop only six blocks away on Calle Insurgentes. The shop sold cell phone accessories and computer supplies, and had a small digital printing operation in the back room.

Miles handed the shop clerk the flash drive. While he waited for the cards to print, he checked his emails and found an important one from Agent Drummond.

"Ryan's theory is spot on. We have confirmed that Hollins Properties is a Reese entity. Unfortunately, that information has not yielded any additional information at this point."

Miles and Ryan had arranged to meet around the corner at Café Catedral for coffee and a strategy session once Miles had finished at the printer. When Miles arrived thirty minutes later, business cards in hand, he immediately congratulated Ryan on his finding the now-confirmed Hollins connection. Ryan explained he had spent his morning sifting through online ads for local real estate brokers and came up with a list of six he felt were substantial enough to take an interest in their fake search for development properties.

"All six of these have four or more brokers, specialize in larger properties, have impressive websites, and purport to have personnel fluent in English. I think we should start with them," Ryan suggested.

"Makes sense. I'm concerned we don't have a real estate background and may not be convincing." Miles was always focused on credibility when doing undercover investigations.

"Valid point, but I think when these people see the big dollar potential of the type we're asking them for, they'll likely do all the talking. I'm more concerned about them trying to find information on Get Real Properties and coming up empty."

"I emailed Carl and asked him to register the company as an LLC. It's not much, but a quick search would turn that up and it would show that the business exists. As long as they don't dig deeper, we should be okay." Miles hoped these basic maneuvers would be sufficient to keep them from being detected.

"Okay. Let's give it a shot," Ryan conceded.

"Which one is first on your list?"

"Premier PV Properties. They're close by on Olas Altas. The website shows a Manuela Ibanez as the manager."

They finished their coffee and walked a few blocks west to the real estate company's office on Olas Altas. The storefront was floor-to-ceiling glass with pictures of numerous properties displayed on billboards in the front window. Inside was a modern office layout with six desks and a large conference table. Only one person was there, likely because it wasn't yet ten o'clock.

"Hola, I'm Manuela Ibanez. How can I help you?" she asked, motioning for them to come in and have a seat in the reception area.

"My name is Michael Martin and this is my partner, Richard

Daniels. Our firm, Get Real Properties, has been retained to find prime investment properties in and around Puerto Vallarta."

"While existing buildings are included in our search, undeveloped properties are our priority," Ryan added.

"Do you have any minimum or maximum price range or property size?" Manuela now appeared fully engaged in this potential sales opportunity.

Ryan smiled, having prepared well for the charade. "No real maximum. As for a minimum, any buildings would have to be at least twenty-four high-end units. Vacant land possibilities must be able to at least accommodate a building of that size or larger. We want to look at all viable opportunities. Our client has substantial funding and wants to get in on the rapidly increasing real estate values in this area."

Manuela asked them to join her around the front of the conference table so they could face the large-screen TV hanging on the back wall. Using her laptop, connected to the TV via Bluetooth, she took them through pictures of numerous available properties, explaining details about each as they went through the slides.

"A number of these look promising," said Miles. "We're not all that familiar with the geography, so can you fill us in on the various locations of these properties?"

"Of course," she said, putting a map up on the TV screen. The northernmost was in Bucerías, a small seaside town about fifteen miles north of Puerto Vallarta. Mismaloya was about twelve miles to the south.

"We've been told to look at a number of properties owned by another US company, Hollins Properties, Ltd. Do you represent them?" Miles was hoping to establish a quick connection.

"All the properties I've shown you are offered through a

multiple listing service. A few of them are clients of ours, the rest are represented by other real estate companies. Once you select the properties you're interested in, I'd be glad to provide you with the details we have for each, which may or may not include their ownership, as some companies requested that to remain confidential. To get started, I'll print out the list of the properties I've shown you here. Please review them and let me know which ones you would like to know more about and visit."

Manuela made a few keystrokes on her laptop, and the printer on the far wall launched into action. She retrieved the printouts and handed Miles a folder with all the documents. "Thanks. We'll review these and get back to you," Miles said.

After they left the real estate office, Ryan suggested they try one more place nearby. It produced almost the exact same results. They adjourned to their condo to sift through the paperwork to look for any information that would lead them to something owned by Hollins Properties. After four hours of googling, they discovered the ownership of six out of the fourteen properties. None were owned by Hollins. They decided to call Manuela Ibanez and ask her about the other eight properties. She immediately offered to pick them up the following morning for a tour of the properties they had selected. A tour wasn't really necessary for their investigation, but they hoped spending time with her might help reveal some valuable details about the owners.

Armando Delgado, Reese's operations manager, was on his way to Versalles to inspect the location for the trailer sales office. As he turned onto Calle Lisboa, his cell phone rang.

When he saw Reese's name on the caller ID, he took a deep breath. Every phone call he had with his demanding boss had been tense. His job had been a positive move financially, but it was taking a substantial toll on his personal life. His wife and children had grown silent around him to avoid invoking his newfound temper. As he answered his phone, he wondered if this call would only add to that stress.

"Yes, Mr. Reese," Armando said.

"Listen carefully. I've decided, in addition to a trailer for an office at the property, you're going to set up an additional sales office in the heart of Old Town at a storefront I've rented at 292 Calle Madero. I expect you to make this happen immediately. The landlord will meet you there at nine tomorrow morning to give you the keys and show you around. My projects in Mazatlán and Ixtapa are already operational, so I need you to have the office there ready to go in a week, without fail," Reese commanded in his no-nonsense, confrontational manner.

"Which type of development have you selected for the preconstruction sale?" Armando asked.

"I will email you all the details tonight. The packages with all the displays and sales materials will arrive on Monday. Have you hired any salespeople?" Reese asked impatiently.

"I've hired one who is perfect. Her name is Maria. She's been selling time-share units for three years, so she'll have no trouble with making empty promises. I have an interview set up with another former time-share salesperson, which I will now have to reschedule." He gulped.

"Why?"

"Because it's scheduled for nine tomorrow." Armando hoped his flippant response wouldn't be met with Mr. Reese's often-volatile temper. Thankfully, it wasn't. Reese simply hung up.

As they walked to dinner, Ryan asked Miles what he thought of Puerto Vallarta.

"It's wonderful," Miles exclaimed. "Amazing weather, incredible food, beautiful beaches, and a variety of great live entertainment."

"And one of the gayest places on the planet," Ryan teased.

"There is that," Miles conceded. "The gay-friendly thing is great, but why is that such an anomaly?"

"Because we live in a narrow-minded world. And not just as it applies to gay-friendly," Ryan pointed out.

The conversation continued over a whole red snapper dinner at Joe Jack's Fish Shack and finished with a decision to take in one of the city's famous drag reviews. They proceeded to the Palm Cabaret and purchased two tickets for that evening's performance.

"So, what did you think?" Miles asked as they walked back to their condo after the show.

"It rocked! At the only other one I've been to, the performers lip-synched and told bad jokes. These queens actually sang the songs and had genuinely funny one-liners." Ryan was bubbling over with enthusiasm.

"I agree. A definite step-up from anything I've seen. Changing subjects, any ideas on how we get Ms. Ibanez to divulge the names of the property owners who may have requested anonymity?"

"Great question. At some point we may just have to demand it," Ryan offered.

"I trust we can be more cunning about it than that," Miles assured him.

When Miles and Ryan walked out of their building the next morning, Manuela was waiting for them next to a black Chevy Tahoe SUV.

"Buenos días, gentlemen. This is Octavio. He will be our driver for today." She motioned for them to each take a seat in the rear.

"Nice to meet you," they said.

"*Mucho gusto*," Octavio replied.

Once the SUV was able to leave the curb and merge with the traffic, Manuela filled them in on the itinerary.

"We'll first head to Bucerías to look at one of the properties you selected. It's the farthest north. Afterward we'll look at the one in Nuevo Vallarta, and we'll finish with the last six, all in Puerto Vallarta."

Miles and Ryan played along throughout the tour, asking what they hoped were pertinent questions and commenting about the favorability of each location. Once their three-hour expedition was complete, they returned to Manuela's office to review details for each property they visited.

"So, what did you think of the properties overall?" Manuela asked.

"All good possibilities," said Miles. "Do you have some additional details to share, beyond the information on the sell sheets?"

She nodded and picked up a small pile of file folders from her desk.

"Here's what I've come up with for each of them in addition to the information I gave you yesterday." She laid the pile of eight folders in front of them.

Miles and Ryan each grabbed a folder and reviewed its contents. They pretended to analyze each detail, when in actuality they were only looking for the name of the owners. Six of the eight folders showed their ownership. All were Mexican companies.

"These two are the most interesting," Ryan said, and handed her the six they were rejecting. The remaining two they had selected were both in Puerto Vallarta and had no mention of ownership. They were both undeveloped properties. One was on the eastern edge of Old Town and the other was in Versalles. Ryan's preliminary work on his essay had already identified Versalles as an up-and-coming neighborhood with a rapidly increasing population of expats with permanent-resident status. The demographic information in the folder for that property would also be helpful once he turned his attention back to the essay.

"Other than what's contained in these two folders, is there anything more you can tell us about the two we've selected?" Miles asked, continuing to probe.

"Is there something specific you'd like to know?" she asked.

"If we're going to pursue a business arrangement with the owners of these properties, we'd like to know who they are," he explained.

"I'll see what I can find out. Anything else I can research for you?" she asked.

When they answered no, she offered her hand, indicating the meeting was over.

"Let's hope one of the two properties we picked will turn out to be a Hollins property," Ryan said.

"If it is, it would sure give us a clear path to Reese," Miles pointed out.

CHAPTER 21

When they returned to the condo, Ryan organized all the information he had gathered for his essay, including the information on the property in Versalles. Even though his primary focus was the hunt for Reese, he still owed Ted at the *Times* his series of essays on the migration of telecommuters to Mexico, and the clock was ticking.

Miles used the time to catch up on his emails. After deleting a bunch of solicitations and spams, he went about answering the important ones. The one from Peter Gonzales was of particular interest.

"Miles, my visit with Pancho was, as you predicted, very enlightening and a relief. He and I now have an understanding regarding full disclosure and how we will operate going forward. Thank you for your excellent work, and for guiding us to a positive outcome. Feel free to send along your invoice. Regards, Peter."

It wasn't often when his cases resulted in the happiness of all parties. It was highly unlikely his current investigation in Mexico would end that same way. He tallied up his hours and emailed the information to Anne, who would create the invoice for PG Parts along with the applicable expenses from his credit card.

The other important email was from Agent Drummond asking for a progress report on the investigation into the whereabouts of Jonathan Reese, and included the line, "All is well in Miami," which confirmed Ken was safe. He wrote her back, thanking her for the news about Miami and detailing the initial progress he and Ryan had made looking for Reese.

"I don't feel like going out to eat tonight. Do you mind if we bring something in?" Ryan asked.

"Works for me. How about pizza?" Miles suggested.

"The restaurant guide I picked up at the real estate company says L'angolo di Napoli has the best pizza in Old Town, and they deliver. I'll check out their online menu and let you know the options."

"Assuming they have a cheese, sausage, and mushroom pizza, order it for me. If you order a second one of your choice, we'll have some leftovers."

"Agreed." Ryan decided on his pizza and placed their order over the phone.

"No leftovers," Miles lamented after they devoured both of their pizzas.

"C'est la vie. What is our next step in the investigation?" Ryan said, turning the conversation to the matter at hand.

"I say we chum the water a little."

"How?" Ryan asked, sounding confused.

"We hire a subcontractor."

Ryan looked puzzled. "I'm not sure I understand."

Miles shrugged. "Rather simple, really. We get someone local to look for Reese in places we'd never think to look. While it's possible they won't actually find him, if he becomes aware someone is actively looking for him, it may cause him to make a move that will expose his whereabouts."

"How so?" asked Ryan.

"He may run, or maybe even close down his operation," said Miles. "Maybe nothing will come of it, or maybe something will. Anyway, I think it's worth a try, particularly since our 'someone local' will be the one looking. If we can at least confirm he's operating here, the FBI will have sufficient evidence to warrant engaging with the local authorities."

"Wouldn't that put the local subcontractor in harm's way?"

"It could, so we need to come up with a plan that protects them while still getting Reese to take the bait."

"How do we do that?"

"Still working on that part, buddy boy." Miles had an idea germinating in his mind about how they might pull it off, but he needed time to think through all the likely complications before he shared it with Ryan. In the meantime, he decided to email Bobbie to see if she was aware that the PG Parts case was now closed. She responded immediately.

"Peter called me as soon as his Mexican partner left Sun Prairie. He was extremely pleased with your work and the outcome. THANKS! Please say hi to Ryan for me."

As instructed, Miles shared Bobbie's comment with Ryan. "Bobbie says hi. Watch out, I think she's falling for you." Miles was ribbing him a little, but cautioning him at the same time because he knew how vulnerable Ryan was at this juncture. Not that Bobbie wasn't wonderful, but getting involved in something new while Ryan was still extricating himself from a bad situation could produce its own set of problems.

"I'm not rushing into anything at this point, but thanks for the warning," Ryan reassured him.

"Good. I'm going to bed." Miles retreated to his bedroom.

"Good night." Ryan didn't even look up from his computer.

"I have a deadline looming for the first installment of his essay. It's just beginning to take shape, and I want to keep at it while the words are still flowing."

When Ryan emerged from his bedroom the next morning, he found Miles standing over the sink, busily doing dishes in his underwear and an apron.

"Nice outfit!" Ryan teased.

"It's after nine. The scrambled eggs I made for breakfast are cold by now," Miles scolded without acknowledging Ryan's comment.

"Is that your best 'good morning' greeting?" Ryan asked as he poured himself a cup of coffee.

"Yep. That's all you get for now." Miles continued to clean up the small mess he'd made while preparing breakfast.

"I knocked off around one in the morning. Thankfully, I made some decent headway on my essay."

"Killing two birds with one stone, you might say."

"I'd say that's an apt description. Have you made any progress on your subcontractor plan?"

"I have, actually. After mulling it over for a while last night, I decided to pursue an unusual alliance to flush out Reese. I called Pancho Alvarez this morning to ask for his help."

"That's a surprise. How do you think he can help us?" Ryan could not have anticipated the answer he got.

"I asked him to arrange a meeting for us with his cartel contact."

Miles's bombshell answer made Ryan explode out of his seat. His face turned beet red and he screamed, "The cartel? That's fucking crazy! Have you lost your mind? Why in the world would you do that?"

"Simple," Miles replied calmly. "They can go places we can't and have the extensive resources we'll need to find Reese. I'm suggesting to use one criminal to help us find another."

The answer actually made sense. It also made Ryan shiver with fear of the possible deadly consequences. "Agent Drummond will be furious and will certainly pull us out of Mexico by our balls if she finds out." Ryan was stating the obvious.

"She won't find out. We won't tell her, and the cartel certainly won't."

"What could possibly be in it for the cartel if they help us?" Ryan wondered.

"Eliminate a criminal competitor and potentially take over his enterprise in the process." Miles's self-assured tone belied his own fears about what getting into bed with the cartel might lead to.

"Did Pancho actually agree to help?" Ryan asked.

"Yes, reluctantly."

"Reluctantly? I wonder why," Ryan replied sarcastically.

"I realize his asking a favor of the cartel could further complicate his situation, but he is also fully aware he owes me, big time. Besides, if this goes down according to plan, the cartel will owe him, big time." Miles was doing all he could to mask the danger by spinning all the positive possibilities he could think of.

"When do things go according to plan?" Ryan asked, not really expecting an answer. Then he added, "How soon does Pancho expect to chat with his cartel contact?"

"He said it may take a while. While he's in the States to reconcile with Peter, he decided to take a week off to visit some relatives in Texas. He promised to attend to it as soon as he returns to Guadalajara."

"So, I guess we're out of the line of fire for a little while then."

Miles interpreted Ryan's sarcasm as an attempt to mask his fear.

CHAPTER 22

Miles decided to shift into full vacation mode and relax now that the harrowing possibility of getting into bed with the cartel was postponed for at least a week. Ryan needed the time away from the investigation to finish the first installment of his piece for the *Times*, but he promised to be at least a limited participant in the vacation.

The whale-watching season would be ending in a few days, so Miles booked a tour for Tuesday morning with WhaleWatch PV. Miles shared with Ryan the information he'd found on the company's website about their focus on conservation, and the company's promise to always observe from a safe distance so no whales would be harmed during their tours. With that, Ryan agreed to come along.

When they arrived at the pier adjacent to the Mexican Naval Base, they met two other people who happened to be waiting to join the same tour.

The two-man crew of the tour boat eventually joined the four passengers. One of the crewmen took a seat in, presumably, the captain's chair, and the other introduced himself as their guide, Victor.

They boarded the boat and were soon underway. As promised, Victor began their education by explaining that the whales who populate Banderas Bay each winter are Humpbacks who migrate there to mate. They then return the following year to have their babies or to make more babies.

For the next four hours, the tour went back and forth from Victor's class to numerous amazing whale sightings. The whale sightings included males showing off to attract females, others fighting for supremacy to win the females, and a couple of females training their calves how to be grown-up whales. They even saw one of the males spectacularly lift himself totally out of the water, which Victor described as a full breach.

Once back at the pier, Miles and Ryan thanked the crew for the great adventure and said goodbye to their tour companions.

"All in all, an unbelievably exciting experience," Ryan exclaimed. "Well worth taking time off work for."

"It was so much fun, except for my sunburned nose," Miles lamented.

"You're supposed to reapply the sunscreen every couple of hours," Ryan reminded him.

"Now you tell me."

In the cab, Miles checked his phone for messages. His inbox showed he had received an encrypted email, which could only have come from Agent Drummond. Since the software to open the encryption was on his laptop, he would need to wait until they were back at the condo before he could read it.

Miles assumed the email was important, so he immediately fired up his laptop once they returned to the condo. The encrypted email simply said, "Call me when you're in a secure location. Audrey."

"What do you think this means?" Miles asked Ryan.

"Apparently, she doesn't want whatever she has to say to be overheard. There's one way to find out for sure."

Strange she signed the email so informally, Miles thought as he placed the call.

"Hello, Miles. How are things in Mexico?" Agent Drummond asked.

"Fine, thanks. What do you have for me?"

There was a moment's pause, which frightened Miles.

"Ken's been injured in the line of duty." Agent Drummond's normally calm, professional voice was halting as she delivered the news.

"What? Is he okay? What happened?" Miles's questions shook Ryan as well. He motioned for Miles to put the call on speakerphone.

Drummond explained, "His team was involved in a confrontation during the seizure of a drug shipment. Ken sustained a bullet wound to his abdomen just below his bulletproof vest. He's at the hospital in critical condition."

"Oh my God. I need to go to him. I'll take the first flight out. Is he in Miami?"

"Yes. I'll have an agent pick you up at the airport. Send me your flight information as soon as you've booked it. Miles, he's a really strong guy and the doctors are saying he is holding his own." She sounded reassuring as she said goodbye.

Miles, with tears running down his face, turned to Ryan, who was typing something on his phone. "Why the fuck are you on the phone right now?" Miles shouted.

Ryan walked over and gave Miles a big hug. "I was reserving you a spot on a United flight leaving in three hours. I just sent you the confirmation. Pack up your stuff and get moving. Oh, and don't forget to leave your gun in the safe. Like Audrey said, Ken's a strong guy. He'll pull through."

"He'd better." Miles mumbled as he went to his room to pack.

When Armando arrived at the new office location, the landlord was already there. The door was open, the lights were on, and there was an unmistakable fish smell the moment he walked into the building.

"Good morning. My name is Roger. You must be Armando." The landlord spoke in English without an accent. Clearly an expat, Armando decided, particularly given his American attire of a button-down dress shirt and khakis.

"Nice to meet you. Was this place a fish market?" Armando asked, cutting right to the heart of the matter.

"Yes, but don't worry. Our crew will be here this afternoon to get rid of the smell and give the entire unit a fresh coat of paint," Roger promised.

"I sure hope so. There is no way we can use this space as a sales office if it smells like dead fish." Armando wasn't optimistic but took the set of keys from Roger anyway.

Armando walked out with the landlord. He couldn't stand to be in the place a moment longer, given the smell. It surely would be a turnoff for the prospective salesperson he was supposed to interview in twenty minutes, so he waited for the interviewee outside. Thankfully, the smell of breakfast tacos from the stand on the corner provided immediate relief from the odor he had endured inside the building.

While he waited, he called Decoración de Oficinas PV to postpone the delivery of the furniture and accessories for a week. Thankfully, Mr. Reese had the foresight to ship the displays and sales materials to them as well. With any luck, the landlord's crew would have everything remediated by then, so Armando could have the office open in a week as promised.

Disappointing Jonathan Reese was not something that would be tolerated.

The candidate for the sales position showed up just as Armando finished his call. During their brief phone interview a few days before, Sidney had proven to be equally fluent in Spanish and English, an absolute must. At first glance, his appearance fit the job description as well. He was good-looking, well-dressed, and had a warm smile. Perfect for a con man.

"Hello, Sidney. Since the office is empty and there's nowhere to sit, let's walk to the coffee place across the street and talk."

Once they were seated at the restaurant, Armando began the interrogation. "So, Sidney, when we spoke on the phone you told me you previously worked for Pueblo Del Mar Resort selling time-shares. Tell me a little more about that."

"It was high-pressure, both for me to perform, and the pitch we were instructed to use on the prospective buyers. With so many units and time-share weeks in their inventory, there was endless stress," Sidney lamented.

"So, pressure bothers you?" Armando wondered if he had the right candidate.

"The only part that bothered me was, no matter how well I performed, they were never satisfied. There was never a finish line. Motivation by intimidation didn't work for me."

"This job has one goal and one goal only. Sell forty-eight preconstruction units in ninety days. There will be three of us working together to meet that singular objective," Armando reassured him.

"I like that. Will there be other projects or is this a temporary position?" Sidney asked.

"Good question. If you perform well, there will definitely be other projects."

Their discussion went on for another hour discussing compensation, the specifics of the building, the units, and the price points. Armando was satisfied he had the right person for the job but had one important final question.

"Let's say the project ultimately falls short of what you promised your customers. Could your conscience handle that?" Armando asked.

"Remember, I sold time-share," Sidney answered without hesitation.

He got the job.

CHAPTER 23

The flight to Miami was sheer torture. Miles's apprehension over Ken's possible condition coupled with the uncomfortable middle seat he secured due to his late booking made the flight almost unbearable. Further compounding his unhappiness was the lack of a distraction. The plane's entertainment system was out of order, and he'd forgotten to pick up a book or magazine before boarding. Even the airline's own magazine was missing from the seat pocket. All he could do was sit there and stew.

Mercifully, the flight arrived on time at 9:15 p.m. It took forty-five minutes for Miles to clear customs and leave baggage claim. As soon as he exited, a tall man approached him, showed Miles his badge, and introduced himself.

"I'm Agent Conrad. Please come with me."

They exited the terminal where a car was waiting right outside the door. Agent Conrad introduced the driver, Agent Jeffords.

"Do you know what Ken's condition is?" Miles asked.

Agent Conrad responded apologetically. "Sorry. We're not part of his team and haven't been given anything other than orders to pick you up at the airport and transport you to the University of Miami Hospital." Fortunately, the ride was just a little over ten minutes.

When Miles arrived at the intensive care unit, Ken was

unconscious with multiple tubes coming out of his chest, an oxygen mask covering his face, and an IV and numerous wires attached to various locations on his body. The attending nurse told Miles they deeply sedated him to alleviate his pain and to avoid sudden movements that might put stress on his wound.

Miles texted Ryan to give him an update, kissed Ken's forehead, and settled into the bedside chair for the night. Normally, he would have had trouble sleeping sitting upright in an armchair, particularly with the chorus of beeps coming from the collection of devices attached to Ken. But the long trip and the anxiety of what he would find in Miami had left Miles so exhausted he fell asleep almost immediately.

Early in the morning, he was awakened by a familiar voice.

"Good morning, Miles." Agent Drummond gave Miles's shoulder a light touch.

Miles quickly opened his eyes. "Audrey, I didn't expect to see you here. So nice of you to come."

"Ken's one of my agents, and a close friend. Besides, I recommended him for this duty, so . . ." Her voice trailed off, signaling she felt partially responsible.

"You picked the right person for the job. This job is inherently dangerous. Just an incredibly unfortunate outcome." Miles did his best to be comforting even though he was equally in need.

"I know." She paused briefly to collect herself, then asked, "How is he doing?"

"No change, really." Tears welled up in Miles's eyes. "The doctor who was in late last night said he felt optimistic about Ken's recovery, provided they can avoid any infection setting in. So, I guess we just sit and wait for now."

"Then I'll wait with you," she said, and pulled up a chair next to the bed.

Ryan put the finishing touches on the first installment of his essay and sent it off to the *Times*. His focus returned to the hunt for Jonathan Reese in hopes that one of the two remaining properties from their list would provide a connection. He decided to revisit each property to look for any clues on-site. The property on the east side of Old Town was within walking distance, so it would be first up.

The walk along the uneven, broken sidewalks on Calle Lazaro Cardenas took him past the Central Market, which was buzzing with activity. Fresh fruits and vegetables were displayed in several open-air stalls. The meat, fish, and deli products were housed inside the covered pavilion. Ryan passed by, vowing he'd stop back on the way home to pick up some food for his evening meal.

He found the vacant lot he was looking for in a prime location overlooking the Río Cuale right where it turned due west toward the ocean. The property was fenced off with no visible signage or evidence of activity. Ryan decided to see if any of the businesses close by could provide a lead. He stopped at a bar ironically called Qué Pasa and ordered a beer.

"Know anything about that vacant lot on Aquiles Serdán at Madero?" he asked the bartender.

She shrugged. "All I know is some company bought the building there and tore it down. Nothing since."

"Since when?"

"Been almost two years now, I'd guess."

"It's strange to go to all the trouble to tear it down and then do nothing with it, don't you think?"

"Maybe, but my guess is they're looking to add something more before moving ahead."

"Makes sense," Ryan conceded.

Before calling it a day, he went back to check out each property adjacent to the vacant lot. The property to the north was a fairly modern apartment building, which didn't seem to be a cost-efficient acquisition target if you simply wanted to tear it down to make room for a larger building. The other property to the south would be a much more sensible option. It housed a single-story home with an attached *lavandería*. The family living in the home likely also operated the laundry.

Only one way to find out. So, he approached the woman behind the counter to see if the building was for sale. "*¿Se vende?*" he asked, using his limited Spanish.

"No. *¡Vete!*" she said angrily, and used the universal two-handed wave to tell him to go away.

Her feisty response gave Ryan the distinct impression it wasn't the first time she'd been asked that question. The bartender's speculation might well have been correct. This property was likely not owned by Reese, whose history clearly showed he wouldn't go into a venture without all his ducks lined up. This situation was not buttoned up at all.

After a stop at the Central Market to pick up some food for dinner, he decided to call Miles for an update once he had successfully navigated the treacherous sidewalks and returned to the condo. "How is Ken doing?" Ryan asked hopefully when Miles picked up.

"No change yet. Audrey was here this morning. Nice of her to come all the way from Chicago just to visit for a couple of hours." Miles spoke as he walked into the hall outside Ken's room to talk. "What's happening there?"

"A couple of things. First, I just sent off the initial installment of my series to the *Times*. With that out of the way for now, I can concentrate on finding Reese. I've made some progress on that already. If my theory is correct, we can now eliminate the Old Town property from our list of those owned by Reese."

"Glad you were able to submit your essay. How did you eliminate the Old Town property from consideration?"

Ryan relayed the information he had uncovered and how it did not fit Reese's modus operandi.

"You're right," said Miles. "Reese is anything but patient, let alone willing to depend on something he can't control. So, now we can focus on the property in Versalles. See what you can dig up on that one. If nothing comes out of that, we're back to square one."

"I'm on it. Please keep me updated on Ken's condition," Ryan said.

"I will, of course. I'll call you tomorrow."

Nothing changed with Ken's condition, so after a long day of watching Ken's caregivers parade in and out of the room, Miles asked the agent standing guard when he would be relieved.

Agent Crowder looked at his watch. 10:50 p.m. "Should be in about ten minutes if Wayne is on time," he said. "Why do you ask?"

"Would you be able to drop me at my hotel on your way?" Miles answered.

"Happy to," the agent agreed with a smile.

As if on cue, Wayne arrived for his shift, so Miles and Agent Crowder were able to leave. On the way back to the hotel, it occurred to Miles he hadn't eaten since 7:00 a.m. when he had a quick breakfast at the hospital cafeteria. After Agent Crowder dropped him off at the hotel, Miles walked across the street to a delicatessen, which was mercifully still open. He needed comfort, and nothing comforts quite like a bowl of matzo ball soup and a pastrami sandwich.

CHAPTER 24

R yan left the condo early. After a quick stop for coffee and a cinnamon bun at the Paris bakery, he hopped into a taxi and instructed the driver to take him to the Versalles property on Calle Lisboa. The cabbie had dropped him off at the entrance to the mobile home park just across the street from the empty lot. Ryan had thought it was a strange location for a modern upscale condo building when he and Miles saw it on their real estate drive-by tour.

Just like the property he visited yesterday, the empty lot had nothing but a chain-link fence surrounding it. No signage, not a piece of construction equipment to be found anywhere on-site. However, there was one important difference. This lot was large enough to accommodate a substantial building without needing an add-on property. It dawned on Ryan that it made perfect sense. The location across the street from the mobile home park would have lowered the acquisition cost of the lot compared to any other lot in this up-and-coming neighborhood. Reese would certainly know this would increase his per-unit profit.

If this was in fact Reese's property, Ryan imagined the location would allow the sales personnel to suggest the mobile home park would eventually disappear and be replaced by another luxury condo project. This would give the buyers an instant jump in the value of their new unit. If Reese had a property in Puerto Vallarta, this was it.

On the way back from his site visit, he placed a call to Manuela Ibanez.

"Hola, this is Manuela."

"Hello, Manuela. This is Richard Daniels. I've revisited both properties we discussed having an interest in, and we've decided to pursue the one in Versalles. What is the next step?"

"Well, unfortunately we've just been informed the property is no longer on the market. The owner has decided to develop the property themselves." Manuela's voice dropped off in disappointment.

"We'll just have to keep looking," Ryan conceded. Before ending the call, Manuela promised to keep him up-to-date on anything new that came on the market.

Ryan did his best to mask his excitement. Now that the property was going to be developed, information about the person behind the project would soon emerge. If it turned out to be Reese, they had him.

Ken's doctor approached Miles, who was staring out the window, and tapped him on the shoulder. "We will bring Mr. Caldwell out of sedation shortly. We'll do it slowly, but be aware he will be disoriented and possibly agitated for a while."

Miles smiled. "Then he must be doing better."

"So far, so good. Once he's awake we should be able to assess his situation more precisely. When the nurse arrives, we'll need you to step out of the room."

"Of course. Thanks, Doctor Roth."

Shortly thereafter, the nurse who had been on duty since Miles arrived entered the room, carrying a tray with a hypodermic needle, an IV bag, and a covered cup, which Miles assumed was filled with water for Ken once he awoke.

As Miles stood up to leave the room as the doctor instructed, the nurse motioned for him to sit back down.

"The doctor said—" Miles began, but she stopped him.

"He was just following standard protocol. My nonstandard protocol is for a familiar face to be here when we bring him out of the sedation." She assured him this was best for Ken.

"How long will it take before he regains consciousness?"

"Generally a patient will start to awaken in about ten or fifteen minutes." She used the hypodermic needle to clear the IV line. Then she exchanged the IV bag feeding the sedative drip with a new one. As she attached fabric restraints to Ken's arms and legs, Miles lost his cool.

"Why are you tying him down like that?" he shouted.

"Because if I don't, he's liable to tear out his IV or worse." Her straightforward, professional delivery made Miles regret his outburst.

"Of course the restraints are a sensible precaution. I'm sorry I yelled at you." His embarrassment was evident in his voice.

She went about her work without acknowledging Miles's apology. She finished and then, just before she left the room, turned to Miles. "Please buzz me the minute he begins to stir."

Miles nodded and returned to his chair at Ken's bedside.

When Armando's phone rang, he knew without looking that it was Reese demanding a progress report. He reluctantly stopped humming along with the Mariachi music, turned off the radio, and pulled his car to the curb before he answered. "We're on track to open by the end of the week, I assume." Reese expected only an affirmative answer.

"It will be if they get rid of the fish smell so we can move everything into the office on Friday," Armando explained.

"Fish smell?" Reese asked angrily.

"I suspect the landlord didn't mention the storefront was previously a fish market. That, coupled with the fact that it created quite a mess when nothing was done during the six months it was vacant." Armando knew bad news did not sit well with his boss. He hoped the fact that the problem wasn't of his making would deflect Reese's wrath. He was wrong.

"Problems are always bound to come up. I expect you to fix them immediately. That's what I pay you for." Reese would not tolerate having his timetable thrown off.

"I'm on it," Armando promised, knowing no other response would be acceptable.

Immediately after he hung up, Armando called the landlord and read him the riot act.

"Roger, if you don't have the place ready to receive our furniture and supplies on Friday, we're done with this place." Armando delivered his ultimatum with all the force he could muster.

"Don't worry. Everything will be fine," Roger promised.

Armando was more than a little skeptical.

About thirty minutes after the nurse left the room, Ken began to stir. At first there were only slight movements of his limbs and some eye twitching. As soon as Miles noticed the movements, he signaled the nurse. It took her a few minutes to arrive. By the time she walked in, Ken's movements had become erratic and fitful. He wasn't really awake, just agitated like he was having a nightmare.

"Mr. Caldwell, can you hear me?" the nurse asked.

She only got a moan in response. Watching Ken's struggle to regain consciousness was heart-wrenching, particularly since Miles could do nothing about it.

As Ken's disorientation waned, the pain of the wound took over. He struggled to free his hands, pulling them in an attempt to grip his injured abdomen. The nurse motioned for Miles to try to help calm Ken. "Hi, there," Miles said, taking Ken's hand. "Can you hear me?"

The sound of Miles's voice caused a marked change in Ken's movements. They slowed dramatically. His head turned toward Miles as he tried to focus. After a few seconds, he replied with a barely audible, "Hi."

Miles kept talking to Ken, doing his best to keep his emotions in check. As the minutes passed, Ken became more and more lucid. However, accompanied with his increased awareness came the pain the sedation had withheld.

Now that Ken was awake and no longer needed to be tied down, the nurse released him from his restraints. He immediately held out his arms as an invitation for Miles to give him a hug. Of course, Miles complied and added a kiss on the forehead.

CHAPTER 25

R yan was having his morning coffee at the condo when he received a text.

"Ken's awake. He's in pain, but his condition has definitely improved. I'll call tonight to catch up."

Ryan sent a text back with just a thumbs-up emoji, even though he knew how much Miles hated them. A little lighthearted needling was definitely in order.

Returning to his plan for the day, Ryan decided to revisit the property in Versalles hoping to uncover anything that confirmed Reese as the property's owner, and if so, when development would begin. He and Miles only had the condo for a few more days, so he hoped to have some concrete evidence of Reese's involvement before they left. He gathered up his notes and his laptop, placed them in his rucksack, and left to hail a taxi. In less than a minute, he was on his way.

Once again his phone dinged. This text was from Ted at the *Times*. Its intent was not subtle in the least.

"Your first installment was excellent. Looking forward to receiving your next one on Friday."

Ryan decided to wait until he returned to the condo before he replied. Typing out a text in a taxi zigzagging through traffic was a futile exercise, and besides, Ted was only interested in delivering messages. Regardless, the only response that would satisfy Ted would be Friday's installment, and it wasn't ready.

As Ryan exited the cab, he smiled at what he saw. A small mobile home sat at the front of the lot on Calle Lisboa.

Looks like someone is setting up a sales office. If Ryan's instincts were correct, it would be Reese's organization. He decided he would return in a couple of days to check for a sign out front, or if he got really lucky, someone already stationed inside the trailer. He had seen everything there was to see, so he hailed another taxi and returned to Old Town in search of some lunch.

Miles kept Ken company at the hospital all day. Fortunately, he had bought a book at the hospital gift shop to read when Ken was sleeping. When Ken was awake, Miles did his best to keep him engaged by making small talk. Miles did most of the talking, as Ken's airway tube left his throat raspy and his speech diminished. Around eight, Ken motioned for Miles to come to the bedside.

"It's time for you to get out of here," he said in the strongest whisper he could muster.

"I can stay a while longer," Miles offered.

"Go," Ken demanded.

Miles realized Ken was right. It was time to return to the hotel and call Ryan to get a progress report. They still hadn't found Reese, and their time in Puerto Vallarta was running out. Thankfully, Pancho would return to Guadalajara in the morning, so the cartel connection—if there was one—needed to be discovered soon.

"How's Ken?" Ryan asked without even saying hello.

"He's making slow but steady progress. A long way to go though."

"I've made some progress on this end as well." Ryan went

on to explain all he had uncovered since Miles left, ending with that morning's activity at the Versalles property.

Miles's melancholy morphed into renewed resolve and a singular focus. "Since Ken seems to be out of the woods," he said, "I'm comfortable returning to Puerto Vallarta as soon as I can find a suitable flight. We really need to step things up and hopefully engage with the cartel to augment our forces."

"I don't get why we still need to get into bed with the cartel. We've likely found the connection to Reese we've been looking for. Don't you think we can flush him out into the open by ourselves?" Ryan reasoned.

"I see your point, but what if Reese gets wind that we're looking for him? He could go into hiding, or worse, have us eliminated. The cartel is our buffer in either scenario. They can find Reese without him knowing they're looking for him, and if there's any eliminating to be done, it would be without us in the line of fire. Besides, what if we're wrong about Reese owning the Versalles property?" Miles's logic was sound.

Given the obvious dangers involved, Ryan again pushed back against engaging with the cartel. "Okay, I see what you're saying, but I really feel like we're going to break this thing open very soon and we haven't even gotten to first base with the cartel yet."

"So, rest up. The next few days are likely to be action-packed. Ryan, remember our assignment. Find Reese and let the authorities take over. If the cartel finds him first, then we won't be going beyond the assignment. They may well choose to go beyond, which frankly would be fine with me. Oh, and please check on the Versalles property one more time before I get there. I'll send you my flight information before the night is over. See you tomorrow."

Immediately after they finished their call, Miles searched for flights. The best he could come up with was a 1:15 p.m. departure the next day, and a 7:45 p.m. arrival, with one stop in Mexico City. The departure time worked perfectly, as it gave him a chance to stop by the hospital to check in on Ken before his flight to Puerto Vallarta. His scheduled arrival time would allow him to reach the condo in time for a nightcap.

He sent out two emails before calling it a night. The first was to Ryan, which included his flight information and another assignment.

"Find out what you can about the cartel that controls Puerto Vallarta, and then see if they have any connections to local law enforcement. DO NOT ENGAGE!"

The second email went to Pancho Alvarez.

"Pancho, our time here is quickly running out. Please make the connection with your friends as soon as possible. Again, thank you for your help."

CHAPTER 26

W hen Ryan returned to the condo he decided to check in with Bobbie to, at the very least, express his continued interest in their relationship.

"Hi, Ryan. I'm glad you called. "Are you and Miles enjoying Mexico?" she asked, accepting Ryan's explanation.

"Yes and no."

"I don't understand."

Ryan explained, without being explicit, that Ken had been injured and Miles had left Mexico to be with him. He knew she would freak out that Ken had been shot, so he was intentionally vague about what exactly happened. He didn't mention what he and Miles were actually busy doing in Puerto Vallarta until Bobbie surprisingly brought it up.

"Peter Gonzales mentioned Pancho Alvarez was doing a favor for Miles without elaborating on it."

Wanting to end the line of questioning, Ryan answered with a half truth. "He's helping Miles with some information on a property."

Ever the attorney, Bobbie began the cross-examination. "Investment or second home?"

"It's just something one of his clients is interested in," he answered, continuing his subterfuge with a plausible explanation.

Bobbie suspected there was more to the story but decided she'd probed enough and changed the subject. "So, how long will you be staying there?"

"Miles is coming back here to Puerto Vallarta tonight. We plan to stay for another few days. Miles needs to head home soon to attend to his business. Anne's been holding down the fort back in Lakeville, but you can only turn down so many cases before the phone stops ringing."

"Will you be returning with him?" she said hopefully.

"Yep. I need to find a new place to live." Ryan's voice clearly expressed his lack of enthusiasm for the task of relocating.

"In New York?" she asked, hoping he would say no.

"I haven't figured that out yet. Miles offered to let me stay at his place until I come up with a plan. Looks like I'll be there a while."

Seizing the opportunity, she asked, "Let me know when you get back to Lakeville. I'd like for us to get together again."

"I'd like that too."

Miles had a two-hour-and-forty-five-minute layover in the incredibly busy Mexico City Airport. It afforded him plenty of time to clear immigration and customs with time to spare for a bite to eat. He also had time to place a call to Ken's hospital room. He was surprised when a nurse answered the phone.

"Mr. Caldwell's room. Nurse Hoffman speaking."

The surprise of a nurse answering the phone unnerved Miles, but he replied calmly. "Hi. I'm Ken's friend Miles Darien. Is he able to come to the phone?"

"Not at the moment, he's in the bathroom. Can you hold?"

"Yes," Miles replied with a sigh of relief.

His wait was short.

"Hey, are you back in Puerto Vallarta already?" Ken asked.

"Almost. I'm in Mexico City waiting for my connecting flight to board. Glad to see you're able to get to the bathroom. Bedpans are the worst."

"No shit!" Ken laughed at his own joke, which caused him to wince in pain.

Miles heard Ken's painful grunt and joked, "Whoever said laughter is good for what ails you must not have had a hole in their belly."

"Very funny. Travel safe and call me tomorrow."

"I will. Keep getting better!"

Just as he ended the call, there was an announcement that he assumed meant his plane was boarding. The only words he understood were "Puerto" and "Vallarta," but he knew he was at the right gate, so he followed the other passengers who were forming a line at the door to the jetway. Again, he lamented that the only languages he had ever studied, other than English, were Hebrew and Latin.

When Miles walked through the door of the condo at ten thirty, Ryan was at the high-top dining table busily typing away on his computer.

Before Miles could speak, Ryan put up a hand, clearly asking for his train of thought not to be interrupted. Taking the hint, Miles retreated to his bedroom to unpack. He hadn't been able to do any laundry in Miami, so he gathered up his dirty clothes and took them to the washing machine in the hall closet. Just as he turned the machine on, Ryan spoke.

"Welcome back. How was the travel?" Ryan said, looking up from his computer.

"Smooth, thankfully."

"What's the update on Ken?"

"I'm happy to say he's improving and was particularly excited that he was able to get up and go to the bathroom." Miles's disposition had come full circle from where it was when he left for Miami.

"I can imagine. Thanks for giving me a few minutes to continue working when you walked in. I was just putting the finishing touches on the first draft of my next installment for the *Times*. It's not due until Friday, so I have two days to edit it, which is more than I'll need." Ryan sounded genuinely relieved. "I'll also have plenty of time to work on our assignment."

"Good. Any news on the Versalles property, or information on the local cartel?"

"Nothing yet on the local cartel or their ties to law enforcement. As for the property, the only change I found was an electrical line running into the trailer. I'd say they're getting ready to open for business. Condo sales, I would guess."

Ryan's assumption was hard for Miles to argue with. "That's my guess too. It wouldn't surprise me a bit if they make an effort to seem like they've begun construction by the time they open the office. More buyers will believe their pitch if they see evidence of progress. I hope they're just as anxious to begin selling as we are for them to be. Once they're open we can pose as prospective buyers and finally talk to someone who could lead us to Reese."

"Or prove the property isn't his after all."

"True." Miles agreed. While the logic that Reese owned the property was sound, he had to be realistic about the chance that having that information would successfully uncover his whereabouts.

Before calling it a night, Miles checked his phone again but still nothing from Pancho. If need be, he and Ryan would do it alone, but having the cartel onboard would certainly speed up the process and increase their chances for success. It would also increase the chances for a violent confrontation.

CHAPTER 27

Ryan and Miles plotted out the day's activities over breakfast at Casa Nicole, a modern but decidedly Mexican place Ryan had discovered while Miles was in Miami. The walls were covered with a unique collection of self-portraits by Puerto Vallarta's hometown artistic hero, Frida Kahlo.

Miles jumped right into their tasks for the day. "Let's split up. I think it would be wise for me to go check out the Versalles property alone. You've just been there, and too many visits by either of us before they're operational might raise suspicions. Any thoughts on how you'll dig up information on the cartels and find out if they have connections to local law enforcement?"

"Actually, I do and it won't even require some elaborate cover story." Ryan had obviously anticipated Miles's question and had a plan ready to go.

Miles was intrigued. "Do tell."

"I plan to walk into the offices of Vallarta Newsday, the local online English-language news outlet, and introduce myself as a journalist on assignment from the *New York Times*. Which, of course, I am. I'll truthfully explain how I'm working on a story about the influx of expat telecommuters to the city and, assuming they'll talk with me about it, I'll eventually steer the conversation toward the local crime scene."

"I love it," said Miles. "You being you to get the information we're after is the perfect cover. As one professional speaking to another, you should be able to easily gain their confidence and really find out what they know."

They each downed one more cup of coffee and went off on their respective assignments.

Miles's visit to the site on Calle Lisboa proved to be enlightening, both figuratively and literally. When he arrived at the site, the trailer door was open with the unmistakable sound of someone working inside. He poked his head in the door and saw a man installing a light fixture.

"Hello," Miles said to let the man know he was there.

"Buenos días, señor! Can I help you?" the man asked.

Miles was elated the man spoke English.

"I live nearby and I'm just curious about what is going on with the property," Miles explained.

"I don't really know. Just putting in lights so they can be open on Friday."

The brief visit had given Miles what he came for. He and Ryan would return on Friday as prospective buyers of whatever they would be selling in that trailer. He had no doubt whoever worked there would provide information that would either lead them to Reese or turn their search in the right direction.

It only took a five-minute taxi ride for Ryan to reach the offices of Vallarta Newsday on Río de la Plata. Ryan introduced himself to the receptionist, who asked him to take a seat while she retreated to a large room filled with several rows of desks filled with people hidden behind their large computer monitors. It gave the appearance there were no people at all. The walls were covered with large TV screens displaying live webcam images from across the city, which gave the place a certain Orwellian feel. The offices of the mighty *New York Times* seemed quite antiquated by comparison.

After a short wait, the receptionist returned with another woman who introduced herself as Maria Rosales.

"*Mucho gusto*," Ryan replied, holding out his hand.

"What can I assist you with?" she asked without taking it.

Ryan explained his assignment from the *Times* and wondered if she would be willing to provide him with some perspective on the local crime scene, particularly how the growing expat population might impact it.

"Let me see if Ramón has a few minutes for you," she replied. "He covers that subject matter for us." She turned and walked to the back corner of the room, leaving Ryan to wait at the front desk. After a couple of minutes, she motioned to Ryan to join her.

"Ramón, this is Señor Ryan Duffy from the *New York Times*. Please help him any way you can."

The two men shared a handshake.

"Maybe someday we'll need his help in return," she added with a wry smile, then turned and left the two men to talk.

Ramón brushed the shaggy black hair away from his face and pulled up a chair from an empty workstation, inviting Ryan to sit. He then asked Ryan to explain his assignment.

Ryan did so in detail and added, "I'm curious if there are actually two different realities here. The reality of crime affecting the locals and those that affect the expat and tourist population."

"In some respects you are correct. There are different realities. For example, the police are much more, shall I say, tolerant of the gringos than they are of locals. The cartel also tries not to mess with the gringos." Ramón's diplomatic description caught Ryan off guard.

"Why not?" he said.

"Two factors. First is money. If the visitors leave out of fear of the cartel, their money stops flowing. The cartel is better off leaving the visitors alone and doing their dirty work to intimidate the native population and local businesses. The second reason is the politics of money. If crime against foreigners increases, more police presence will be required, which means the already-tight police budget will need to be increased to keep the money flowing. Remember, money has a way of ending up in the pockets of the powerful, regardless of which side of the law they're on. Right now the police and the cartel have an unwritten alliance. Don't mess with the money and we'll let everyone do their thing, so to speak."

Ramón's analysis made perfect sense. Ryan continued with a question directly related to his article. "Has the rapid growth of tourism and expat relocation changed the scenario to any great degree?"

"Most of the increase in crime we've seen is best described as petty stuff. Pickpocketing, purse-snatching, car theft, that kind of thing. Police Chief Renaldo sends out extra squads whenever that sort of activity spikes. Sure, there are some issues with white-collar crime, like real estate fraud, but the cartel is behind most of that."

The last comment reaffirmed what Ryan thought. If it turned out Reese was, in fact, a competitive threat to the cartel's real estate interests, they might well be interested in helping Miles and Ryan draw him out. He decided to seek out a connection that could engage the powers that be.

"You mentioned before there was an unwritten alliance between the police and the cartel. Is there any direct interaction between them?"

"I'm told the chief and the head of the Velasco cartel

communicate in secret whenever things need to be calmed down. Strictly unsubstantiated, but a widely accepted likelihood."

"One last question. As you've said, there's a lot of money floating around. Are there rival cartels vying for a piece of the action?"

"There have been from time to time, but remember the unsubstantiated alliance?" Ramón asked with a wink.

"Sí." Ryan got the point.

He now had much of the information he needed for both his assignments, so he thanked Ramón and caught a taxi back to the condo.

When Ryan arrived at the condo Miles was on the phone with Ken, so he retreated to his room, flipped open his laptop, and typed up his notes from his visit to Vallarta Newsday. Just as he finished transcribing his notes, Miles ended his call.

"How's Ken?"

"He's still in quite a bit of pain. He tries to hide it, but I can hear it in his voice." Miles's voice was clearly pained as well.

"Any idea how much longer he'll be hospitalized?"

"They're transferring him to a rehab facility tomorrow afternoon. They'll do an evaluation and then decide." Miles didn't want to dwell any further on his anxiety over Ken's condition, so he shifted the conversation. "What did you uncover at the news outlet?"

"I got exactly what I'd hoped for." Ryan went on to detail what he'd learned. In turn, Miles shared the information he had about the opening of the sales office in Versalles.

"Hopefully Pancho's contact will be on speaking terms with someone high up in the Velasco cartel hierarchy," Miles offered.

If nothing substantive were to come from their visit to the condo sales office on Friday, the cartel angle would be their only remaining lead at present.

"Any news from Pancho?"

"Just an email saying he's working on it."

Both men knew they were running out of options, and time. If they didn't come up with something soon, they would have to return home empty-handed.

CHAPTER 28

S ince they had to wait a day before the Versalles trailer office would be open for business, Ryan suggested they have a beach day. They decided to try La Palapa, an upscale but traditionally decorated place on the beach Ryan had uncovered on his way back from the news office.

The setting at La Palapa was ideal. They had front-row seats on the beach with an unimpeded view of the water, a collection of pangas floating just offshore waiting to be hired for a fishing trip or an excursion to Los Arcos National Marine Park. The constant flow of interesting people walking on the firm sand where the sea met the beachfront completed the show.

"I'm amazed how incredibly unselfconscious all these people look," Miles noted as he sipped his mango margarita.

"If you can't let it all hang out at the beach, where can you?" Ryan said, raising his glass in agreement.

After they shared an order of guacamole and a plate of fish tacos, they engaged with the beach vendors. Ryan opted for a foot massage while Miles got involved in an intense negotiation over a colorful tablecloth with one of the vendors roaming the beach, hawking their wares. The couple sitting next to them joined in, hoping there would be an additional discount for a two-tablecloth purchase. The man had his Hawaiian-style shirt unbuttoned, revealing his more-than-ample belly. In contrast, his slender female companion wore a tasteful, age-appropriate one-piece bathing suit. Once the negotiations were successfully completed, they introduced themselves.

"Hi. I'm Gregg Samuels and this is my wife, Claire. We're from Toronto. And you are?"

"Nice to meet you. I'm Miles Darien and this is my friend, Ryan Duffy. He's from New York City and I'm from Wisconsin. What a great place for a vacation!" Miles declared.

"Agreed," said Claire. "In fact we've come to love it so much over the years that this time we're here looking to buy a vacation getaway. That is, if we can find something that fits our budget and wish list."

The mention of real estate brought Ryan quickly into the conversation. "Have you come across anything?"

"Nothing we've fallen in love with," said Gregg. "We've started to look at preconstruction opportunities. The prices are lower, and the ability to customize a unit is appealing. That said, the uncertainty on whether it will actually be built, and when, makes me nervous."

"We happened to hear there's a new project about to go on sale in Versalles," said Ryan. "Have you seen anything about it?"

"Not yet, but I wonder if it's the same building in Versalles advertised in the window of that storefront they're working on over on Madero," wondered Claire.

Miles gave Ryan a wink. If this were, in fact, the same project it would be a lot easier to check it out in Old Town on foot.

Just then, another beach vendor selling Hawaiian-style shirts approached. Gregg jumped to his feet and waved the man over. "Love these shirts, and they're only 200 pesos."

"The perfect costume for a visit to the real estate office," Miles whispered to Ryan.

Ryan nodded as he sorted through the vendor's inventory

of colorful prints in search of the perfect tourist shirts. He finally settled on a bright-green one with yellow fish swimming around on it. Miles bought a blue one with a more subdued geometric print for himself, and a similar gray one as a gift for Ken. After one more round of drinks, they paid their bill, collected their purchases, and said goodbye to Gregg and Claire.

"Perfect beach day!" Ryan declared as they walked back to the condo.

"I agree. By the way, do you plan on wearing that shirt to your next meeting at the *Times*?" Miles joked.

Ryan responded, as he always did to Miles's needling, by giving him the finger. When Miles and Ryan got back to the condo, Miles decided he would take a nap.

"I'm a lousy day-drinker," he confessed. "I need to lie down for a little while."

Ryan yawned. "I could use one myself, but my piece for the *Times* is due tomorrow. I need to add the information I got yesterday about the local crime scene to put the finishing touches on it. Enjoy your nap."

When Miles awoke and checked his watch, he was amazed to see he had slept for two hours. He shook out the cobwebs, washed his face, and went to see what Ryan was up to. The screen on Ryan's laptop was down, which Miles took to mean the piece for the *Times* had been completed. Ryan's bedroom door was closed, so the relief of finishing his work coupled with the day at the beach had apparently taken its toll on him as well.

Miles grabbed a bottle of Topo Chico sparkling water and went out on the balcony to call Ken. His call went right to voicemail. He left a message, and spent a few more minutes enjoying the view before going back inside to take a shower.

When he emerged from his shower all clean, refreshed, and dressed, Ryan was on the balcony engaging in an animated phone conversation.

"Let me repeat, there is no chance of me changing my mind. Please let Hank and his crew in on Saturday morning. I've given them the list of things we agreed are mine. You're welcome to make sure they only take those things. There is nothing more to say." Ryan hung up without waiting for her agreement.

Miles gave him a minute to calm down before asking, "She wants another chance, I assume?"

"She says she's worked out her issues with the help of her therapist and is supposedly ready to make a commitment to monogamy. The thing is, even if she has changed, so have I. The feelings I had for her have vanished." Ryan's voice showed no sign of sadness.

"Glad to hear you've come to terms with it." Miles acknowledged, then realizing it was a good time to switch subjects, added, "So, what should we do tonight?"

"There's a seven o'clock show at the Incanto piano bar featuring a Latino group that looks interesting. Along the way, we'll pass the real estate office the folks at the beach mentioned." Ryan had obviously had time to scope out a plan for the evening while Miles was in the shower.

"Food?" Miles's one-track mind spoke up.

"Yes, they serve food. Any more questions?"

When they got to the sales office, several workers were busy unloading a truck filled with office equipment: a couple of desks, a conference table, an assortment of chairs, and several posters with building images affixed to mounting boards. Miles approached the worker who appeared to be in charge.

"Perdóname," Miles said, using one of the few Spanish expressions he knew.

"Sí, señor?" the man replied.

Miles had no alternative but to continue in English. "When will the office be open?"

"Mañana," the man answered, apparently understanding the question.

"Gracias!" Miles said, and motioned to Ryan it was time to move on.

"How come you didn't ask that guy any more questions?" Ryan asked.

"Simple. He was obviously just part of the delivery and setup crew. If he had been one of the office staff, he would have responded in English and likely even started a sales pitch. At least it looks like things will start to get interesting first thing tomorrow."

CHAPTER 29

A fter filing his article with the *Times*, Ryan joined Miles over breakfast to plot their strategy for approaching the real estate office on Madero, each adding details derived from years of experience in their respective disciplines.

"I think we need to pose as a gay couple excited to become permanent members of the LGBTQ community here," Miles recommended.

"Why a gay couple?" Ryan asked.

"It seems logical that two guys wanting to buy a place together would be a couple, doesn't it? Don't worry, it's just a cover story," Miles teased.

"Very funny. It actually does make sense, but I had another concept in mind," Ryan offered.

"What's your angle?"

Ryan collected his thoughts for a moment before offering his alternative plan. "Rather than use your story or the one we told Manuela Ibanez at Premier PV Properties, my idea is for us to pose as real estate investors looking to acquire multiple units to rent out on Airbnb. The size of the sales opportunity and the fact they will be dealing with the actual buyers might help us quickly get to someone higher up in the organization, maybe even Reese."

"Okay, we'll be a married gay couple looking to purchase multiple units to rent out. How's that!" Miles proposed.

Miles's proposal made Ryan laugh so hard he had trouble catching his breath. "Won't we need wedding rings as part of our disguises?" Ryan asked sarcastically once he collected himself.

"All right. Not married," Miles conceded with a fake frown.

The lighthearted exchange took the edge off their nervousness, as they both had the sense something significant was about to happen.

On their way to check out the real estate office, Miles and Ryan rehearsed their story. They would be posing as a gay couple from Chicago who had been coming to Puerto Vallarta for a few years and had fallen in love with it. They wanted to buy four or five nice units to rent out on Airbnb with a few weeks of vacation for themselves thrown in. They'd prefer to pick out their own furnishings, so purchasing preconstruction "white box" units would be ideal.

"That pretense should make us their ideal target client," said Miles. "Let's hope we don't have to go through all these motions only to find out this property isn't one of Reese's." His comment drew a nod from Ryan.

The first thing they noticed when they arrived at the real estate office on Madero was the sign over the door reading, "Banderas Bay Villas." Inside the office, three people whom they assumed were staff members were busily arranging the furniture. A well-dressed man who appeared to be in charge looked up. "May I help you?"

"Quite possibly. I'm Michael Martin and this is my partner, Richard Daniels," Miles said.

"*Mucho gusto*. My name is Armando Delgado and I'm the manager of this office. How may I be of service?"

Miles proceeded to recite, in great detail, the backstory he and Ryan had concocted.

Ryan interjected a few tidbits as well. "We've checked with a number of other local companies, and they just did not have the type of units we're looking for. Also, it would be ideal if we had all of our units in the same building. It will make managing them so much easier." Ryan was giving Armando the perfect answers to questions he hadn't even asked yet.

"Well, señores, I think we may just have exactly what you're looking for." As he directed Miles and Ryan to join him at the conference table in his glass-enclosed private office, Armando was already counting the pesos his commission would bring, not to mention the forthcoming accolades from his demanding boss.

Miles caught Armando giving a look to his two salespeople, suggesting they should kick themselves for not being the one who greeted the two gringos in the funny shirts.

Once they were all seated, Armando shifted into full pitch mode. "The six stories of apartments will have a total of forty-eight units. Each floor will feature five two-bedroom units and three one-bedroom units. Since we are in the preconstruction stage there is the ability to combine a one-bedroom and a two-bedroom unit to create a three-bedroom unit. Our two-bedroom units range from $425,000 US dollars to $595,000 US dollars. The one-bedroom units start at $330,000 US dollars to $360,000 US dollars."

"I assume which floor and configuration will determine the specific unit price?" Miles speculated.

"That is correct. Here are the layouts for each unit. Feel free to take your time to study them. I need to excuse myself for a few minutes to meet with my team." Armando closed the office door and joined his team in the main office area.

"What's our next step?" Ryan asked.

Before answering, Miles stood with his back to the door to be sure he wasn't heard. "First, we express interest in two one-bedroom and two two-bedroom units. Then we ask about terms, and so on. At that point, I think we'll need to move to the big deal of the day. Who are we actually doing business with?"

"I think we may need to slow play this a little bit," Ryan suggested. "Maybe even suggest we need to think things over and then maybe schedule another meeting. Serious buyers wouldn't just jump in all at once."

"Good thinking."

Armando was on his way to rejoin them, so they shifted their conversation to critiques of the various condo layouts.

"I like the two-bedroom corner units," Ryan said as Armando reentered the room.

"Yes. Those are the most desirable. Two different views with a wraparound balcony," Armando explained.

Miles rose from his chair, walked around to Armando's side of the table, and picked up the building plans.

"Armando, Richard and I have another meeting in thirty minutes, so here's what I'd like you to do for us. Please write a proposal including these four units." Miles laid down the plans in front of Armando and pointed to the layout of each unit they wanted and the floors they would consider. "Include all the financial details and timing for each step in your proposal."

"Of course. I can have it for you on Monday afternoon, if that works," Armando replied.

"It does," said Miles. "One more thing. Before we'll even consider moving ahead, it's important the financial details include information about the entity we'll actually be doing business with. Please see that your proposal provides that information."

"I understand. Shall we say two o'clock on Monday afternoon then?"

"We'll be here," Miles confirmed as they got up to leave.

The meeting had gone about as well as they could have possibly hoped. If Armando delivered on their last request, they would be well on their way to learning if Reese was, in fact, the person behind the Banderas Bay Villas project.

As they walked back to the condo, Miles's phone beeped with a text. It was the long-awaited text from Pancho.

"My contact has arranged the meeting you requested for tomorrow morning. Please call me for details."

They now had a Saturday morning meeting with the local cartel contact followed on Monday afternoon with what figured to be an enlightening discussion with Armando about the condos and their ownership. This was shaping up to be the perfect one-two punch.

CHAPTER 30

A fter putting away some groceries, Miles announced, "I'll call Pancho to get the details on the meeting he's arranged. Then I need to check on Ken. I'm worried about him since he hasn't returned my call."

Ryan grabbed a couple of beers from the refrigerator. "Sounds good. I'm going up to the pool. Join me when you're done?"

Miles accepted Ryan's invitation and then placed a call to Pancho.

"Hello, Miles," said Pancho. "Here's what I have for you. At nine tomorrow morning you need to be at a place called the Salty Caesar. There will be a man sitting alone at a table outside. His name is Stefan. All I know is that he's willing to talk to you. I did not get any indication from my contact how much help he will offer." Pancho almost sounded apologetic.

"Pancho, I really appreciate what you've done." Things were quickly escalating. While he was grateful Pancho had arranged the meeting, Miles couldn't help but feel apprehensive about engaging with the local criminal element.

"Miles, I am forever in your debt. If there is ever anything more I can do for you, all you need to do is ask."

"Thank you." Miles ended the call and turned his attention to Ken, who hadn't returned his call from the night before.

"Sorry I didn't return your call," Ken said when he answered. "I've been on the move for the last day or two."

"What do you mean 'on the move'?"

"They sent me back to the hospital to do some tests to measure my progress. The healing process is right on schedule. They did, however, discover a little something they're concerned about." It was apparent by the way he said it that he was downplaying the circumstances.

"If they're concerned about it, it's unlikely to be only a little something," Miles said.

"The x-ray showed some form of mass near my pancreas. There is no definitive diagnosis and it's likely nothing. I have some additional tests scheduled for Monday. Hopefully we'll get to the bottom of it then."

While Ken was obviously doing his best to minimize the serious possibilities, Miles could hear the trepidation in his voice.

"I sure hope you're right it's nothing," he said. "You've been through quite enough already."

Miles decided it might be best for both of them if he changed the subject, so he shifted the conversation to a report on the progress of their hunt for Reese.

"Have you updated Agent Drummond on what you've learned?" Ken asked.

"Not yet. I'm hoping to have more concrete evidence before I do."

"Makes sense. Call me tomorrow?"

"Of course," Miles said.

The scene at the rooftop pool was a refreshing change from Miles's serious phone calls. As usual, there was an eclectic gathering of gay and straight, American and Canadian, all accompanied by copious quantities of beer, wine, cocktails, and snacks. Afternoons on the rooftop were always a nonstop pool party.

"How's Ken?" Ryan asked innocently as he handed Miles a bottle of Modelo Especial.

"He shared some scary news with me. They found something unrelated to his gunshot wound." Miles tried his best not to sound panicked, but his concern was hard to mask.

"What did they find?" Ryan's lighthearted tone shifted to one of concern.

Miles went into detail describing Ken's x-ray, and that more tests were scheduled for Monday. Their subdued conversation offered a sharp contrast to the revelry going on around them, so they finished their beers and returned to the condo. Neither felt like going out that evening, so they picked up tacos from the stand around the corner and looked for a movie on Netflix, hoping to find something silly that would provide a real distraction. They settled on *Dumb and Dumber*.

CHAPTER 31

The walk to the Salty Caesar was only a few short blocks from Miles's condo. He liked to think of himself as a cool customer, but his anxiety grew with each step. His many years as a private investigator, and experience in the Lakeville Police Department forensic lab hadn't properly prepared him for this encounter. Getting into bed with a Mexican cartel rose to a whole new level of intrigue.

As expected, when he arrived at The Salty Caesar there was a man seated alone at one of the outdoor tables. None of the other tables were occupied. Inside the bar, other patrons were drinking, smoking, and conversing. It was as if they knew to keep their distance, like he had a forcefield surrounding him. While the man was small, he had the look of a person in total control of his surroundings.

"I'm Miles Darien." Miles held out his hand, unsure if it was the right move.

"Hola, Señor Darien. My name is Stefan. Please have a seat." Stefan did not offer his hand in return.

Miles sat down somewhat relieved by the informal greeting delivered in perfect English.

Stefan waved to the bartender. *"Dos cafés*, por favor." He waited for the coffee to arrive before addressing Miles. He casually lit a cigarette. "So, I understand you're looking for a man named Jonathan Reese. What makes you think we have knowledge of this man and his location?"

"It is my understanding that your organization has a handle on all activities in Jalisco of the nature Reese is typically involved in." Miles did his best to mask his uneasiness by getting right to the point.

"And if we had such information, why do you expect we would share it with you?"

"Because his operation has substantial value and is likely active in other cities nearby as well. He is, in a sense, in competition with you. There are millions of dollars to be gained by the elimination of a competitor if you were able to, shall we say, assume control of his enterprises." Miles counted on that rationale to deliver a worthwhile incentive to Stefan and his associates.

Stefan didn't acknowledge Miles's takeover concept. "I must ask. Why are you looking for this man, Reese?"

"He owes me. Big time. Besides my personal stake in this, which is substantial, his cruelty has resulted in so much unnecessary pain and suffering for many others, including people I'm close to."

"So, you plan to kill him if you find him?" Stefan asked matter-of-factly.

"No, that would be letting him off easy. I plan to ensure his operation is dismantled and he's turned over to the authorities who will surely see to it that he spends the rest of his life suffering in prison." Miles's anger bubbled to the surface.

"You obviously know the kind of activities we're involved in. Why do you think we care one bit about him or his operation?"

"Simple. He's different from you. He hurts people just for

the sake of hurting them. He wants what they have, and when he gets it he disposes of them. You take care of those who elect to go along with your various propositions. While it's not the way I would choose to do business, I understand you have a different set of rules. People only get hurt if they don't follow directions." Miles hoped his tacit approval of the cartel's methods would score a few much-needed points.

Stefan leaned back in his chair and nodded in approval. "I like you. You've got enormous cojones coming here to ask us for help of this kind. This is not the way we usually do things, but here's what I will do for you. I will see if our people know anything. If we have something, we'll talk again. Now I need to get going. You can pay the check, and be sure to tip generously." With that, Stefan got up, walked across the street, and got into his late-model Cadillac Escalade. As he drove off, Miles noted the vehicle had no license plates.

Miles paid the check and, as instructed, left a hefty tip. When he got up, he realized his whole body was wobbling. While he had been able to keep it together during the meeting, the fear he had been suppressing was now shaking his entire body. After taking a moment to collect himself, Miles starting walking. He reached for his phone to call Ryan but thought better of it, realizing it would be unwise to have a conversation of that nature where it might be overheard. It also gave him some extra time to calm down before he filled Ryan in.

Just as Miles walked through the door of the condo, his phone rang. It was Ken.

"Hi there. Did you have the biopsy?" Miles asked, hoping for the best.

"I did. And it turns out you won't be getting rid of me anytime soon."

"So, it was nothing serious?" Miles asked hopefully, putting Ken on speaker phone so Ryan could hear.

"Just a cyst they removed. I'm hoping to move back to rehab tomorrow, and home a couple of days after that. What's going on there?"

"Hi Ken, it's Ryan. We're still hunting for Reese."

"Details!" Ken demanded.

Ryan explained the specifics of what he had uncovered at the news agency, and the progress they made at the real estate office.

Miles took over. "I just came back from a meeting with a representative of the Velasco cartel—"

Ken interrupted Miles mid-sentence. "What the fuck are you doing messing around with those people?"

"Calm down. Let me explain." Miles first took Ken through his original concept for involving the cartel in the investigation, and how he initiated contact through Pancho's connection. He then took Ken and Ryan through the details of his meeting that morning with Stefan.

"I say stay focused on the real estate angle," said Ken, noticeably unnerved. "Hear me on this, involvement with the cartel can only mean big trouble."

Ryan held up his hand so Miles would let him respond. "I totally agree with you, Ken. We have a meeting with the real estate guy on Monday afternoon. Hopefully he will lead us to Reese, and we can let the idea of involving the cartel die on the vine." Ryan immediately regretted the "die-on-the-vine" comment. Thankfully, neither Miles nor Ken commented on it.

"Whatever you do, do not tell Audrey what you're up to," Ken instructed.

Miles laughed. "This is not my first rodeo, you know."

"I do know, but I want to be sure you protect yourself, even if it means not completing the mission."

Ken was obviously concerned, and well he should have been. These guys played for keeps, and Miles was no match for this ruthless criminal enterprise, even with Ryan at his side.

"I want you to stay away from the cartel," Ken demanded.

Miles appreciated Ken's concern, but he had no intention of complying.

CHAPTER 32

"Since we have no investigation activities planned for the day, I'm suggesting we go to Yelapa," Ryan recommended as they cleared their breakfast dishes.

"Yelapa?" Miles asked.

"Yes, my guidebook says it's a cute little town with a couple of amazing waterfalls, some good food, and artsy stuff to buy. Besides, it's a beautiful day for a boat ride."

Somewhat reluctantly, Miles agreed to take the journey. They gathered a few essentials, like towels and sunblock, and went down to Los Muertos Pier to catch the water taxi. The pedestrian-only pier jutted out into the bay and provided an unobstructed view of the coastline for miles in each direction, blanketed in a colorful array of beach umbrellas and lounge chairs. It was also a launching point for yachts, Jet Skis, tour boats, and water taxis.

Miles was surprised to learn their water taxi was merely one of the small pangas he'd seen floating beside the pier during their last visit to the beach. There were six passengers on their boat, two on each of the three flat board benches. The boat started off slowly, and after about a minute shifted into high gear, bouncing hard off every wave and causing the passengers to frantically reach for something to hold on to.

"I guess I should have asked before we left, but how long is the ride?" Miles asked, almost screaming to be heard over the noise of the motor and pounding of waves.

"About forty-five minutes," Ryan replied.

Miles was not happy with the answer. He eventually settled into the erratic tempo of the rise and fall of the boat and enjoyed the seaside landscapes they passed along the way. Mountains covered with lush jungles, pristine sand beaches sprinkled with palapas, and an occasional small fishing village, dotted their route.

As soon as the water taxi deposited them at the pier in Yelapa, Miles led the line of passengers making a beeline to the nearest *baño*. Nothing like forty-five minutes of bouncing along the water to stimulate the bladder.

The famous waterfall was their first stop. They decided to climb up the steep, meandering pathway without pausing to shop, or for refreshments. The trail wound through a beautiful green jungle of tropical plants, many with exotic, multicolored birds nesting among them. Along the way, they passed several groups on guided tours. They walked by them slowly, hoping to overhear a few tidbits of information the guides were passing out.

Their climb was rewarded when they reached the top. The cascading waterfall with its natural pool at the bottom was incredibly beautiful. The tranquility of the rhythmic flow of water was a wonderful change of pace from the pounding surf they had battled on the boat.

An older couple was talking about a place on the beach that had great food and rented kayaks and Jet Skis by the hour.

"C'mon, sounds like fun," Ryan urged.

"I'm all in for the lunch on the beach. I'm reserving judgment on the water sports for now." Miles was not nearly as adventurous as Ryan, except in the crime-solving area.

They made their way back down the path to the beach, and located the restaurant the older couple had touted, El Barracuda. Miles suggested they opt for seats at a table just inside the door next to the large open-air window.

"I need a little break from the sun," he pointed out.

"Me too. Particularly since I'm thinking about renting a Jet Ski after we eat." Ryan knew Miles wasn't likely to join him, given he had another bumpy water taxi ride to contend with later in the day.

Just then, a waiter approached their table. "Hola! What can I get for you, señores?"

"I'll have the grilled shrimp diabla," Miles requested.

The waiter turned to Ryan, who ordered, "The fried fish tacos, please. And a Corona."

"A Corona for me, too," Miles added.

While they waited for lunch to arrive, they turned their conversation back to their investigation.

"How do we get Armando to divulge the ownership of the condo project if he resists?" Ryan asked.

"The only card we have available is to tell him we'll buy the units, but only if we get the information. We'll just have to convince him we're prepared to make the deal."

After the big lunch and a couple of Coronas each, Ryan decided the Jet Ski idea would not be a wise one, so he suggested they take the next water taxi back to Puerto Vallarta. When they arrived at the pier, the older couple from the waterfall were also waiting for the water taxi. The man was having trouble removing his backpack. Since she was so much shorter than he was, she appeared unable to assist him. Miles stepped in and helped him remove the backpack, then introduced himself.

"Hi. I'm Miles and this is Ryan. We saw you at the falls. The restaurant you were talking about was excellent. Sorry about eavesdropping."

"No problem. I'm Sam and this is my wife, Sophie. We've spent a couple of days here as a break from our house hunting."

"Seems like everyone we've run into is looking to buy some type of property. Are you looking to move to this area permanently?" Ryan asked.

"Yes and no. We're looking for a place where we can vacation and also rent out when we're not using it," Sophie explained.

"A common practice, we're told," Miles said. "Any luck?"

"Well, we've ruled out Old Town and Cinco de Diciembre," said Sophie. Not much available in our price range with the amenities we're looking for. We've shifted our search to Versalles, which is getting more popular by the minute. In fact, we found a preconstruction opportunity that looks promising."

"By any chance, is the place on Calle Lisboa?" Miles asked, hoping for a connection.

"Yes. Are you interested in that property as well?" Sophie asked.

"We have an appointment at their sales office in Old Town to learn more about it," Miles admitted.

Sophie smiled. "We met with them on Friday at their Versalles office—actually, it's just a trailer—and got some preliminary information."

"Did they, by any chance, mention the name of the developer?" Miles asked.

"They didn't mention it," said Sam. "But they told us their firm is also developing properties in Ixtapa and Mazatlán, so they seem like a substantial company."

Miles couldn't help but think this was sounding more and more like the type of enterprise Reese would be behind. Lots of down payments for multiple properties in multiple cities, none of which would likely ever be built.

CHAPTER 33

Miles awoke at six-thirty Monday morning and decided to take a walk for coffee without waking Ryan. It took a while to find one open as Puerto Vallarta's day begins later than what he was accustomed to. As he began adding some milk to his very strong café Americano, his cell phone rang. The caller ID showed a number he recognized.

"Hi, Audrey. You're on duty early this morning." Miles tried to sound cheery, but he knew an early-morning call from Agent Drummond could only mean something was wrong.

"Unfortunately, I just received an edict from my superiors in Washington to cut off funding for your mission," Agent Drummond said. There have been some recent cutbacks, so the mandate going forward is to only fund specific 'hot' cases, and while finding Jonathan Reese is a 'hot' case to you, unfortunately it's not on Washington's 'hot' list. Your expenses to date will be reimbursed, but nothing after today. I'm truly sorry to cut your investigation short."

Miles sighed. "The condo has been prepaid till the end of the week, and so has our airfare, so if we choose to stay we'll only have our out-of-pocket expenses to cover. Correct?"

"Yes, that's correct. Since the rest of your trip is on you, please focus on enjoying the last few days there as a vacation," she proposed. "We'll hopefully find another way to locate and capture Reese when some funding reappears." Her tone was not at all encouraging.

"Or if he resurfaces in the States," Miles offered.

"Of course. By the way, I believe they'll release Ken from rehab in a couple of days, so I suspect he'll be back home in Chicago when you return. Miles, thanks for taking this on. I hate to have to pull the plug on you before you've had a chance to see your search through to its conclusion."

As the call ended, Ryan entered Miles's room. He had obviously overheard some of the conversation.

"So, we're done?" Ryan asked.

"Not totally. They're only ending our per diem a few days early. It's unlikely it would have been extended beyond the condo rental period anyway. We can certainly choose to continue on our own dime. Let's not throw in the towel just yet. I'm inclined to motor ahead, particularly if we learn something significant this afternoon at the real estate office."

"Works for me." Ryan added.

After breakfast, Miles decided he'd better check in with Anne to see how things were going at the office.

She answered on the first ring. "Hi, boss. How are things going in sunny Mexico?"

"It's beautiful here," he said, the disappointment cracking in his voice. "Although our current investigation has yet to yield any meaningful results. I suspect we'll be home this weekend as planned."

"Sorry about the investigation. On the bright side, you have a number of potential cases waiting for you here. That is, if you get back before the prospective clients get impatient and decide to look elsewhere." Anne was doing her best to encourage Miles's timely return.

"Keep them on the hook as best you can until I get back. Any other news?"

"Not really, unless you consider the six inches of snow we got yesterday to be news."

Miles had almost forgotten the unpredictable hazards of Wisconsin's weather as winter turned to spring. He concluded the call by thanking Anne for taking care of everything in his absence, then joined Ryan on the balcony to strategize their approach to their meeting at the Banderas Bay Villas sales office.

"Enjoy the beautiful sunshine and warmth while you can, buddy boy. Anne just told me Lakeville got six inches of snow yesterday."

"Not excited to return to that. Before we leave I'd really like to accomplish something meaningful here other than simply getting a sunburn," Ryan said sarcastically, but his frustration showed through.

"You did get your research for the *Times* series done, didn't you?" Miles reminded him.

"Small consolation. We came to find Reese, and so far we've got bupkis."

"True, but we're not done yet. We need to push Armando into divulging who's behind their operation." Miles was doing his best to cheerlead.

"And if he doesn't?"

"Then we leave town with only our sunburns to show for it."

Miles and Ryan walked to the meeting in silence. They had

rehearsed their lines over and over as if they were in a one-act play. Miles would play the good cop with Ryan playing the bad one. Their plan included introducing some conflict into the negotiations that they hoped would sufficiently rattle Armando into divulging information in order to preserve the sale.

When they arrived at the Banderas Bay Villas sales office, two other sales presentations were in progress. Obviously, the rapidly growing popularity of the Puerto Vallarta area, coupled with the lack of available inventory, had made this new development a hot commodity.

Armando was waiting at the door when they arrived. "Buenas tardes, señores. Please join me in the conference room."

Once Miles and Ryan were seated, Armando handed both of them file folders with proposals for each of the four units they had selected. The proposals contained detailed descriptions along with several artist renditions of the building, and the layouts and notations of each unit with its floor number.

"Looks complete, except where is the pricing?" Miles asked.

Armando seemed surprised by the question. "The pricing for each unit is as shown on the first page of the sell sheets."

"I see that, but where does it show the discount if we buy all four units?" Ryan raised his voice slightly to underscore his disbelief.

"Those are the prices." Armando was obviously playing hardball.

"So, you're suggesting we pay full price for a four-unit purchase of almost two million US dollars. Are you nuts?" Ryan had now shifted into full bad-cop mode.

"These units are in high demand, as you can see by the activity in the outer office, so we're not typically offering any discounts." Armando wasn't blinking.

Before Ryan could respond, Miles took over. "Richard, let me ask Armando a question. Are you willing to allow us to at least make an offer at a price we feel is fair?"

Ryan winked at Miles, approving of his good-cop intervention as well as for remembering his alias.

"Of course. I can't promise my superiors will accept an offer for anything less than what we've advertised, but feel free to do so," Armando offered.

"I assume you have a special offer to purchase form we should fill out with our proposed pricing?" Ryan asked, resuming his role.

Armando took a moment before answering. "How about this? I will fill out those forms for you once you supply me with the details of your offer along with copies of your passports and credit card information for the 10 percent down payment as earnest money."

Armando's request was reasonable enough if they had actually been who they said they were. Miles had to think fast since they had no way of providing either the passports or a credit card in the name of his alias. He got up from his chair and walked around the table, stroking his chin in deep thought. He stopped suddenly as if he had been hit by lightning, and addressed Armando.

"I'm uneasy about supplying all that information to you until we know your bosses are comfortable receiving a counteroffer. How about this? You confirm with your superiors that they will entertain a less-than-asking price offer. If they agree, we will provide all the required information to you when we return to make our formal signed offer. As for the earnest money, I can do better than what you've requested. We'll give you a cashier's check for 50 percent of the total purchase price within twenty-four hours after the time the agreement is signed by your superiors, who, by the way, we'll need you to identify. That should be adequate incentive to work with us on the purchase price, considering the down payment would be nearly a million US dollars."

Miles figured the large cashier's check would be an effective stall and provide a big incentive to reveal the name they were looking for.

Miles's offer made Armando smile. "I'm confident I will receive their approval to let you make an offer at a price you choose. Will you be able to return tomorrow with the information we need so we can formalize an offer?" His reply provided the opening they had been looking for.

Ryan resumed his bad-cop alter ego. "Yes, and one more thing. Be sure the offer to purchase document clearly spells out who we will be doing business with. Make sure it's not some fake corporation. We're shelling out a ton of money, and we want to be damn sure we're doing business with a reputable organization."

Ryan had really taken to his new role, which provided an effective cover-up for the fact that he and Miles were the real fakes.

"Two o'clock again?" Armando offered enthusiastically.

"Two o'clock it is," Miles agreed.

CHAPTER 34

W hen they got back to the condo, Ryan grabbed a beer and adjourned to the rooftop pool. Miles stayed in the condo to call Agent Drummond to see if she could assist them, even though they had been officially cut off by the FBI.

"Hi, Miles," answered Agent Drummond. "Has something come up since we spoke this morning?"

"Actually, yes. Is it possible for you to supply us with passports using a couple of assumed names?" Miles knew he was asking for a big favor.

"I could, but why would I?" Agent Drummond asked, somewhat perturbed by the request.

Miles explained the situation that had just unfolded at the real estate office. Since supplying the passports would not actually require the FBI to make any additional cash outlay, he hoped she would see the value in granting his request. He reasoned that by supporting this last-ditch effort to find Reese while they were still in Mexico, it would give Miles and Ryan a chance to provide a payoff on the investment the FBI had already made.

"What names do you want to use?" she asked, which Miles took to mean she had reluctantly bought into his logic.

"I'm going as Michael Martin. Ryan is Richard Daniels. We're both supposedly from Chicago. You can make up the other stuff. Our meeting is tomorrow afternoon at two, so we'll need them before that."

"Gee, thanks. Let me see what I can do." Agent Drummond offered. It wasn't a firm commitment, but it was all he needed to hear.

When Miles joined him at the pool after his call, Ryan was clicking away on his phone. After finishing his message, Ryan asked Miles how his call with Agent Drummond went.

"She didn't say no, so hopefully she'll make it happen." Miles was cautiously optimistic.

"And if she doesn't?"

"Still working on that contingency, but quite frankly, if Armando isn't forthcoming with the information, we may not even need them. Anything newsworthy going on with you?"

"Bobbie wanted to know when we'd be back in Lakeville. She has an appointment there at the end of next week and would like to get together."

"With just you, I assume," Miles said, feigning hurt feelings.

"Yes, but don't worry. She still loves you," Ryan assured him.

They shared a laugh and then turned their attention to a heated discussion between a security guard and a woman lying on a lounge chair on the other side of the pool. Soon everyone else at the pool was staring at the confrontation. Suddenly, the apparently intoxicated woman stood up to reveal her bare chest and the reason behind the confrontation. She had apparently been sunbathing topless, which was a clear violation of the condo rules. When the security guard handed her a towel she refused it, so he called for reinforcements on his walkie-talkie. A couple of minutes later two other security guards arrived.

The female guard picked up the towel and forcibly wrapped it around the woman while the other two guards gathered up the woman's things. The three guards then escorted the woman off the pool deck and down the elevator.

Miles shook his head. "Hard to believe getting rid of a couple of tan lines is worth ejection from the pool deck, not to mention her possible expulsion from the building altogether."

"True, but seems like much ado about nothing. Who gives a shit if she wants to sunbathe topless?" Ryan asked rhetorically.

"Obviously, whoever makes the rules around here. Also, it's not like we're in Europe where it's commonplace. This staunchly Catholic country frowns on such things."

"We do in the States as well. But it's just silly." Ryan turned back to his phone. "I'm texting Bobbie to tell her your feelings are hurt and to see if you can join us when she comes to Lakeville."

Miles grabbed a pillow from the empty chair next to him and threw it at Ryan. Ever the athlete, Ryan caught it mid-flight and sent it back whence it came, striking Miles squarely in the chest.

"We'd better call a truce or the security guards will come back and escort us out." Miles was only half kidding.

After they had both showered and dressed, they walked down to the beach to join the throngs of people who had gathered for the nightly ritual of watching the sunset.

"Isn't it fascinating how alluring it is to watch something that happens every night?" Ryan wondered.

A young woman standing next to him chimed in. "It does happen every night, but it subtly varies each time. A cloud here, a passing sailboat there, and differing shades of orange, pink, and blue make this spectacular picture something totally new each evening."

Once the sunset show was over, they walked over to Twisted

Palms for a drink and to decide on a place to eat. It turned out to be Martini Monday at the bar, so they joined in. After they each had two vodka martinis, they decided it would be wise to move on to food, so they asked the bartender for a recommendation. He steered them to Il Pesce, an Italian seafood restaurant just three blocks away.

"It's incredible how many Italian restaurants there are in Puerto Vallarta." Ryan commented.

"It is, and it's even more fascinating how good they all are," Miles pointed out.

"Likely this one will be too," Ryan predicted.

It was.

Shortly after they arrived back at the condo, Miles received a call from Agent Drummond.

"Miles, those passports you requested will be available at ten tomorrow morning. You will need to go to the US Consulate office in Nuevo Vallarta. You can find the address online. When you get there ask for Benjamin Watts. He's been briefed on your request. These passports should work fine for your meeting, but do *not* try to use them as real passports. They will not register as valid with any Mexican or US governmental agency."

"Don't worry. We only need them for our meeting," Miles assured. "Thanks for making this happen. With a little luck they'll help us locate Reese."

"Hope so. Keep me posted on any developments. Have a good night."

Before going to bed, Ryan checked on the location of the Consulate. Based on the map information he found, it appeared to be about a forty-minute cab ride each way. They made a plan to leave the condo around nine thirty to ensure they would be back in plenty of time for their two o'clock meeting at the Banderas Bay Villas sales office.

CHAPTER 35

A s planned, Miles and Ryan arrived at the Consulate shortly after ten o'clock. They walked through the metal detectors and into the lobby, where there was a beehive of activity. It took several minutes in line before it was their turn at the information desk.

"How can I assist you?" said the woman behind the desk.

Miles noticed her name badge, which read: "Nancy Shore."

"We're here to see Benjamin Watts, Ms. Shore."

"May I see some form of identification, please?" she politely asked.

Thankfully Miles and Ryan had thought to bring along their real passports, which they handed to her. Ms. Shore picked up the phone and informed the person on the other end, presumably Mr. Watts, that they had arrived. She then returned their passports.

She pointed to a set of chairs on the far wall. "Please take a seat over there."

Just as they sat down, a studious-looking young man approached them. "Mr. Darien and Mr. Duffy, I'm Benjamin Watts. Please follow me."

He led them though a doorway and down a short hall to a sparsely furnished office. The nameplate on the desk identified the office as his.

"Please have a seat," Mr. Watts requested, pointing to the

two chairs opposite to his desk. "It's not often this office receives a special request from the FBI. Come to think of it, I don't recall us ever receiving one. You must be on a special assignment."

Mr. Watts was obviously fishing for an explanation, which neither Miles nor Ryan would give him.

"Your assistance is most appreciated," Miles acknowledged. "We really need to be on our way. Here are our passports to establish our identities."

"Thanks. Everything seems to be in order. Here is the package I was charged with delivering to you." Mr. Watts handed a manilla envelope to Miles, who immediately examined its contents.

"If there is anything else I can help you with, just ask," said Mr. Watts. "Anything at all. Always willing to help out another agency of the US Government."

"Thanks so much. If we need anything, we'll be in touch," Miles promised.

The three men left the office and walked down the hallway back to the reception area. Once they reached the door, Miles and Ryan shook hands with Mr. Watts and left the building.

As they walked to the corner in search of a cab, Ryan broke out laughing. "That young man was really itching to volunteer for duty as an FBI agent on a dangerous secret mission."

"I suspect his brief encounter with two guys he wrongly perceived as federal agents was about the most exciting thing that's happened to him in a very long time," Miles said as a cab pulled up.

They had some time to kill after the cab dropped them off at their condo, so they decided to pick up a few groceries. Ryan volunteered to go to the Emiliano Zapata farmers market in search of some avocados and bananas. Miles would go to the Ollin Market for some milk and a loaf of bread.

They met back at the condo about an hour later and had a snack before walking to their meeting with Armando. When they arrived at the sales office, they were told Armando wasn't there at the moment. Ryan checked his watch, which said 2:05 p.m. "Looks like we've been stood up," Ryan said.

"Let's wait a few minutes and see if someone shows up," Miles suggested.

A moment later a young woman came rushing out of the back office and approached them.

"Hola, I'm Maria. I work for Armando. He's been detained at our Versalles office and asked me to let you in to the conference room to wait for him. While you're waiting, I can provide you with the forms for your offer to look over. He promised he won't be delayed for long. Will you be kind enough to wait?"

"We can wait for a little while," Miles agreed. She handed him the forms and invited them to each take a seat in the same conference room where they had met with Armando. They each declined the bottle of water she offered, so she left them alone in the room and retreated to a desk at the front of the office.

"How long do we wait?" Ryan asked.

"We'll give him thirty minutes. If we leave, we leave with nothing. Hopefully he's just as anxious as we are to conduct our business. I assume they have agreed to allow us to make a counteroffer or she wouldn't have given us the forms, so let's fill them out." Miles grabbed a pen on the desk and entered the information from their new passports.

Armando appeared fifteen minutes later. He rushed into the conference room and apologized.

"I'm so sorry to keep you waiting. My Versalles salesperson was late showing up for work, so I had to stay there. He had some car trouble, and he had to wait for a tow truck to take it to the repair shop. Thank you for your patience. Did Maria give you the forms?"

"Yes, she did. And we've filled out the passport information. I noticed all your information is missing, however." Ryan did his best to sound irritated.

"Yes, the form Maria gave you was blank. I'll fill it in with the name of the company and its address, and so forth." Armando took the form and entered the information. Miles and Ryan exchanged a glance that said, *Keep your fingers crossed.*

Armando finished entering the information and handed the form to Miles. There it was. The name filled in on the seller line was Hollins Properties, Ltd. Miles needed to muster as much self-control as he could to not disclose his excitement. Now that they had what they wanted from Armando, he inserted their low-ball offer of $1,740,000. He showed it to Ryan, who nodded, and then gave it back to Armando.

"Your offer is quite a bit lower than we had hoped and is likely to be countered," Armando said. "Regardless, I will make a few copies for each of us to sign, and I'll submit our copy to my superiors, who will evaluate it and send me their response. Once I have it, we can make a time to meet again to go over the status of your offer, and discuss the next steps."

"Armando, I'm curious. Who are your superiors?" Ryan probed further, hoping to hear Jonathan Reese's name.

"My contact is Juan Ramirez. He works out of our Mexico City office. His address is the same as the one on the form." Mr. Ramirez was obviously either Reese's alias or an intermediary.

Even though Armando didn't name Reese as his contact, they had received the confirmation they had been seeking. This condo development was undoubtedly a Reese enterprise. They had everything they would get from this afternoon's charade.

With any luck, it would be compelling enough to motivate the FBI to continue their pursuit.

Armando told them he would contact them by phone as soon as he heard from his home office regarding their offer. They thanked him for his help and left, finally feeling they had accomplished at least a portion of their assignment.

Once back at the condo, Miles called Agent Drummond.

"Did you get the passports?" she asked without a greeting.

"Yes, and they were instrumental in our establishing that, as we suspected, the property here is in fact owned by Hollins Properties, Ltd. That ties it directly to Reese. While the paperwork doesn't specifically locate him, there is a strong likelihood he's in Mexico City."

Miles shared the balance of what they had learned from Armando.

"Good work, Miles. That's important information to have if I can interest anyone in Washington to reopen the case. It's fucking cold here, so go enjoy the rest of your time in Mexico," she advised.

"We will. Stay warm."

After he hung up, Miles noticed he had received a text from Pancho:

"Same time. Same place. Same guy. Tomorrow."

Apparently their search was not yet complete.

CHAPTER 36

Miles suffered through another mostly sleepless night. His mind was at full speed, imagining what Stefan might have for him. The possibilities had given Miles renewed hope of actually finding Reese, not merely locating the center of his operation. He finally gave up trying to rest, and got out of bed just before sunrise.

The sound of the percolating coffee maker woke Ryan. "You're up and at 'em early this morning."

"Couldn't sleep. I kept thinking about the possibility that our cartel contact might actually help us find Reese before we leave."

"It better be something we can act on quickly since we only have a couple of days before our flight leaves on Friday." Ryan grabbed a cup and filled it.

Now that the sun was up, Miles opened the door to the balcony and motioned for Ryan to join him outside. "Of course, but it's also possible we get some additional information to pass along that further incentivizes the FBI to renew our pursuit of him."

"I hope so, but I must admit it'll be great to get back to the States. Remember, I need to decide what I'm doing with the rest of my life." Apparently the reality of what was ahead of him had now taken center stage.

"Not really. You just need to decide on the next chapter," Miles reminded him.

"Semantics. You're going back to your dog, your house, and your work. I'm going back to an uncertain future." Ryan was always so buttoned up, but now he appeared uncharacteristically unnerved by his future's lack of clarity.

"It's a wonderful opportunity, buddy boy. While you have numerous decisions to make, they all come with enormous upside." Miles was doing his best to spin it in a positive light.

"Are you charging me for this session?" Ryan asked sarcastically.

"Yes. You're buying dinner tonight."

———

When Miles arrived at the Salty Caesar, Stefan was seated outside at the same table as last time. Again, none of the other tables were occupied. As he approached the table, Stefan motioned for him to again sit in the chair across from him. Once Miles was seated, Stefan waved the waiter over. Miles ordered coffee although he had already had plenty. The waiter returned immediately with a cup for Miles and a refill for Stefan.

"So, have you been enjoying your stay in Puerto Vallarta?" Stefan asked innocently.

"Yes. I love it here," said Miles. "Unfortunately, our investigation has not been as successful as I would have liked."

"Maybe I can help you with that."

"How so?" Miles asked as offhandedly as his excitement would allow.

"You see, the information you provided regarding Jonathan Reese's activities here, and in Ixtapa and Mazatlán, will most definitely turn out to be useful to us."

"How so?" Miles asked again.

"Let's just say we and our counterparts in those other cities are not pleased that your Mr. Reese is working in our communities with the help of an organization similar to ours from Mexico City." Stefan once again avoided using the word "cartel."

"I see. You're saying an organization like yours based in Mexico City is using him as a way of disguising their activities on your turf." Miles had gotten the drift.

"You are a good detective, Señor Darien."

"You said you could be helpful with our investigation. In what way?" Miles was looking for the payoff.

"Turns out we have the same goal, eliminating Mr. Reese and his operation. I have some information that your friends in the FBI will be most interested in."

Miles suddenly felt a chill run through his body. How did Stefan know he was working with the FBI, and more importantly, would there be consequences?

"The FBI?" Miles asked.

"Don't worry. We know all about your relationship with them. As long as you cooperate with us and stay out of our affairs, we will all be fine." Stefan's reassuring words were delivered with a smile.

Miles's chills suddenly vanished. "You said 'cooperate.' How?"

Stefan went on to explain that while Reese's operation was, in fact, located in Mexico City, he was seldom there. The cartel using Reese's operation as a front had arranged for him to obtain a Mexican passport and a Cuba Tourist Card. Stefan's group found out that Reese spent the majority of his time in Havana, out of the reach of the American authorities and any entanglements between the factions in the cities his operation did business.

"That's most interesting, but how does this information help me assist you?" Miles wondered.

"Simple. I will give you his exact location in Havana. The FBI can eliminate him there without worrying about upsetting your country's relationship with the Mexican government." Stefan's matter-of-fact use of the word "eliminate" reminded Miles how these people so routinely resolved their disputes.

"And without your counterparts in Mexico City blaming you for eliminating him," Miles added.

"Like I said, you're a good detective."

"Okay, then. Provide me with the information and I'll pass it along immediately."

Before responding, Stefan excused himself and went inside the restaurant. He returned with an envelope in his hand. "All the information you need is in this envelope. I wish you good luck." He handed it to Miles. "My associates and I are counting on you to make this happen."

Miles took it as a warning, not a form of encouragement. Stefan then excused himself, leaving Miles and the envelope alone at the table. Knowing what "counting on you to make this happen" meant gave Miles a chill. The server stopped by a few moments later to leave the bill, which Miles gladly paid.

Miles waited until he was safely back in the condo before opening the envelope. His theory was confirmed about it being a warning. Included with the documents regarding Reese's whereabouts was a picture of Miles's home in Lakeville. His chills returned.

A short time later, Ryan walked into the condo and found Miles at the high-top kitchen table, studying the contents of the envelope. "What ya got there?" he asked.

Miles relayed his encounter with Stefan and the assignment they, and the FBI by proxy, had been given. He decided not to mention the obvious threat should they fail.

"Wow. Looks like we can deliver a lot more than just the confirmation of Reese's involvement here," Ryan exclaimed. "Have you contacted Audrey Drummond yet?"

"I haven't. I'm thinking about running this by Ken first to get his take," Miles suggested.

"I don't see the value in that. You have to give the information to the FBI immediately. What could Ken possibly advise you to do that would be different?"

Of course Ryan's logic was sound, but Miles had been spooked by the picture of his house and was evaluating every option. "First of all, Ken is the FBI, so I am informing them. Second, I did some checking and we could easily make arrangements to go directly to Havana from here if we choose to pursue Reese on our own."

"Have you gone mad? This is a job for the professionals. Why in the world would we take on Reese ourselves? Besides, he's liable to have an army of his own security people protecting him, not to mention any assistance he might be getting from his cohorts in the Mexico City cartel." Ryan was now pacing, holding his head in disbelief.

Miles decided to show Ryan the picture. "Don't you see if Reese isn't brought down, they'll come after me and maybe . . ."

"Me? That's a stretch."

"If they know where I live, they certainly know about you. Particularly since you've been here with me the whole time. I'm not crazy about doing this, but if the FBI decides not to spend the money or the resources to get rid of Reese, Stefan's folks might well get rid of us unless we take care of it ourselves." Miles's frightening scenario was certainly a possibility.

Ryan placed his hand on Miles's shoulder. "Here's what I figure. Stefan was merely doing everything to strengthen your resolve in getting the FBI to take care of this business. If you don't, it would be more beneficial for him to have his people take care of Reese than it would be to take care of us."

"Your logic fails in one important way. He can't take care of Reese directly or he'll start a war with their rival cartel in Mexico City. Given the size of their respective territories, I suspect the Mexico City guys have substantially more firepower." Miles's reasoning was hard to argue against, and scary at the same time.

"Okay, I buy that, but what does eliminating us do for them?" begged Ryan.

Miles's eyes narrowed as he replied through clenched teeth, "It sends a message to the FBI."

"Sounds far-fetched to me. Why are we the key figures in this hunt? Your thirst for vengeance has put us right in the crosshairs of some scary people. We need to leave this in the hands of the FBI."

"Maybe. But do you suggest we sit back and take the risk that the FBI does nothing and Stefan's associates come after us?"

Ryan didn't answer.

CHAPTER 37

A s they walked back from dinner at Bravos, Miles noticed he had missed a call from Ken. Once they were back in the condo, he returned the call.

"How are you two amigos doing?" Ken asked innocently as he answered the phone.

"We're fine, but it appears our future is somewhat cloudy," Miles replied ominously.

"Tell me," Ken demanded.

Miles went on to explain, in detail, the dilemma he and Ryan had found themselves in as a result of the cartel's demands. He also laid out the option of taking care of things themselves if Ken's associates at the FBI decided not to go after Reese.

"Talk to Audrey about this," Ken told him. "Tell her everything you know and give her the chance to get approval to go after Reese. I cannot emphasize enough that you must not take this on yourself. Miles, you're a talented sleuth, not a trained assassin. Leave the 'eliminating' to those who are." Ken's warning could not have been sterner.

"I'll call Audrey and see what she says," he agreed. He did not, however, say what he would or would not do based on her response.

"Call me as soon as you hang up from that call," Ken demanded.

"I will. Now on to your report. When will you be released from rehab?"

"Tomorrow, I hope. I expect to see you back home this weekend." He emphasized the last part.

"My place or yours?" Miles asked playfully, hoping to deflect Ken's concern.

"Either is fine as long as it's not in Havana."

Before he called Agent Drummond, Miles spent considerable time trying to figure out how he could protect Ryan if things didn't go well and Reese remained at large. He concluded that Ryan absolutely should not remain in Lakeville once they returned home to the States. He figured the cartel didn't have a beef with Ryan directly, and if they did it wasn't likely to warrant a wide-ranging manhunt. Once he had his mind made up about that, he placed the call.

"Hello, Miles," answered Drummond. "Are you packed and ready to return to the frozen North?"

"Almost, but that's not the reason for my call. I have some new information that I think you'll be interested in."

"Out with it."

Miles realized it was time for full disclosure, so he recounted what had transpired with Stefan and the information in the envelope that included Reese's hideout. He held back any mention of the implied threat also contained in that envelope.

"First of all, how in the world did you get involved with the cartel?" She simultaneously sounded flabbergasted, upset, and impressed.

"As I may have told you, the original motivation for my trip was to do some work for a client down here, and it involved his dealings with the cartel. Once that situation was successfully resolved he was able to connect me with one of the cartel's representatives who provided the information about Reese. Turns out they want him gone as much as we do."

Miles went on to explain the angle about Reese's involvement with the Mexico City bad guys, which meant the Puerto Vallarta bad guys couldn't mess with Reese for fear of starting a war.

"So, now you're suggesting the FBI find Reese in Havana and eliminate him for the benefit of the Velasco cartel?" Agent Drummond's response sounded more like a request for clarification than a rejection of the idea.

"Remember, you had us searching for Reese in the first place, and not for the benefit of the cartel. It's for the FBI's benefit. Any additional value for the cartel is coincidental, and now, unavoidable."

"'Coincidental' is an interesting way to describe it. May I also assume that if we don't take care of this you're somehow on the hook for Reese's demise?"

Agent Drummond had astutely reasoned the outcome if her superiors decided not to act. Miles knew he now had to come clean or he'd risk becoming persona non grata in the eyes of both the US Government and the cartel.

"If he doesn't go down, Ryan and I are likely to be the ones taking a fall," he admitted, hoping it would add some sort of extra incentive for the FBI to act.

"And if I can't get our people to move on this . . ."

He sighed. "Then we may have no alternative but to go to Havana ourselves."

"That's preposterous. Even in the unlikely event you're able to find and eliminate Reese, you stand an excellent chance of getting killed or even worse, spending the rest of your days doing hard labor in a Cuban prison." Agent Drummond's voice was filled with both anger and trepidation.

"So, Audrey, I guess that leaves the ball in your court. I hate to put you in this position, but remember the objective has always been to find Reese. Now that we have located him, I'm confident the US Government has sufficient motivation to act, and the necessary assets in Cuba who could handle this job. Even quite possibly returning Reese in one piece to stand trial for his crimes. After all, isn't that the reason you asked us to locate him in the first place?"

"I can't deny your logic, Miles," Agent Drummond said. "I'll see what I can do on my end, but hear me loud and clear. Under no circumstances are you to go to Havana to find Reese. If you do and somehow get out alive, I will see to it that you are arrested the moment you try to reenter the US. Do we understand each other?" She wasn't asking, she was mandating.

"Of course I understand. We'll be home Friday evening as planned." Miles had now done all he could to enlist the FBI in going to Cuba to apprehend Reese. He realized that Agent Drummond's warning had effectively erased any thoughts he had of doing the job himself. What still hung over him, however, was if Agent Drummond's superiors said no, he and Ryan would be destined to live their lives in constant fear of the cartel's reprisals.

CHAPTER 38

The morning of their last day basking in the warmth of Puerto Vallarta's tropical weather, Miles called George to confirm the details of their pickup at O'Hare on Friday evening.

When he finished the call, he and Ryan decided to start their final vacation day with a return trip to Casa Nicole for breakfast. Ryan again ordered the famous crunchy French toast. Miles opted for the Machaca. They planned their last day of fun in the sun over their second cup of Chiapas coffee.

The flight the next afternoon to Chicago was uneventful, on time, and—thankfully—not particularly full. Agent Drummond's arrangements to transport Miles's weapon were still in place, so they were whisked quickly and without event through security in Puerto Vallarta as well as US immigration and customs in Chicago. Miles was particularly relieved that his pistol had only been excess baggage on his trip.

The ride back to Lakeville with George was as uneventful as the plane ride had been. Once they had collected Molly and arrived back at the house, Miles decided he would text Anne to see if she would meet him at the office in the morning. She answered immediately and suggested nine o'clock, to which Miles agreed.

"I'm meeting Anne at the office at nine tomorrow, so you'll be rid of me for a few hours."

"Thank God!" Ryan replied with a heavy sigh of relief.

After walking Molly, Miles spent the rest of the evening unpacking and returning a few emails. As he was trying to fall asleep, he could hear Ryan on the phone in the other bedroom. He assumed he was talking to Bobbie. The thought of his two friends getting together made him smile, both because he felt they could bring each other happiness and, selfishly, because it was possible, once this Reese business was over, his best friend might stay in the area permanently.

Before he went to sleep, Miles wanted to check in on Ken. It was late, so he sent him a text instead of calling. "We made it home safely. Hope you have as well."

The response came in immediately. "I'll be home tomorrow afternoon. I'll call as soon as I arrive."

"Thank goodness you're back!" Anne blurted out as Miles walked through the door to the office.

"Nice to see you too," he replied to her somewhat frazzled greeting.

She went straight to informing him. "We've had close to twenty inquiries while you were gone. The three that remain are summarized on fact sheets in the file folder on your desk. I solved two of them and the rest have gone elsewhere."

"You solved two of them?" Miles exclaimed in disbelief.

"Don't worry, there were only basic internet searches, so your license is still intact," she assured him.

"You seem a little on edge this morning. You're usually, shall I say, more relaxed. Is something wrong?"

She took a deep breath. "I'm fine. Just glad I can stop saying no, or 'Can your case wait a few days?' and for things in general to return to normal."

"I had no idea my being gone for a couple of weeks would be so difficult for you," Miles admitted. "I'm really sorry."

"No problem. That is, if you remember that when my annual review rolls around." Anne's droll sense of humor had instantly returned.

Miles acknowledged her jibe with a smile and walked into his office. Shortly after he settled in behind his desk, Anne came in and laid a pile of mail down in front of him.

"I pulled the envelopes that I knew were either bills or junk mail. Just the usual stuff. The rest of it is in this stack."

"Thanks," Miles said without looking up.

As he made his way through the letters, he came to one that was hand addressed and without a stamp. Someone had apparently dropped it through the mail slot in the front door of the office instead of mailing it. Inside there were two pictures, one of the frosted glass panel of his office door, which read "Miles Darien Investigations," and the other was the same picture of his house that Stefan had given him in Puerto Vallarta. The foreboding feeling he had when he opened the envelope in Puerto Vallarta had returned. The two pictures were surely intended to remind Miles, in no uncertain terms, that the cartel was expecting immediate action, and had someone locally who was keeping a watchful eye on him. It gave him a sick feeling in the pit of his stomach.

He debated whether to immediately call Agent Drummond or wait to get Ken's advice on how to proceed. Since Ken was due back that afternoon, Miles decided to wait and divert his attention to the three cases Anne had held at bay until he returned. One in particular piqued his interest.

A local accounting firm, Abernathy & Kromm, was concerned that a recent ex-employee may have taken some valuable client information with her. Since they couldn't confirm

the theft with absolute certainty, and since none of the clients
had reported any misuse of their information, there was nothing
criminal to report to the police.

The rundown Anne had supplied noted for him to call the
firm's managing partner, Bill Abernathy, on his cell phone.

"Hi, Mr. Abernathy, I'm Miles Darien."

"Mr. Darien, thanks for getting back to me. I assume your
assistant filled you in on our predicament." Mr. Abernathy's
deep baritone befit his big-name stature in the business
community.

"Yes she did, and please call me Miles."

"Good. So Miles, what do you think we should do?" Mr.
Abernathy asked.

"I'll need a lot more information in order to figure that out.
When would be a convenient time for us to meet? Preferably at
your office."

Miles knew in order to find any evidence of wrongdoing,
he would most likely need to conduct a thorough search of the
company's records and systems.

"How about six o'clock Monday evening after everyone
has gone home? That way we can talk freely and you can have
access to everything without raising any eyebrows. Oh, and
please call me Bill."

"That makes sense, Bill. In the interim, can you send me the
personnel file for the ex-employee you suspect may have stolen
the confidential information?" Miles intended to do a little
homework before the meeting on Monday.

"Of course."

They exchanged email addresses, with Bill opting to use
his personal email account for their correspondence to avoid
alerting anyone else in his organization that an investigation
was underway.

"See you Monday at six," Miles confirmed as they hung up.

Ken's text read, "Just landed. I'll call you when I get home."

Miles texted a thumbs-up emoji, knowing how much Ken also detested emoji. Just the perfect little welcome-home tease, he thought.

Miles finished sorting through his mail and left for home to wait for Ken's call. On the way, he decided to stop at the grocery store to pick up a few things to replenish his refrigerator. As often happens in a small town, he ran into someone he knew, Laura Rathburn, the wife of his coroner friend, Jim.

"Hi, Laura. How are you?" he asked.

"Danny's in trouble," she said softly, holding back tears.

"What happened?"

"He got into a fight at school. A kid called him some derogatory slur for a gay person, so he punched him. Broke his jaw. He's been charged with assault and we'll probably be sued by the parents." She was no longer holding back tears. "It just happened yesterday. Jim bailed him out and now we need to find a good lawyer."

Miles offered one possibility. "I highly recommend Carl Rafferty. We're good friends and he's a heck of a good lawyer."

Just then, her phone rang. "Hi, honey. I'm at the store and I just ran into Miles. He has a lawyer to recommend." She handed the phone to Miles.

"Hi, Jim. So sorry to hear about what happened."

"I don't condone violence, but the kid called Danny a 'fucking fag,' and not surprisingly, Danny lost it." Jim's voice was sad and angry all at the same time.

"Understandable, but now he'll need to mount a defense. Have you hired anyone yet?" Miles asked.

"Not yet. Laura said you have someone?"

"Carl Rafferty. He's excellent, and a good friend who I know will mount the best possible defense. I'm also quite confident he'll be someone Danny will be comfortable with."

"Text me his number."

"Will do, and please use me as a reference."

Jim agreed. Miles handed Laura's phone back and said goodbye. He started into the store to shop, but paused at the entrance and reflected on how he had just, a couple of weeks prior, counseled Danny to stand up for himself. Now standing up for himself had gotten Danny arrested. For a moment, Miles questioned whether he had done the right thing. In the end, he concluded that he had, in fact, given Danny sound advice, and Danny had been right to stand up for himself. Unfortunately, not in the way he chose to do it.

Miles waited anxiously for Ken to call, so he was elated when it finally came through.

"Glad to be home?" Miles asked.

"Sure am. Are you glad to be home as well?" Ken replied.

"Well . . ." Miles's one-word answer trailing off was an answer unto itself.

"What's wrong?" Ken asked.

Miles explained the additional threat he had received via the envelope dropped off at his office.

"Tell Audrey about it. Maybe she's already arranged for action to be taken in Havana. If that doesn't happen, she owes you protection." Regrettably, Ken wasn't speaking in an official capacity.

"Any protection she might provide could only be for a short time. The cartel could simply wait until the coast is clear and then . . ." Miles's voice again dropped off, leaving Ken to imagine the rest of the sentence.

"Call Audrey," Ken insisted.

"Okay, I will. When can I see you?"

"Friday night. Here?"

"Works for me. And yes, I'll call her right now." Miles was concerned about what Agent Drummond might have to say. What if she hadn't gotten authorization to pursue Reese in Havana? Miles set his worries aside and called her.

"I was just about to call you," Agent Drummond said without so much as a hello.

"What news do you have?" Good news, he hoped.

"We sent a team in to find Reese at the location you provided. Someone must have alerted him that we were coming, because the place was completely deserted, and it had been left as though the inhabitants made a hasty retreat. No one in my organization had enough notice or knowledge of the mission to be the one to tip him off. It's likely someone in your cartel contact's organization is really working for their rival."

Her supposition made perfect sense, but it sure complicated matters.

"I guess my next move is to contact my guy down there and tell him what happened," said Miles.

"Contact him, tell him what you've learned, and let me know what he says." Agent Drummond hung up.

Miles figured the new information would likely shift the cartel's focus off him temporarily, and cause Stefan to look inside his own organization. The question became whether Stefan could still muster the wherewithal to find out where Reese had escaped to. If not, the hunt would have to shift back to Reese's real estate operations in Mexico. That would create a huge dilemma for Miles. Should he leave his business again to assist the FBI in pursuing Reese a second time, or should he sit back and wait for either the cartel or the FBI to act?

Unfortunately, Miles did not have any way to contact Stefan directly, so he was forced to call Pancho and ask him to act as intermediary once again.

"Hola, Miles. *¿Qué pasa?*" Pancho answered cheerfully.

"I need to get word to 'our friend' immediately."

"What's the message?" Pancho asked.

"Try to speak to him directly and tell him this exactly: 'No one was home when we stopped by. Do you or someone you know have a forwarding address?' Be sure you get an acknowledgment that he definitely understands the meaning of the message."

Miles wanted to be sure the message was cryptic enough that it wouldn't create suspicion should any unauthorized persons or authorities be listening, but send an unmistakably clear message to Stefan at the same time. "Got it. I'll get the message to him right away and report back any response. Stay safe, Miles."

While Miles waited to hear back from Pancho he immersed himself in the Abernathy & Kromm case. While he was making notes for his Monday meeting, his phone beeped with a text. It was from Pancho.

"Our friend is looking for a forwarding address and will send it along as soon as possible."

So, now Stefan knew they had followed through as promised and had earned, at the very least, a brief reprieve.

Armando's caller ID showed it was his boss on the line. "Hello, sir. I haven't heard from you for a while."

"I've been traveling," said Reese. "Why haven't you closed any deals since we last spoke? My patience is wearing thin."

"I have several clients preparing offers," Armando answered unconvincingly.

"Let's hope so. Whatever happened to that possible four-unit sale you were negotiating? Did they reject our counteroffer?"

"They never showed up for the next meeting. In fact, they didn't respond to any of the follow-up emails I sent them either." Armando knew his boss was not going to be satisfied with that response.

"I will send you a picture of a man. Please let me know immediately if he is one of the guys who made the original offer. In the meantime, close those other offers. I will not tolerate any additional failures." Reese was literally screaming into the phone.

"Yes, sir," Armando promised. He shuddered with the feeling that more than his job was now at stake.

CHAPTER 39

A t their Monday evening meeting, Miles and Bill Abernathy discussed the specific job responsibilities of the suspected former employee, Elaine McDowell. The confidential information she had access to during her employment included clients' names, addresses, social security numbers, business entities, credit card numbers, investment account details, and bank records—a virtual treasure trove of exploitable financial data. Miles cautioned that her access to the information didn't prove she stole any of it.

They uncovered the suspected theft during their routine audit of their server logs. Ms. McDowell had accessed a large number of client data files minutes before she unexpectedly and unceremoniously resigned and walked out the door. The fact that, to their knowledge, the breached data had not been used meant Miles still had a chance to come up with a way to stop any potential crimes before they were committed. It would require him to set a trap for Ms. McDowell and do so before any damage was done. Miles advised Bill Abernathy not to alert his clients just yet. Miles wanted Ms. McDowell to believe she had gotten away undetected so she would continue implementing her plan, which would give him the chance to catch her in the act.

As Miles drove home he decided to enlist the services of Brent Fogerty, an IT professional who knew his way around both the traditional and dark webs. Brent had first assisted Miles while Miles was on the Lakeville PD's forensic team and Brent was an outside contractor. They had also worked together occasionally after Miles established his detective agency. After he walked into the house and gave Molly a quick belly rub, he called Brent.

Brent answered on the first ring in a voice that sounded as if Miles had awakened him. "Mr. Darien, it's been a while."

"It has. How have you been?" Miles asked casually.

"Just fine. I assume you're not calling to simply inquire about my well-being. What's up?"

Miles filled him in on the suspicion of theft, and that the stolen client information was possibly being offered for sale online.

"Pretty common crime, unfortunately. The thieves seldom use the information they acquire directly. By selling it anonymously on the dark web, they build a barrier between themselves and the persons who actually use the information in a crime."

Miles had thought of the same possibility. "Can you help?"

"I can try. Please send me what you have and I'll see if I can uncover anything. If necessary, am I authorized to purchase some of the data if it will firmly establish the connection?"

Miles agreed and gave Brent carte blanche to do whatever was necessary to connect any attempted sales of the purloined data to Ms. McDowell. Given the valuable information he might uncover, Brent promised to send Miles a signed nondisclosure agreement and to update Miles immediately if he made any connections.

After hanging up with Brent, Miles received a text from Carl Rafferty.

"Thanks for referring the Rathburns. I'm confident we'll get the charges against Danny dropped. If they file the civil case, that will be a little more difficult. I'll keep you posted."

Miles replied with a thank you and made his way to the kitchen. He found Ryan at the table on his computer, munching on some fried chicken.

"How did your meeting with the accounting firm go?" Ryan asked.

"I am now in pursuit of a suspected data thief," Miles said, and explained the details of the case.

"So, you're in a race against time."

Miles sighed. "Like always."

Miles spent the next forty-eight hours working his way through the other two cases Anne had presented when he returned home from Mexico. One involved finding out if a man being sued for divorce had hidden some assets from his soon-to-be ex-wife. The other was attempting to find the biological father of a woman who, after her mother's death, found out she had been conceived at a fertility clinic using sperm from an anonymous donor.

The first case was relatively easy to solve. Using the clients' credit card account login information, Miles was able to discover that the husband, Stuart Jasperson, had made a one-day detour to the Cayman Islands while on a business trip to Tampa, Florida. He had used rewards points to pay for his flight. The only reason anyone goes to the Cayman Islands on a day trip is to make a deposit into one of the banks offering an untraceable account. Using rewards points would make uncovering the ticket purchase a little more difficult.

Finding the money he had taken with him was a bit more

challenging. Among the assets Mr. Jasperson's attorney had documented in the divorce proceedings, was a collection of classic cars, which gave Miles an idea on where the money might have come from. Miles had met Riley Metcalf on one of George's fishing outings. Riley owned a garage that serviced all forms of exotic and collector cars. If anyone in Lakeville would know about Stuart Jasperson's cars, it would be Riley, so Miles gave him a call.

"Sure, I've worked on all of Stuart's cars over the years. What do you want to know?" Riley replied in his straightforward style.

"Do you know if he sold one recently?"

"Actually, he sold two. One was a 1970 Mustang Boss 429 in mint condition, the other was a beautiful 1961 Mercedes-Benz 190SL." Riley spoke almost reverently about the two cars.

"Any idea what they would have sold for?" If the amount was substantial and not included in the financial information the attorneys had exchanged, Miles would be on to something.

"Each one was probably worth between 150 and 200 thousand. Sold them out of state, I was told. But I don't know any specifics about the sales."

"Thanks, Riley. Hope to see you out on George's boat once the weather warms up a bit."

"Looking forward to it!"

Calling Riley had definitely paid off. Since the inventory of cars Mr. Jasperson had included in his list of assets did not include either vehicle or any record of the proceeds from their sale, Miles had substantial evidence as to where the missing money likely came from. It would now be up to Mrs. Jasperson's attorney to take over confirming the details surrounding the sale of the cars and the current whereabouts of the money that was unaccounted for. The jaunt to the Caymans would strongly suggest to her attorney where that money currently resided.

Finding Tracy Littman's biological father would be a more difficult assignment, as records from fertility clinics are sealed and almost impossible to access. Relying on his background in forensic science, Miles called his client and asked her to take a complete DNA test workup, which he hoped would reveal a lead. This, along with any information Tracy could provide about her mother's side of the family tree, would be the starting point.

"Hi, Tracy. This is Miles Darien. You've spoken with my assistant, Anne, about your quest to find your biological father. Do you have a few minutes to go over a couple of things?"

"Of course," she replied enthusiastically.

"I have a question about the reasons you want to connect with your biological father. Is this about just wanting to know him, or is it about needing to know him, like for a medical reason?" Miles suspected her motivation to find her father just might be more than a desire to connect with him.

Miles could hear her starting to cry. "Both," she replied quietly.

"Please tell me about it." Miles did his best to sound comforting.

"Obviously, I'm curious about him. Anyone would be, I guess."

"And the medical reason?"

"I told your assistant that my mom passed away and, unfortunately, she was my only living blood relative other than my biological father. I have a progressive liver disease that will eventually require a partial transplant. The lists are long, and matches are hard to find. Maybe he or one of his other children may be able to help." Her answer sounded more like wishful thinking than desperation.

"Okay. First, you must get a DNA test done. Also, I will need any information you can find that could lead us to the fertility clinic your mom went to. I'll also need all the background information you can find on her side of your family. Once we have those puzzle pieces, I will help you find an expert who specializes in these genealogy searches. This could end up being costly, so are you prepared for that?" Miles knew she could be looking at spending tens of thousands of dollars on this investigation.

"My mom left me in a good place financially, so within reason, I have the resources."

"Good. I'll send you the name of the clinic I recommend for the DNA test. You send me anything you have on your mom's family background, and on the fertility clinic she used."

She agreed. Miles promised to begin working to select a qualified genealogy expert. They agreed to speak again as soon as Tracy had received the results of her DNA test.

CHAPTER 40

Miles worked a full day, so after a brief stop at the grocery store, he arrived back home. Shortly after he walked through the front door, Ryan came down the steps from the second floor, dressed for a night out.

"Are you sure you don't want to join Bobbie and me for dinner tonight?" Ryan asked.

"Thanks, but I have some work to do. Besides, I'd like to get to bed early for once. I've been going at it nonstop ever since we returned from Mexico, so a quiet night at home with Molly really appeals to me."

"Good, then we can spend the evening simply focusing on the two of us," Ryan teased.

"Sounds serious."

"Could be," Ryan said as he grabbed his coat and walked out the door.

Miles went to the kitchen and deposited the groceries. He grabbed the leash, which sent Molly scurrying to his side. Taking her for a walk was often as much of a relief for him as it was for her. They walked along the bluff overlooking Lake Michigan. While the lake was not an ocean and the shoreline wasn't a tropical beach, the water lapping up against the shoreline gave him the same soothing sense of well-being he had experienced in Puerto Vallarta. To him, it was certainly compelling evidence of why so many people craved living in proximity to bodies of water.

About a block from home he felt his phone vibrating in his pocket. He waited until they were back in the house before he checked the phone. He had a missed a call and a text, both from Anne. The text read, "Call me!"

He called. "Sorry, I had the ringer off on my phone. What's going on?"

"A woman named Elaine McDowell called. She insisted to meet with you tomorrow morning, so I gave her a 9:00 a.m. appointment. Hope that was okay."

"More than okay. She's intimately involved in that case from Abernathy & Kromm you took for us while I was in Mexico. It's likely what she has to say will break the case wide open. See you first thing tomorrow."

Any hope Miles had of a quiet evening at home had instantly evaporated. His mind shifted back and forth from theory to theory about how she knew about his investigation and why she wanted to meet. Realizing he needed to wait until the morning to learn what revelations Ms. McDowell would provide, and still in a holding pattern waiting for a message from Pancho, he made a sandwich, poured himself a beer, and turned on the TV to watch the news.

"Did you enjoy Mexico?" Bobbie asked.

"Yes, but glad to be back in Lakeville," said Ryan. "Every aspect was amazing. The weather, the setting, the food, on and on. I even wrote an article for the *Times*. The only negative was that Miles's investigation came up empty."

"Is the investigation over then?"

"No, he's waiting on a new lead of some sort." Then Ryan dropped the big news. "Did you hear about Ken being shot?"

"What?" Her dramatic exclamation caused the entire restaurant to grow quiet. "Sorry. Tell me what happened," she whispered.

Ryan explained all that had happened to Ken, finishing with his safe return home. Having brought Bobbie up-to-date on current events, he switched to his predicament.

"All of my stuff is out of the condo in Manhattan and in storage at my friend Hank's warehouse. Miles has been great about allowing me to stay with him as long as I want, but I really do need to start looking for a permanent home," Ryan lamented.

"I totally get it. As luck would have it, I have something along those lines to tell you about that might interest you. Last Saturday night I was invited to a dinner party at my friend Alice's home. She is an English professor at the university. I got into a conversation at the dinner table with Dennis Collins, the head of their School of Journalism and Mass Communication. I casually mentioned, without your permission of course, that I have a friend who writes for the *New York Times* and might be looking to relocate."

"Is this your way of luring me to come to Madison?"

"Partially. I'd love to have you close by, but the really interesting part of the story was his response." She paused for his reaction.

"Go on," Ryan implored her.

"He told me they have an assistant professor position available which, in addition to teaching classes, is the primary adviser to the student newspaper, the *Daily Cardinal*. Given your practical experience, I think you would be well suited for the position. I have his contact information if you'd like it." She handed him a slip of paper with the information on it.

"I'm not a teacher," he insisted, placing the piece of paper on the table.

"Yes you are, but obviously not in the traditional sense. Your articles teach people about a subject and help them formulate a point of view about it. Besides, your parents were both college professors, so you have an understanding of what goes on there. Also, what could be a better teaching platform than your experiences working with arguably the number-one news-paper in the free world?"

"You should do the interview instead of me," he joked.

"Well, I kind of did," she admitted sheepishly.

On Friday morning, Miles awoke refreshed. It had been some time since he had slept so soundly. The progress he'd made on his cases, coupled with a "time-out" in his search for Reese, had relaxed him considerably. He had showered, eaten breakfast, and taken care of Molly before Ryan even made an appearance. He drove to the office with his window open a crack, letting in some of the crisp morning air. When he arrived just before eight, Anne was already at her desk.

She greeted him with a smile and a "good morning."

"Hi. Can you come into my office? I want to bring you up-to-date on the progress I've made on our three open cases."

Without answering, she picked up her steno pad and followed Miles into his office. He began with the details on the trail of the missing assets in the Jasperson-divorce case.

"Do you expect that will be the end of it?" she asked.

"I think so, but let's wait for confirmation from our client."

The search for the anonymous sperm donor was next. Miles

asked Anne to begin researching which fertility clinics were operating in the area thirty years ago, and to see if any were still in existence.

Finally, he brought her up-to-date on what he'd learned about the Abernathy & Kromm data breach. "Please put a note in the file that I've engaged Brent Fogerty on this. You should receive a signed NDA from him as an email attachment. If he sends it to me, I'll forward it along to you."

"And our nine o'clock appointment?" Anne probed.

"Could be a confession or some new revelation. I'm also interested to find out how she knows we're involved in the case. I'll see her alone and fill you in after she leaves," Miles promised.

Anne returned to her desk. Miles used the time before his meeting to search his contacts for the name of the DNA clinic he had used a while back. Once he found it, he emailed the information to Tracy Littman. He straightened his desk in preparation for his meeting with Elaine McDowell. When he looked up, Anne was standing in the doorway to his office.

"Ms. McDowell is here," she announced. Miles rose from his chair and motioned for Anne to show Ms. McDowell in. She was a tall woman about forty years old, with reading glasses hanging from a beaded chain around her neck.

"Mr. Darien, thank you for seeing me on such short notice."

"Since I have been hired to find you, this is certainly my pleasure." Miles offered her a chair at his small conference table and decided to forgo any of the usual formalities. "If I may ask, how did you find out about my involvement with Abernathy & Kromm?"

"Let's just say I still have some friends there," she replied coyly.

"Fair enough. You called this meeting, so please enlighten me on the reason." Miles couldn't hold back his curiosity.

Ms. McDowell straightened up in her chair before speaking. "You have been hired, I assume, to gather evidence that I stole client information and intend to use it for profit. Let me assure you, the opposite is true. I have suspected for quite a while that someone was, in fact, stealing client information and using it illegally. When I found out who it was, I had to leave and then take some time to decide what to do about it."

"What's to decide? You go to your boss and turn that person in," Miles pointed out.

"Not the right approach when the person you suspect *is* your boss," she fired back.

Miles almost fell off his chair. "Bill Abernathy?" He blurted out.

"No. His son, William Abernathy, Jr., who goes by Will. He's Executive VP, and I reported directly to him. Once I had the proof, I just couldn't stay there. I've wrestled with what to do about it, and then when I found out you were hired to find me, I realized I might be framed by Will for his crime. That's why I went into hiding."

Miles was confused. "What convinced you to come to see me then?"

"I felt my options had come down to going to the police or coming to see you. Going to the police would likely lead to a scandal that would hurt a lot of people I care about if the firm is implicated. Coming to you might contain the damage to the one person who deserves to be punished." The rage she'd kept inside now bubbled to the surface.

"I assume you feel that if you went to Bill Sr. with your evidence, it might backfire."

"Absolutely. I could still be made the scapegoat, or at the very least be fired. It would be easy to find ways to wrongly implicate me if the thefts ever came to light. The only way I saw to escape the cage I find myself in, is to have you expose the real culprit in the course of your investigation."

Miles thought her logic was sound. "If what you've laid out is the truth, your reasoning makes a lot of sense. Are you sure you weren't a detective in a former life?" Miles hoped a little humor might put her at ease.

"Actually, there is a lot of detective work in my area of accounting. In fact, it's called forensic accounting. It's the methodology I used to look into what I suspected was going on at the firm."

Her explanation authenticated Miles's supposition. "What was Will doing specifically?"

"There's plenty of evidence showing a suspicious pattern of payments from clients' accounts where the firm handles all their bookkeeping. Setting up fake vendors, and then submitting fake invoices from those vendors for payment, is quite easy to do if you have control of both the checking accounts and transaction records."

"How do you know it was Will?"

"All the clients with the suspicious transactions were his personal clients. He had all the access and approval authority he needed to make it work." Her explanation made perfect sense.

"Any idea why he might be stealing the money? I assume his father pays him well."

"He is paid well. I suspect gambling problems, but I have no proof of that," she admitted.

"Well, you've given me a lot to go on. Please go back into

hiding and leave Anne with a secure way to contact you." They shook hands, and Elaine went out to the front office to give Anne the contact information.

Miles had a big decision to make. Turn his investigation 180 degrees and delve into Will Abernathy's misdeeds, or go directly to Will's father with what he already knew. Regardless of which alternative he chose, his first order of business was to contact Brent Fogerty to cancel his search for Elaine McDowell's nonexistent criminal activity. Then it occurred to him that Brent might still be able to help with the case.

CHAPTER 41

A s lunch approached, it occurred to Miles that he and Ryan hadn't spent much time together the last few days. Since he was leaving later that afternoon to see Ken in Chicago, he decided to invite Ryan to lunch.

They traded updates over lunch at the Blackhawk Diner. Miles began with the latest on his three new cases. Ryan filled him in on his possibilities in Madison.

"Do you have an interview for the UW job lined up?" Miles asked.

"I have a preliminary online video interview tomorrow with the department head. Assuming that goes well, they'd like me to come to Madison for another one in person on Monday." Ryan sounded genuinely excited.

"What about transportation?" Miles asked.

"The solution for that will be achieved after lunch. You will drop me off at Bixby Mazda to pick up my new car—or should I say my new used car. I bought it online yesterday. Regardless of where I end up, I'll definitely need it." Ryan had never owned a car in New York City, so this purchase was a significant step in a whole new direction.

"So, a return to NYC has been eliminated from consideration?" Miles had a firm grasp on the obvious.

"I've at least figured that much out." Ryan appeared genuinely relieved.

Miles's ride to Chicago to visit Ken was filled with emotion. They had both been through so much since they last saw each other. The fact that Reese was still at large made him feel as if he'd let Ken and his associates down, even though they hadn't fared any better in their hunt for Reese.

Just as his car turned off the Interstate and on to the Edens Expressway, his phone rang. It was Ken.

"Hi. I'm almost there but the traffic is horrible." Miles answered Ken's question before it was even asked.

"Take your time and don't park the car. Just pull up front and call me. I'll come right out," Ken instructed.

"Where are we going?"

Ken refused to elaborate, simply saying Miles would have to wait until he arrived. As he told Ken, the late-afternoon traffic heading into town was extremely heavy, barely moving at a crawl. Miles realized how lucky he was that he didn't need to deal with this mess on a daily basis. Many people do, but it was definitely not for him. The drive on the expressway to Ken's place in Andersonville took more than an hour and a half even though it was less than a twenty-mile drive. He was used to dealing with stressful situations, but this one really had his nerves on edge.

As Miles finally approached Ken's building, his traffic-induced anxiety had mostly subsided. Following Ken's instructions, Miles called him as he pulled up to his building. In a matter of seconds, Ken was out the door and scurrying down his front steps. His rapid movements were welcomed evidence that his recovery from the bullet wound and cyst-removal surgery was nearly complete.

After a warm embrace, Miles asked, "Where to?"

"We're meeting some friends at Willy's in Rogers Park. It's a casual bar-and-grill-type place. Good food, mature crowd. I think you'll like it." The Cheshire-cat look on Ken's face told Miles something was up.

"Who are the friends?" he insisted.

"Just some of my work buddies," was all Ken would divulge.

When they walked into Willy's a short time later, it took a few moments for Miles's eyes to adjust to the dimly lit restaurant. As his vision cleared, he saw a couple of familiar faces seated around a large rectangular table filled with half-full cocktail glasses and bottles of beer. One face in particular stood out. It was Agent Drummond.

"Thanks for allowing us to intrude on your reunion week-end," she said.

Miles thought about saying something flippant about not having been consulted, but he decided to be cordial instead.

"Nice to see all of you," he simply said.

"I planned this little get-together to officially welcome Ken back to his post, and to thank you for finding our fugitive," Agent Drummond said, raising her glass. The others at the table did as well.

"But, unless I missed something, he wasn't actually found." The puzzled look on Miles's face highlighted his confusion.

"Good point," said Drummond, "except you did locate him and force him to flee. A criminal on the run is a criminal who isn't likely committing other crimes while they're fleeing. Besides, our chances of catching him are far greater now as he becomes visible and likely travels through international checkpoints."

"Okay then, what should we eat?" Ken asked, effectively pausing the shoptalk.

After they ordered some food to share and another round of drinks, the casual conversation that followed moved to their favorite places to escape winter. Miles chimed in, extolling the virtues of Puerto Vallarta.

"You can't beat the combination of perfect weather, incredible food, top-notch entertainment, and of course, the pristine sandy beaches," said Miles.

"You should handle the marketing for their tourist bureau," Agent Clayton mused.

"Sign me up!" Miles declared. His inclusion in both the shoptalk and in the lighthearted conversation that followed made Miles feel that he had been accepted by Agent Drummond's team as a peer. It was a feeling he loved.

Key West, Hawaii, and Jamaica were offered up by other members of the group. Just then the food arrived. Between bites, Miles and Ken caught up. Ken beamed about how well his rehabilitation had gone, and how thrilled he was to return to work on Monday. Miles told him all about the progress he'd made on his three new cases and the exciting new possibilities that had arisen for Ryan in Madison.

"Do you think he'll take the job in Madison if they offer it?" Ken asked.

"I think it's quite possible," said Miles. "It's a natural fit given his talents and experience. It would also solve his dilemma on where to reside going forward."

"And the Bobbie thing?" Ken wondered.

"It would certainly force the issue, don't you think?" Miles was supportive of those two getting together, although he worried it was driven by Ryan's unsettled circumstances.

"I do. And I think they'd be great together. I like them both very much and fully endorse the notion of them becoming a couple."

"Quite possibly, but we don't get votes," Miles pointed out.

Once the empty plates had been removed and a third round of drinks had been ordered, Agent Drummond pulled Miles aside.

"Miles, you and Ryan did the FBI a great service with your work in Mexico. It was dangerous and took real ingenuity to accomplish what you did. It's unlikely we would have ever located his whereabouts in Cuba without your help. Like I said before, his being on the run gives us a good chance at tracking him and ultimately capturing him."

Miles beamed. "I was happy to help. I must confess that my typical cases now look pretty dull by comparison, but I'm good with that. I'll gladly leave the powerful cartels and career criminals to you and your cohorts."

"Good plan," agreed Agent Drummond.

***

Miles woke up Saturday morning to the sound of soft music playing and the smell of something delicious cooking. Ever the investigator, he hurried to the kitchen to find the source of the wonderful smell.

Ken was clad in a bright-blue apron over his jeans, looking quite the domestic as he stood at the stove. "Coffee's ready to go, so help yourself. Eggs sunny-side up or over-easy?"

"Sunny-side up, just like my mood," Miles replied suggestively.

"Bacon crispy or soft?"

"Crispy," Miles answered matter-of-factly, his provocative tone having vanished.

Ken broke out laughing. "I couldn't resist ignoring your innuendo. Truth be told, no one has ever made me feel like you did last night."

"Okay, you're forgiven," Miles conceded as he walked over and gave Ken a huge kiss. Then adding in mock anger, "Don't overcook my eggs!"

Now they were both laughing. They hadn't yet discussed

plans for the day, so they focused on their options over breakfast, ultimately deciding on spending the first part of the afternoon at the Art Institute of Chicago followed by shopping on Michigan Avenue, and finally dinner on Randolph Street.

"You understand we're taking a big risk by expecting to get into a restaurant on Randolph Street on a Saturday night without a reservation," Ken warned him.

"Sure, but we'll go early before the hordes arrive. If that doesn't work, you can just flash your FBI badge at the host." Miles was kidding, but at the same time thought it might not be such a bad idea.

"Funny. How soon will you be ready to go?" Ken asked, pointing to his watch.

"If you do the dishes, I can be ready in about an hour." Miles loved evading chores.

"Get moving then!" Ken commanded.

Ryan couldn't wait to share the latest development about the university job with Bobbie.

"Professor Collins has invited me to come to Madison on Monday for a ten o'clock follow-up interview with members of his department," Ryan announced, sounding pleased.

"So, your call with Professor Collins obviously went well. When do you plan to arrive in Madison for the follow-up interview?" Bobbie asked.

"Miles is in Chicago for the weekend, so I'll either have to wait until he gets back sometime tomorrow or come in on Monday morning. If you're offering accommodations, I could leave here tomorrow as soon as he gets back." After the words left his mouth, Ryan felt he had possibly overstepped.

"*Mi casa es su casa,*" she replied without any indication he had crossed a line.

"I'll call you once I have a better idea of my arrival time," Ryan promised. His worry turned into excitement over what might lie ahead for the two of them.

"You do know this is actually a selfish plot I've cooked up," she confessed.

"That's what makes it so intriguing," he said.

CHAPTER 42

"**H**oney, I'm home," Miles shouted cheerfully as he entered the house. No response. Ryan was nowhere to be found. Molly wasn't around either, which was solid evidence they were either out for a walk or had taken a ride in Ryan's new car.

Miles took his overnight bag up to his room and, after unpacking, logged onto his computer where he found an encrypted email from Brent Fogerty. Given the work Brent did, he was always careful when using email.

"I believe I've found someone local peddling the type of financial information your client was concerned about. At this point I can't be certain who it is. Do you want me to engage?"

Miles told him to proceed. He decided not to update Bill Abernathy until he was sure the information offered online was from Abernathy & Kromm and, if it was, that he could confirm the identity of the culprit.

The sound of the front door closing and Molly's unmistakable squealing as she bounded down the stairs confirmed Ryan had returned. Miles met Molly at the top of the stairs and, after a quick "hello," went downstairs.

"Thanks for getting home so early," Ryan said. "It will be much more pleasant driving to Madison in daylight." In the past, Ryan had been primarily a passenger on his visits to

Wisconsin, so he appreciated he didn't have to find Bobbie's place in the dark. "I'll just grab my stuff and go."

"Hope both interviews go well." Even though he was being tongue-in-cheek, Miles hoped Ryan would secure both the job and the relationship.

"Me too. I'm planning to be back sometime on Tuesday," Ryan said, not acknowledging Miles's inference tease.

As he drove to Madison, Ryan's mind shifted back and forth between the two possibilities that lay ahead. The more he thought about the position at the university, the more it appealed to him. Professor Collins had discussed how they encouraged their journalism school staff to continue publishing while performing their teaching duties. The thought of having a steady income with benefits and still continue his own essay work seemed like the ideal setup. A relationship with Bobbie was also most appealing, but the pieces of that puzzle were not nearly as well-defined.

Bobbie's house on Madison's East Side was a good-sized bungalow. It was situated on a quiet, tree-lined street much like the one in Lakeville where she grew up. As he drove into town, he passed Lake Monona, one of two large lakes that bookended Madison. Ironically, it also reminded him of Bobbie's childhood home, which was situated only a few blocks from Lake Michigan. He removed his suitcase from the trunk of the car and walked up to her front door. Before he had a chance to ring the bell, the door opened. Bobbie was standing in the doorway dressed as if they had some fancy plans for the evening.

"Have you been standing there long?" Ryan asked playfully.

"For hours!" she declared.

After a quick chuckle they hugged, and he walked into the

house. She waved for him to follow her upstairs to the empty bedroom across the hall from hers. Ryan was pleased that she wasn't rushing things. While he hoped something romantic might develop, he thought it wise for them to take it slow. They were on the same wavelength.

"It looks like you have plans for us to have a night out somewhere upscale," he guessed.

"We are. I made a seven o'clock reservation at Merchant, a really lovely restaurant close by. Hope you don't mind that I went ahead and booked it."

"I don't mind at all. I'm glad you did. Would you like to go somewhere for a drink first?" Ryan asked.

"I know just the place."

After Ryan changed his clothes, they drove to Gib's Bar, which was only a few short blocks away. From the outside it appeared to be an ordinary house, just like the others in the neighborhood. Inside it was a comfy bar with craft cocktails and a relaxed vibe.

"So, are you excited about the prospects of becoming a college professor?" Bobbie asked, not revealing the real question on her mind.

"The job sounds interesting, particularly with the addition of being adviser to the student newspaper. I did some research on both the school and the city. Both are impressive." Ryan decided not to mention how impressive he thought Bobbie was. Go slowly, he kept telling himself.

After a round of drinks and small talk, they hopped into Ryan's car and drove another few blocks to Merchant. Ryan was already seeing Madison as the kind of place he could potentially see himself living in.

Their meal was excellent, but it was their growing connection that made the night special. Ryan had to remind himself to slow down several more times during the evening. When they returned to Bobbie's after dinner, they spent a couple more hours talking, and then decided to call it a night. They shared a short hug and a kiss on the cheek before adjourning to their respective bedrooms. It appeared that Bobbie had given herself the same directive.

When Ryan arrived on campus at the University of Wisconsin the following morning, he was stunned by the enormity and beauty of the place. His meeting was at Bascom Hall, appropriately located on Bascom Hill. The well-worn lecture hall where Professor Collins set up the interview was huge with stadium-style seating for at least two hundred students.

Once Ryan arrived at the front of the room, the five professors stood and introduced themselves.

Professor Collins began the interview. "Don't worry, Ryan. Our interrogation does not include waterboarding." The laugh they all shared immediately relaxed Ryan. The interview went on for about thirty minutes before Professor Collins raised his hand as a sign to stop.

Again, they all exchanged handshakes, and left Ryan feeling even more enthusiastic about the opportunity than he was going in. The interview had energized him, so he decided to take a stroll around campus before driving back to Bobbie's.

After about fifteen minutes, his phone pinged. He saw two texts, each with the same basic message, "How did the interview go?"

He would reply to Bobbie's inquiry in person that evening, so he called Miles.

"Hi. The honest answer to your question is, I don't know. It was cordial, and I feel like my answers were well received, but I'm just not sure."

"I assume there are other applicants." Miles's assumption was likely the case.

"Most likely, but it was never mentioned."

"Well, good luck. I know you'd be great at it. Are you coming home tomorrow as planned?" Miles's question sounded like more than a casual inquiry.

"That's the plan."

"Good, because we have some work to do."

"What work?" Ryan wasn't aware of any open assignments the two of them had.

"I just got a text from Pancho containing a message from Stefan," Miles revealed.

"What was the message?" Ryan was sure he wouldn't like the answer.

Miles proved him right. "Just one word: 'Chicago.'"

CHAPTER 43

S ince Ryan would have to wait for more information, he spent the rest of the afternoon wandering around the campus and then up State Street to the Capitol, all the while rolling over in his mind all the implications of the one-word text that had apparently pinpointed Reese's current location.

Miles saying they had work to do indicated he believed they would somehow be involved in tracking Reese down. Would the FBI again use them as bait? With all their resources, couldn't they just track him down on their own?

An hour passed with no return call from Miles, so Ryan called him instead.

Miles answered the phone with an apology. "Sorry to keep you hanging, buddy boy, but I was on the phone with Ken and Audrey until a couple minutes ago."

"You said we have work to do. What did you exactly mean by that?"

"It was an assumption. I didn't actually know at the time, but I do now." An air of resolve was evident in Miles's voice.

"And . . .?"

"You and I are supposed to go to an FBI safe house in Chicago, both for protection and in the event they need us to somehow assist in drawing out Reese." Miles seemed to actually be looking forward to such an assignment.

"That's what I was afraid of." Ryan shook his head.

"Sorry to break this to you, but they want us down there this evening. Please get back to my house as soon as you possibly can. The FBI will have armed agents here in a car waiting to take us to the safe house. How soon can you be back?"

"I'll just drive back to Bobbie's house to pick up my things. I'm hoping she can either meet me there to let me in or tell me how to get in without her."

"Good," said Miles. "Update me once you're on the road."

Ryan agreed, and then immediately called Bobbie, first updating her on his interview and then telling her that Miles needed his help on a case in Chicago, which required him to return immediately.

"I don't understand," she said.

"He didn't go into any detail, but he said it was urgent so I told him I'd get back right away. Is there a way I can get into your house without you having to come home?" Ryan asked, wanting to save her the inconvenience.

"Sure. There is a keypad outside the garage. The code is 9259. The door between the garage and the house is unlocked. I do have one question though. Are you really leaving to help Miles or simply to avoid what might transpire between us tonight?" Her question revealed her insecurity about their new relationship.

"If you still want me to, I'll return immediately after this case is over," Ryan promised.

"Good answer. Be careful, and get back here ASAP!" she demanded.

When Ryan arrived at Miles's house, he noticed two unfamiliar cars out front. As he pulled into the driveway, Miles immediately came out of the house to greet him.

"Hi. It's likely we'll be there for at least several days, so pack everything you might need," Miles said.

Ryan pulled his suitcase from the trunk of his car. "Okay, but why are there two cars parked in front of the house?"

"They decided it would be safer if we traveled to Chicago in separate cars," Miles replied, unfazed by the obvious implications.

Ryan's facial expression showed that, unlike Miles, he was definitely not unfazed by those implications. "You mean if one gets fired upon, I assume."

"Go and pack!" Miles said, pointing to the staircase.

Ryan emerged ten minutes later, having been ordered to hurriedly replenish his suitcase. His shoulder bag bulging now with all the work-related notebooks and electronics he hadn't taken with him to Madison.

Given the time of day, the ride to Chicago would be considerably slower due to the afternoon rush-hour traffic. Miles was ecstatic that, unlike his last trip, someone else was dealing with the stress of negotiating the onslaught of cars and trucks.

To make good use of their travel time, Miles and Ryan spoke to each other by phone the entire way. Miles decided to ask Ryan about his budding romance as a way of taking his mind off what may lie ahead.

"So, are things accelerating between the two of you?"

"They might have if you hadn't pulled me away," Ryan shot back.

"Sorry, couldn't be helped. Seriously, is there some there, there?" Miles was hopeful.

"Using the word 'there' three times in one sentence may be your new record," Ryan pointed out.

"Stop avoiding the answer!" Miles demanded in mock anger.

"Yes, I believe there is some there, there," Ryan confessed.

"You've just tied the record." Miles's retort made them both laugh. Laughter would surely be a precious commodity as the danger they faced escalated dramatically. Just then the driver of Miles's car slammed on the brakes, narrowly missing the delivery van that had cut in front of them.

"Chicago traffic never disappoints," Miles exclaimed.

"Did something happen?" Ryan sounded concerned.

"Nothing significant. Just my play-by-play account of the highway action. We had to make a sudden stop to avoid being cargo in the delivery van that cut us off." Miles's explanation was remarkably calm.

"Changing subjects, were you able to resolve that accounting firm case?" Ryan asked.

Miles couldn't wait to share his client's forthright response to the findings with Ryan. "Just did before we left. It turned out the real culprit was the owner's son, who is also an executive at the firm. He was stealing from his clients by manipulating their accounts and using their funds to support a gambling habit. I sent the evidence I had accumulated to the father, and then called him so we could walk through it all. After a thorough review of all the evidence, he immediately promised to personally reimburse the clients for the money his son had stolen. Then, if his son is willing, the father will help him enroll in a gambler's-anonymous-type rehab program."

"Seems like an honorable man. What about the woman who had originally been accused of the thefts?"

"He is an honorable man and the next part is, for me, really the best part of the story. He wants her to come back to work, taking his son's executive position." If Ryan had been in the car, he would have seen Miles beaming with satisfaction.

"Do you resolve all your cases so neatly?" Ryan joked, but with obvious admiration.

"No, unfortunately. That said, we've had a number of positive outcomes lately, but that's not the norm. Usually, someone is at fault and suffers some major consequences for their actions."

"Let's hope that's the case for Reese," Ryan said.

CHAPTER 44

Both cars arrived at the safe house around seven thirty. Calling it a "safe house" was somewhat of a misnomer. It was safe for sure, but not a house. The building was actually a converted warehouse in an industrial park adjacent to Midway Airport. The location made sense for two reasons. First, it was not in a residential area where innocent people could be endangered by a violent confrontation. Second was the setup. The building only had two entrances, with no windows at ground level. One entrance was a single, large overhead door on the front of the building, and the other was the office entrance on the side. Both were fortified with sophisticated security systems and reinforced doors with automatic locking systems. Their visit was definitely not the first time this facility had been used for a similar purpose.

The on-duty agents, other than the ones who brought Miles and Ryan to the safe house, were all dressed as warehouse workers. Whatever they were armed with was well hidden underneath their jackets, which likely concealed bulletproof vests as well. Miles assumed the locked cabinets attached to the back wall housed an assortment of heavy firepower.

The warehouse office space had been redesigned to allow for conversion into multiple bedrooms as needed. It was equipped with several movable partitions rather than stationary walls. This would allow the room to be configured as needed to accommodate the number of people staying there. A large number of cots were stacked off to the side, which could deploy in a matter of minutes. The layout also included a good-sized bathroom which, with its multiple toilet stalls and shower room, resembled a high school locker room. There was also a stove, refrigerator, and a single television. The larger area of the warehouse acted as a garage for the agents' vehicles, and included some long tables and chairs as well as a small exercise area with some free weights and a treadmill.

"Home sweet home," Miles declared, tongue-in-cheek.

"I must say I've never stayed in a place quite like this," said Ryan.

"You must not have been in the armed services," a familiar voice declared.

Sure enough, there was Agent Drummond, who must have slipped through the side door while they unpacked.

"How was your ride in?" she asked in the businesslike tone she always assumed when her agents were present.

"Harrowing, as expected," Miles replied.

"I'm doing everything I can to ensure this will be as harrowing as it gets while you're here. Speaking of which, please remember you are to stay in this building so we can provide you with protection until we get a line on the whereabouts of Jonathan Reese. Understand?" She spoke firmly.

"I have a question," said Miles. "You had to curtail our search in Mexico because of budget restraints, correct?"

"Yes, that's right. Why do you ask?"

"Watching my home and office. Bringing us here, guarding us, feeding us, and going all out to find Reese costs money, doesn't it?"

"Yes, but that's all included in my discretionary budget.

Mexico was money specifically approved by my boss in DC. Does that answer your question?"

"Yes. I get it."

"Anyone have any other questions?" she asked.

Miles raised his hand like he was in school. "So, no news on Reese?"

She shot him a dirty look. "Nothing yet. Assuming your friend in Mexico is right about his return to the area, I suspect we'll get wind of him very soon. I'm not anticipating the need for you to assist in any way."

"And if you do need us . . ." said Ryan.

"Let's cross that bridge if we come to it. For now, you're here for security purposes only." Agent Drummond had deftly deflected the question.

"What about Ken?" Miles asked.

"He'll be working at headquarters and staying at a different secure location," she assured him.

Miles accepted her explanation with a nod although he had hoped for more reassurance about Ken's safety.

"Will we have internet access?" Ryan asked.

"Yes. But you will need to use our VPN and an incognito browser when you do. One of the agents will assist you in setting that up. Any other questions?" Agent Drummond asked, staring directly at Miles.

"What about meals?" Miles's one-track, food-oriented mind had popped up once again.

She cracked a smile as if she knew the question was coming. "There are beverages in the refrigerator and snacks in the cupboards. We'll have each day's meals dropped off every morning. That's it for me." With that, she turned for the door and motioned for the agent standing behind her to follow.

"Kinda like jail, wouldn't you say?" Ryan suggested.

"Yes," replied Miles, "but in this case the walls are there to keep the criminals out."

The night passed uneventfully. Miles awoke in the morning to the sound of a group discussion coming from the large, open area of the warehouse. Miles dressed quickly and went to see what was going on. He found Ryan standing off to the side of the room.

"Just in time to see the changing of the guard," Ryan announced.

"I wondered what caused all the commotion. Did the new shift bring breakfast?" Miles asked, true to form.

"Yep. All properly stowed in the kitchen. By the way, they also left each of us with an untraceable phone to use."

That's all Miles needed to hear. He headed directly to the kitchen and rummaged through the grocery bags that had been deposited on the kitchen counter.

Ryan joined him. "What are you planning to do today to pass the time?"

Before answering, Miles pulled a box of Cheerios and a container of milk from the bags. "I'll see if I can make some progress in my client's search for her sperm-donor father. And you?"

"I've decided to take what I've learned about Puerto Vallarta and turn it into a travel article."

"For your guy at the *Times*?"

"Sure, but he'll likely just refer me to the editor of the travel section. If they turn me down, I'll have to submit it to other publications." After answering Miles's question, Ryan left the kitchen to get to work at the small desk in the bedroom that he had chosen for his workstation.

Miles stayed in the kitchen, positioning his laptop on the table alongside his cereal bowl and coffee cup. He spent about an hour scouring the internet, looking for an expert in genealogy to assist with his research on behalf of Tracy Littman. While he was in the process of editing his list of possibilities, it dawned on him that he and the FBI had left Anne totally exposed should Reese come looking for him at the office. He immediately picked up the phone and, since it was before her normal starting time, called her cell phone.

"Good morning, Darien Investigations," Anne answered in an uncharacteristic monotone.

Miles was relieved to hear her voice. "Hi, Anne. It's me."

"I was so worried about you!" she exclaimed.

"Why?"

"The FBI stopped by the office late yesterday and instructed me to have all the office calls forwarded to my cell phone. Then they told me to leave the office and stay somewhere other than my house and not to call you. They didn't say why, but obviously I did what they said. What in the world is going on?"

Miles felt elated and guilty all at the same time. The FBI had not left Anne exposed like he had.

"Remember when I told you about the Olivia Sims case? Well, the man behind that criminal enterprise has resurfaced, and the FBI believes he may try to exact revenge on me and others close to me, particularly those who were involved in the case. Thankfully, Olivia is in Florida on spring break, and George and Cora are at their place on Rock Lake with Molly. Now that you're in a safe place, everyone appears to be accounted for."

"Where are you?" Anne asked.

"Ryan and I are in a safe place, also thanks to the FBI. I have some work for you to do on Tracy Littman's case, which I suspect will be a welcome distraction. I've uncovered four candidates who appear to have the right credentials to assist us with the genealogical research on Tracy's biological father. I'd like you to interview each of them and give me your recommendation on which one to hire. Then I'll follow up with that person to get things rolling. Do you know if Tracy had her DNA test yet?"

"I don't know but I'll find out. Do you want me to stay in touch with you at this number?"

"Actually, I think it's wiser to use email," Miles advised. "Much harder to use it to pinpoint someone's location. Please send the emails to my personal account, not the business one. I trust you have a personal account as well, and if you don't mind, let's use that on your end."

"I do, and I'll send you an email so you'll have my address. Then email me your list of genealogists and I'll immediately get started on the interviews. As soon as I have the information about the status of Tracy's test, I'll send that back to you. Thanks for trusting me with that assignment. It means a lot to know you have that level of confidence in me." Anne's voice had returned to its normal upbeat tone.

"You've earned it," said Miles, pleased. "Keep me posted on your progress."

"I will," she promised.

Miles had been instructed not to access his office email until advised it was secure. He decided he had to check it once before complying to see if anything important had come in. Depending on the subject and the sender, he would decide whether to respond and how. Only two of the emails were important. The first one was from Carl Rafferty about Danny's assault case. It read:

"The charges have been reduced to a misdemeanor, and they will be expunged in a year if there are no other incidents. Given their son's provocation of Danny, the family of the boy has agreed to settle for reimbursement of their out-of-pocket medical costs, which will likely be limited to their insurance deductible. All in all about the best possible outcome. Carl."

The second was from Jim Rathburn thanking Miles profusely for referring him to Carl. Another positive outcome to add to his recent winning streak, Miles thought. Under the circumstances, responses to both could wait until Miles felt safe using his own phone to call them.

As the last order of business at her afternoon staff meeting, Agent Drummond asked her investigators if they had uncovered anything indicating Jonathan Reese's return to Chicago.

Agent Harmon reported that a small plane had landed at Palwaukee Municipal Airport in Palatine after midnight two nights before.

"What was so unusual about that?"

Agent Harmon handed the report to Agent Drummond. "We have alerted all airports in the area to notify us of all noncommercial flights that land without filing a flight plan in advance. That was the first one to be reported. Particularly interesting about that one was that it landed and dropped off a single passenger who had a car and driver waiting for them. The plane took off as soon as the passenger was clear of the aircraft. We're checking on details of the plane's registration so we can look into its origin and then interrogate the pilot about the passenger."

"Good work. Keep me posted on any additional information you uncover. What else?"

None of the agents had anything additional to add.

"Come on, boys and girls, we have the upper hand here. We have information that he may be in the area, and he has no idea we know it." She adjourned the meeting with an order. "Get after it, people!"

Ken stayed behind to talk to his boss. "Any reason why I can't take a ride out to the safe house to visit Miles?" he asked.

"A big one. We want as little activity around that place as possible. If anyone should spot you going in there, they'll surely know where Miles is hiding."

"Wouldn't they assume the same thing if they see me at my own safe house?"

"Sure, but he wouldn't be there. Listen, Ken, I'm just trying to minimize exposure for everyone involved in this. If Reese is here in town, we'll get him soon enough and then everyone's life can return to normal. Understand?" Her question was more like an order.

"Of course, but I had to ask."

"Now you've asked. Sorry I couldn't give you the answer you wanted. Let's get back to work and find that creep."

CHAPTER 45

Miles reheated the pasta dish that had arrived that morning while Ryan added the dressing to the premade salad mix.

"I've always enjoyed a nice quiet evening at home watching TV, but being locked up in here is painful," lamented Miles. "I now fully understand the term 'incarceration.'"

"I'd almost prefer to be dangled as an enticement for Reese," Ryan added.

"Maybe we should petition for parole," Miles suggested.

"Funny."

"No, I'm serious. If they don't get a line on Reese soon, I'm more than willing to jump into the fray." Miles's suppressed fury about all that Reese had done was showing through.

Ryan simply shrugged. While he likely had some of the same feelings, he surely recognized this job needed to remain solely in the hands of the FBI. They were both well aware that Agent Drummond would only expose them to danger as a last resort.

Having said his piece, Miles finished his meal and opened his laptop. The email he'd been expecting from Anne about progress on the Littman case was there as promised.

"I've talked to all four possible candidates, and I recommend Jeremy Finchem. He sounded knowledgeable, and is available to begin the search immediately. He mentioned he would like to meet directly with Ms. Littman to learn more about her family. I also received the DNA test results from Ms. Littman. Should I engage Mr. Finchem and send over those results along with Ms. Littman's contact information?"

Miles decided to let her proceed. "Yes, absolutely. Good work (as usual). Please let Tracy know Mr. Finchem will be reaching out to her."

Having finished with email, Miles went to the website of the *Lakeville Examiner* to see what was happening back home. Mostly the same old news about the local politicians fighting over budget allocations, and another bleak weather report. A story on page two of the local news section jumped right off the screen: "Breaking News! Local Office Building Damaged by Fire. Arson Suspected."

It was his building. He yelled for Ryan.

"You have to notify Audrey immediately!" Ryan declared.

"I'm calling her now."

Agent Drummond immediately answered the call. "Hi, Miles. I suspect you saw the news about the fire at your office building early this morning. We're on it."

"Did the fire reach my office suite?" he asked.

"The fire was contained to the basement, but the sprinkler systems throughout the building were activated, which caused extensive water damage to the contents of the offices. I suspect the fire was set by someone connected to Reese."

"Audrey, why start a fire at my office when there was no chance I would be there?"

Before explaining, Agent Drummond set down the phone and put it on speaker. "He surely realizes the risks in watching your house in hopes of getting a shot at you. The chance of being detected was simply too great. By starting the fire, he hoped you would come running, and he or one of his cronies would get a clear opportunity to bring you down. I suspect by now he has figured out it was you who tried to track him down in Mexico, and the one responsible for uncovering his hiding place in Havana. Listen, he could have vanished again to some far corner of the world but chose to come after you instead. You're a massive thorn in his side, and he's decided he needs to see to your removal personally, regardless of the risks. This gives us a chance to get him."

Her theory gave Miles an idea. "If that's the case, don't you think now is the time for me to bait him into forcing his hand?"

"Not just yet. We have gone to great lengths to keep you hidden from him. My strategy is to continue to frustrate his attempts to get at you. The more attempts he makes, the more chances we'll have to catch him." Agent Drummond's logic made sense, even if it would likely further delay Reese's undoing.

"I appreciate what you're saying, Audrey, but don't we have to give him something he thinks will lead him to me?"

"Of course. We're working on that. By the way, I've taken the liberty to dispatch a clean-up team to do what they can to remediate the premises for you. The clean-up crew is something the building folks could have called upon, so that doesn't provide him with any new information. Is there anything you need from your office?"

"Thankfully, both Anne and I have our computers with us. Our other important digital files are all stored on a cloud server, so we're okay there. None of the other stuff in the office is mission-critical at this point."

"Listen, Miles. I know you want to get this over with sooner than later, but time is on our side. For the time being, you're best staying put. Remember, he's the one who's on the run."

Never one to miss a punchline he added, "Yeah, but he doesn't have to eat the food here."

"Goodbye, Miles."

CHAPTER 46

A gent Harmon leaned into Agent Drummond's office and knocked on the doorframe. "I have some information on the passenger in the plane that landed at Palwaukee the other night."

Agent Drummond didn't look up from her paperwork. "And it is . . .?"

"Turns out it was one of the football coaches from Northwestern returning from a recruiting trip." His announcement meant another possible lead wasn't a lead at all.

"Don't those guys fly commercial?" she asked.

"Apparently not when they're going to Scobey, Montana," Agent Harmon pointed out.

"Never heard of it," she admitted.

"Exactly."

As Miles poured his morning cup of coffee, an unfamiliar agent walked into the kitchen and held out a phone.

"Call for you," he announced, handing it to Miles.

"Hello, this is Miles."

"Hello to you too." It was Ken.

"God, I've missed hearing your voice. How are things at *your* secret location?" Miles asked.

"Fine, thanks. Listen, the reason for my call is I've been

asked to monitor your emails, and Ryan's, to ensure there aren't any suspicious ones. Audrey thought you would both prefer to have me do it rather than one of the other agents."

"She thinks of everything." Miles approved.

"So, I'll let you know if I find anything in your emails that requires immediate action. I did see one for Ryan that I think he'll want to know about if he hasn't already seen it. Is he available?" Ken asked.

"Sure. One moment." Miles got up, phone in hand, and walked into the main area of the warehouse where Ryan was using the treadmill.

"Call for you," Miles said, holding out the phone to him.

Ryan had a puzzled look on his face as he turned off the treadmill, briefly toweled himself off, and then took the phone. Ken let Ryan know an email was received from Professor Collins regarding the job at the university. Ken read the email to Ryan over the phone. It was a request for him to come to Madison and speak to a class. Sort of an audition. Ryan was elated that the position was within his grasp, if he could only convince his protectors that the trip to Madison had minimal risk. Ken offered to plead Ryan's case to Audrey, and then asked to speak to Miles.

Ryan handed the phone back to Miles.

"Listen," Ken said. "I've asked Audrey to let me come visit you. She said she'd think about it."

"Keep me posted. I miss you," Miles confessed.

"Same here," Ken replied, signing off.

When he got back on the treadmill, Ryan's excitement shifted his normal walking pace to a run.

When Ryan finally got off the treadmill thirty minutes later, he joined Miles, who was in the kitchen watching television.

"Anything interesting on TV?" Ryan asked.

"Not as interesting as you likely getting the job at UW, and everything that means." Miles did not sound totally supportive of the idea.

"You mean Bobbie, I assume," Ryan replied, picking up on Miles's lack of a full-throated endorsement.

"That and planting roots in a whole new city and lifestyle. Lots of decisions ahead for you." Miles's focus had shifted from the positives to the pitfalls.

"I detect some reservation in your voice. Is there something you're not saying?" Ryan was visibly irritated.

"I just worry that by accepting the job you may also be rushing headlong into a relationship as well. Don't get me wrong, I love both you and Bobbie and would be ecstatic if you found love together. It's just that you've just been through an awful breakup and likely need some time to heal before getting into another relationship. That's all I'm saying."

"Okay, you've said your piece." With that Ryan turned and went to take a shower.

A tall, well-dressed man walked down Pulaski Road and into Montez Dry Cleaning just before the shop closed at seven.

"Hello, sir. I'm Montez. How can I help you?" Montez asked the well-dressed man as he looked up at the clock.

The man handed him a sealed envelope and waited for him to read it, not saying a word.

"Follow me," Montez demanded after reading the letter. He locked the front door and led the man through a maze of dry cleaning racks filled with clothes covered in plastic, then through a laundry workroom to a small office at the back of the store. The office had boxes of various sizes piled to the ceiling, a couple of rickety chairs, and an old wooden desk covered with paperwork.

"So, Jonathan, this letter says some friends of mine in Mexico City want me to assist you in any way possible. Excuse me for a moment while I make a call." Montez walked out the back door of the shop into the alley, speaking rapidly in Spanish.

When Montez finally returned he asked, "How can I help you?" Apparently, the phone call had confirmed the authenticity of the letter of introduction.

"I'm looking for someone," Reese explained.

"Okay, who are we looking for?"

"His name is Miles Darien and he lives in Lakeville, just north of the Illinois-Wisconsin border."

"I'm familiar with it. Why us?" Montez was puzzled by the location.

"Several reasons. First, your friends in Mexico City are also my friends, so we can trust one another. Second, since my assets here have been depleted, you have the necessary resources I need. Third, the Chicago FBI is likely guarding him, and I suspect that means he's likely in hiding somewhere near here."

"It doesn't matter who's hiding them. We will find him." The mention of the FBI didn't faze Montez in the least. "I'm curious. Why are you taking the risk to look for him yourself?"

Reese flashed a wicked smile. "Because now it's personal."

"So, if we locate him, then what?" Montez asked.

"We end him."

CHAPTER 47

R yan was putting the finishing touches on his article about Puerto Vallarta when Ken walked into the kitchen.

"Apparently, Audrey approved your request for a visit," Ryan noted with a big smile.

"Yes, I did," Agent Drummond said. Ryan hadn't seen her walk in behind Ken.

"Miles, we have company," Ryan shouted.

Miles came quickly as if he sensed who the company might be. After exchanging hugs and handshakes, they all joined Ryan at the kitchen table.

Agent Drummond was the first to speak. "This is not just a social visit. We need to talk about Ryan's important off-site appointment next week and some ideas we've come up with to speed up our search for Jonathan Reese."

"I hope this means you'll approve my appointment," Ryan replied hopefully.

"Yes, but with significant restrictions," said Agent Drummond. "You will leave that morning, accompanied by two agents, and go directly to your event. Then return immediately afterward. You will not make any other stops before or after. It is important that you only correspond with your host about your travel plans. May I assume these terms are acceptable?"

"Of course. I can't thank you enough." Ryan couldn't wait

for the conversation to end so he could confirm his plans to Professor Collins.

"Good luck with the job. Now on to finding Mr. Reese. Assuming your information about him being in Chicago is correct, we have to conclude that he, or someone working with him, is watching the places where you might be likely to turn up. We can also assume he may have figured out you are in hiding, possibly with our assistance—"

"What I don't understand," Miles interrupted, "is that if Reese suspects you're guarding us, why would he risk a confrontation knowing he would be greatly outmanned?"

"Because, like you, he needs for this to end. Also, he's not foolhardy. He has, or will have, substantial forces of his own."

"This sounds like a war," said Ryan.

"Very much like a war," Agent Drummond agreed. "So, our challenge now becomes how to have him see you and make a move while, at the same time, mitigating your risks." It was Agent Drummond's job to accomplish missions with the least possible collateral damage, particularly involving civilians. This operation had the potential for collateral damage written all over it.

"I don't see how you can do that," Miles said.

"We will have an agent disguised as you," she announced.

"How will that work exactly?"

"We have an agent who fits your description to a T. A little makeup and a baseball cap and we'll have your doppelgänger." Agent Drummond's explanation drew a look of disapproval from Miles.

"That's all well and good, but how will he take the bait? He's a smart operator. Some guy walking down the street who kind of looks like me won't do the trick." Miles skepticism was well founded, Ryan thought.

"If he's walking down the street holding hands with me, it will," Ken said, adding the clincher.

"This is way too chancy," Miles said.

"Miles, this is what we do. Our job is to find and arrest the bad guys and this is one very bad guy. The fact that he's after you is merely my job and your situation intersecting." Ken was adeptly sidestepping his relationship with Miles and prioritizing his role as an FBI agent.

Miles said nothing as he got up and slowly walked around the room. The other three at the table waited anxiously for Miles to rejoin them and offer his response. After a couple of minutes, Miles returned to his seat at the table.

"It should be me. In fact, it must be me. We can't take the risk that Reese will see through the masquerade and not act." Miles had a point.

"But Miles, you're not trained for this type of thing. My agent is," Agent Drummond reminded him.

"I may not be as highly skilled as your guy is, but I can defend myself. I've done it countless times before. I see no better way to convince Reese to show himself. If we can't draw him out into the open, the threat he poses could go on indefinitely."

Agent Drummond got up from her seat and looked straight at Miles. "Okay then, we'll draw up a detailed plan with you and Agent Caldwell as the operatives. This is not my preferred way to approach this situation, but your point is well taken. Back to your issue, Ryan. Before you send whatever you're planning to your guy at the university, have Agent Caldwell look over it."

Miles and Ryan shared a knowing look. They had found it amusing that Agent Drummond always referred to Ken as Agent Caldwell, even if Miles and Ryan were the only other people in the room.

When Agent Drummond left the kitchen to talk to another agent on duty, Ken waited with Miles while Ryan went off to draft his response to Professor Collins. It gave the two of them a few minutes alone.

"Do you think it was a mistake to have forced Audrey to use me as bait?" Miles asked.

"You made the right call, but I just wish it wasn't."

Miles let out a deep sigh. "Ken, this thing needs to end or I'll spend forever looking over my shoulder and wondering if I'm being hunted and endangering the people around me."

Ken wrapped an arm around him. "Well, let's end it then."

It took Ryan all of five minutes to draft a response to Professor Collins about accepting the offer to speak to the class, in accordance with Agent Drummond's stipulations. He picked up his laptop and walked back into the kitchen to show it to Ken.

"How's this?" he asked as he set down the laptop in front of Ken.

"Looks good to me," Ken said.

After Ryan sent his response to Professor Collins, he noticed another important email in his inbox. It was from Ted.

Ryan laughed out loud.

"What's so funny?" Miles asked.

"Nothing really. Just Ted being Ted. He loved the travel piece but, as always, wondered when I'd have something he could use. Ken, how soon do you think your team will have a plan devised?"

"Soon, very soon. Our tactical team had been working on the problem for a while and came up with the original plan

using a doppelgänger as bait instead of Miles. I promise to let
you know if I hear anything about a revised plan, but it's likely
you'll hear about it first."

CHAPTER 48

A gent Drummond's intercom buzzed, and she picked up the handset.

"Agent Crivello is here to see you," her assistant, Judy, announced.

"Send him in."

An unshaven man dressed in a flannel shirt and ripped jeans appeared at her door.

"Did we have an appointment?" she asked while shuffling the papers on her desk.

"No, ma'am, but I have some information I believe has an impact on a case we've been briefed on. As you know, I've been embedded with the local Mexican Mafia for over a year. Montez called a couple of us in for a meeting last night and told us we have an assignment from our counterparts in Mexico City to assist in a search. He handed each of us one of these." The agent pulled out a piece of paper from his pocket and handed it to Agent Drummond. It was a picture of Miles.

She stopped her other work and gave him her full attention. "This is significant information. What else did he say?"

"Not much, really. We're just supposed to memorize the face of the man in the picture, then destroy the photo, drop anything else we're involved in, and wait for further instructions."

"You need to update Agent Harmon immediately if anything new—and I mean anything—develops." She dismissed Agent

Crivello with a wave of her hand, picked up the phone, and dialed Agent Harmon's extension. When he answered, she simply said, "I need to see you. Now."

Not one to enjoy doing nothing, Miles was elated to receive an email request from Anne asking him to give her a call. It offered him his first opportunity to add something constructive to his otherwise unproductive day.

"The big news is that our genealogy expert has found Tracy Littman's father, sort of," said Anne.

"Sort of?"

"I'll give you some of the key points in Jeremy Finchem's report. The report explains that by cross matching Tracy's DNA with a database of other people living in the US who had registered theirs, he was able to narrow his search, and it eventually led him to identify the father, Raymond Kress. Unfortunately, when he finally discovered Mr. Kress's location, it was in a cemetery in Boulder, Colorado. On a happier note, Mr. Finchem also found the Kresses' had a daughter, Tracy's half sister, Jill Kress Simonton, who lives in Seattle."

"Do you know if Tracy has seen the report?"

"Yes, she has. In fact, Tracy and Jill have been in touch and exchanged some family information. They have also agreed to meet at some point over the summer."

"About the best possible outcome under the circumstances."

"That's wonderful. Mr. Finchem obviously did a great job. Was his fee reasonable?"

"He charged $1,500 which seems fair to me. I have about three hours into the job. How many should I add for you?"

"Fifteen hundred is more than reasonable. I assumed it would be quite a bit more. I have about three hours in as well.

I assume Tracy paid the DNA lab out of pocket. If that's the case, you should be able to finalize her invoice and close the file. Anything else?"

"Just a funny letter from Carl Rafferty. It contained two 50 peso notes he says he found in the pocket of a suit you borrowed." Anne laughed.

"Carl's one of a kind. What attorney returns found money? Thanks again for taking such good care of things. With any luck, I'll be back in the office in a couple of days." Miles hoped it wasn't merely wishful thinking.

"Let me know when it's safe to return to the office and I'll be there," Anne assured him.

Just before the end of the day, Agent Drummond assembled a group of agents that made up the team responsible for finding and capturing Reese. Now that the FBI knew Reese was in bed with the Mexico City cartel's Chicago affiliate, they had a pathway to set a trap for Reese.

The team was charged with devising a scenario that would lure Reese to a location of their choosing by utilizing Agent Crivello, who would be the conduit, as he was still embedded with the local Mexican Mafia. The plan needed to be carefully constructed so that when Reese arrived at the desired location, either alone or with reinforcements, the ensuing confrontation would result in his capture or elimination. She also made it crystal clear there were to be no civilian casualties.

She assigned Agent Harmon to lead the team, and gave them twenty-four hours to deliver a comprehensive plan for her approval.

CHAPTER 49

Armando realized he had no alternative but to call his boss and tell him what had happened to the storefront office on Calle Madero. He had to dial the number twice, as his hands were shaking the first time he tried.

Reese answered on the first ring, "What do you have to report? I trust you've closed some deals by now."

"Unfortunately not. In fact I have some other bad news to tell you. The Old Town office has been vandalized. Our computers and the large TV monitor have been stolen. And the office has been torn apart. Looks like the work of a gang." Armando's voice cracked.

"I expected something like this would happen." Reese must have guessed that whoever had disclosed his whereabouts in Havana was connected to the Velasco cartel in Puerto Vallarta. Knowing he was on the run, this was likely their first step in an attempt to take over his property.

Armando could hear the anger in Reese's voice but was relieved that it was not directed at him, at least for now. "What should I do?" he asked as calmly as his fear would allow.

"For the time being, keep the office closed. And close down the trailer in Versalles. I will be in touch."

Montez was pleased that Reese understood his text message

saying, "Your dry cleaning is ready." arrived at the store promptly at 6:55 p.m. Reese stood off to the side, impatiently jingling the change in his pocket as Montez waited on his last customer of the day. After handing the woman a receipt for the clothes she dropped off, Montez followed her to the door and locked it behind her.

Once again, Montez led Reese through the maze of dry cleaning to his office in the back.

"I have some news from our friends in Mexico," Montez began.

"If it's about my office in Puerto Vallarta being torn up, I've already heard about it. I suspect the local cartel there is responsible for that and for divulging my hiding place in Havana."

"If it is, in fact, the local cartel, it's a bold move on their part. I'm sure our friends are looking into who's responsible, and if they discover that it is the local cartel it will be swiftly dealt with. Now I have another bit of important news to discuss with you. We have reason to believe that one of our guys may actually be an FBI informant." Montez spoke calmly, as if totally unfazed by finding out there might be a traitor in his midst. It must not have been the first time he'd dealt with such things.

"You didn't mention having taken care of him," Reese pointed out.

"All in good time. First, we intend to use him to deliver Mr. Darien to you."

Reese smiled in appreciation. "How do you intend to do that without initiating a major confrontation with the FBI?"

Montez then spelled out his plan in detail with particular emphasis on what Reese's responsibilities were to be. After a short exchange of questions and answers, they adjourned for the evening. The prospect of finally concluding his business with Miles Darien successfully shifted Reese's focus away from the unpleasant events of the day in Puerto Vallarta and squarely onto the task at hand in Chicago.

Miles was watching TV when Ryan walked into the room.

"How is your lecture presentation coming along?" Miles asked.

"I have a draft finished, but it needs a little punching up. I'd like to get it polished and ready to go tonight." Ryan seemed particularly nervous about the lecture. Miles understood it wasn't the presentation itself but rather the impact it could have on Ryan's future. Not to mention Reese being on the loose, which added a whole other dimension to his uneasiness.

"Do you think it needs some jokes?" Miles asked, only half kidding.

"No just some lighthearted observations, I think. Would you read it and possibly give me some suggestions?"

"Sure."

Miles jumped at the chance to help Ryan add some levity to his presentation. It would provide a welcome distraction from the anxiety he, too, was feeling from Reese being at large and likely looking to hunt down the two of them. He spent the next two hours poring over the eight-page presentation, making notes in the margins where he saw places for the type of improvements Ryan had asked for. After handing the pages back to Ryan, Miles went to bed hoping he'd somehow be able to fall asleep.

CHAPTER 50

R yan was up before dawn on Monday morning. The anticipation of what his lecture and job interview would mean for his future had him on edge. There were a couple of hours before he and the agents, who would be his bodyguards, needed to leave for Madison, so he went online to research the rental market for apartments there. He would need to find one a couple of miles from campus, as the ones close by were outrageously expensive. He bookmarked a few options in the hope he would actually need a place.

"Time to go," Agent LaMarca declared.

Ryan knocked on the partition acting as the wall of Miles's bedroom. "I'm leaving. Wish me luck."

"You won't need luck, buddy boy. I know you'll impress the hell out of them." Miles's assurance was a significant endorsement given the cautions he had voiced before.

"Thanks. See you tonight."

Judy appeared at Agent Drummond's office door. "Agent Crivello is here to see you again. Says it's important."

"Show him in," she instructed.

Agent Crivello walked into the office and positioned himself at the front of her desk, and without prompting or saying hello, he announced, "I think something big is going down. A couple of other guys and I have been told to be at the Montez Dry Cleaning shop at seven tonight. I've never been asked to be there before. We always meet at an apartment the gang uses for meetings. This can only mean they're making some sort of move and they need some muscle to pull it off."

"Hopefully, this is the break we've been waiting for. I'm thinking we should have a team following you from a distance just in case something goes awry," she theorized.

"I think that would be a mistake. If they smell that anything is out of place, they may abandon their plan and maybe even blow my cover. I can handle myself and find a way to keep you informed."

"See that you do." Agent Drummond had not completely abandoned the idea of backing up her agent. Knowing where he would be gave her the option to postpone her decision for a few hours.

Ryan and the agents arrived in Madison about an hour and a half before he was due at the lecture hall. After a brief lunch break, the agents left Ryan at the entrance to the building and asked that he call when he was ready to leave. When Ryan arrived at the lecture hall, Professor Collins was waiting for him by the door.

Only a few students were in the lecture hall when they entered. Professor Collins reminded him that most students are typically last-minute arrivals. Ryan placed his notes on the lectern and took a seat next to the professor. Sure enough, the room was full when the bell rang. The audience also included the rest of the interview committee, who were seated in the last row.

The professor gave Ryan a brief introduction and then turned the class over to him.

As Ryan approached the lectern, there was a smattering of applause.

"Thank you, Professor Collins. Does anyone here own a typewriter?" Ryan asked.

One student and all the members of the interview committee raised their hands.

"I also must admit to owning one. It's displayed like an ancient artifact on a shelf in my office just above my computer desk. Can't tell you how many times people ask me, 'What the hell is that there for?'. I suspect that's likely the case for those of you who raised your hands. For me it's a symbol of evolution. It revolutionized the ability of journalists to efficiently produce their work. The computer took that process one giant step further. It provided a vehicle to publish without the necessity of an established media outlet.

"Of course, there are still numerous reputable media outlets, but today's landscape is far more vast than that. Regardless, if you're writing an opinion piece on your personal blog or an article for a widely syndicated outlet, the only way you can differentiate yourself from all the clutter is to do your work using actual facts to tell a truthful and compelling story. Not your truth, but the real truth. Finding that real truth that authenticates what you write is what provides the key element in great journalism. It's called integrity."

Once Ryan finished his talk and all the students had left the lecture hall, the rest of the committee walked down the aisle to join the professor and Ryan on stage. As they approached, Professor Vandenburg gave Professor Collins an affirmative nod, which he acknowledged with one in return.

"Ryan, we are all very impressed with you and feel you'll make a great addition to our faculty. We hope you'll accept our offer to join our department." Professor Collins held out his hand, which Ryan immediately accepted.

"It will be my honor. Thank you all for this amazing opportunity." Ryan was doing his best to hold back tears. Until that moment he hadn't realized how much he really wanted this.

Ryan thanked each committee member individually before following the professor out of the lecture hall and down the corridor to his office. As they walked, all the other implications of his acceptance filled his brain. Where would he live? How would he proceed with Bobbie? Could he actually provide his students with a meaningful learning experience? What about his other essay work?

After spending an hour and a half in Professor Collins's office going over the paperwork, Ryan left Bascom Hall with a contract to review and, more importantly, a real sense of belonging. His parents would be incredibly proud to see he had followed in their footsteps. As he started down the hill, he called Agent LaMarca to let him know he was ready to return to Chicago.

"We have been advised to stay here for a couple more hours," Agent LaMarca announced.

"I don't understand."

"Something big must be going down in Chicago. We're supposed to wait here without attempting to contact anyone in Chicago until we receive word to return."

"Where are you?" Ryan blurted out. Ryan's excitement over his new job had now become anxiety.

"We're at the Wisconsin Veterans Museum. When you get

to the bottom of the hill, walk a few blocks up State Street to Mifflin Street. It's right there."

"Okay," Ryan said as he reached the foot of State Street. Even though it was quite cool outside, he felt beads of perspiration dripping from his forehead. Fear often did that to him.

CHAPTER 51

A gent Drummond had asked everyone involved in the Reese case to remain in place and wait for her instruction. She had decided to take Agent Crivello's suggestion and not have other agents follow him. There were several other unresolved cases that required her attention, so she pored over those files while awaiting word of what transpired at Montez Dry Cleaning.

"There's a call from Agent Caldwell holding for you," Judy yelled from her desk outside Agent Drummond's door.

"Put him through," she yelled back.

Ken didn't wait for Agent Drummond to speak before launching into his appeal. "Hi. I know you've asked everyone to remain in place. Seems to me I could be more useful stationed at the safe house. If there's a confrontation, the extra firepower would surely come in handy." Ken's forceful delivery made it clear he wanted to be by Miles's side if anything were to happen.

"Ken, I understand your desire to help, but I worry your personal involvement might get in the way." In this instance, she was speaking both as his boss and his friend.

"Not happening," he replied. "My first responsibility always has been, and always will be, the mission."

She knew Ken was right about his devotion to duty. "Okay then. Proceed to the safe house and report to Agent Harmon, who's running the operation there."

Agent Drummond had now taken operational advice from two of her agents on this case. She was called upon each and every day to make these types of decisions where lives were held in the balance. She hoped the two she made today were the correct ones.

Agent Crivello—"Victor"—and two other of Montez's cronies were waiting at the back door of the shop at 7:00 p.m. as instructed. Montez let them in a couple of minutes later. They joined him and two other men who were already there waiting in the large work area between the racks of clothes and the office. Agent Crivello immediately recognized one of the men he had been briefed to be on the lookout for. It was Jonathan Reese.

"So, gentlemen. Does anyone have a line on Darien yet?" Reese asked.

"Excuse me. These are my men. I ask the questions," Montez demanded.

"They may be your men, but according to the people you answer to in Mexico City—"

"I don't report to anyone," Montez cut him off. "I cooperate with those people, but I am not their errand boy!"

"They may see things a little differently. Unless you want them to come up here and explain it to you in person, you will do things my way," Reese demanded.

"Are you threatening me?" Montez asked.

"Only if necessary." Reese held his ground.

Then Montez pulled out a gun and fired. Reese grabbed his chest, which was instantly covered in blood. He slowly fell to the ground.

Montez looked at Agent Crivello. "Victor, go out into the alley and make sure no one is there."

Agent Crivello returned moments later and signaled that the coast was clear.

Montez pointed to two of the other men. "Go dump that body someplace no one will ever find it." He tossed one of the men his keys, and then clapped his hands as a signal for them to hurry up.

They picked up Reese and carried him out the back door and down the alley to Montez's car. As ordered, they loaded Reese's body into the trunk and drove off.

"The rest of you, get the hell out of here so I can clean up this mess!" Montez commanded.

Crivello and the other remaining man left out the back door, which Montez locked behind them. Owning a dry cleaning shop was convenient when cleaning up the mess from a shooting. Using the chemicals he had on hand, it only took Montez about ten minutes to erase all evidence of the shooting and dispose of the bloodstained rags.

Agent Crivello got into his car and drove off immediately after leaving Montez Cleaners. He made several turns to make sure he wasn't being followed. When he felt he was a safe distance away and not being pursued, he reached under the driver's seat for his phone and called Agent Drummond, who was in her office awaiting some news from his meeting at Montez Dry Cleaning.

"Agent Crivello, what do you have for me?" she asked calmly.

"They killed him," he told her.

Astonished, she asked, "Reese?"

"Yes," Agent Crivello answered, and then recounted in detail all that had happened at the meeting, starting with the argument and finishing with Reese's body being thrown into the car and driven somewhere for disposal.

"Are you absolutely sure he was deceased?" Agent Drummond asked.

Knowing Agent Drummond wanted absolute confirmation that Reese was gone before deciding to call off the operation, he elaborated. "As sure as I can be without taking his pulse. It appeared the bullet entered the left side of his chest. Based on the amount of blood, I'd have to think it was a direct hit to his heart. When he fell he wasn't moving at all. The other guys were as shocked as I was."

"Okay. I want you to return to the apartment you've been using as part of your assignment. We may need you to reengage with them at some point, so you must maintain your cover. I hope this will actually be the end of this case, but it's my job to be skeptical until we have indisputable evidence."

CHAPTER 52

A fter spending the balance of the afternoon exploring the exhibits at the museum, Ryan and his escorts went down the block to Cento for pizza. Just before their meal arrived, Agent LaMarca received a call.

"Excuse me for a minute," he said as he stood and went outside to take the call. Less than five minutes later, he returned. As he sat down, Agent LaMarca gave them the good news. "Well, it appears things have been wrapped up back home. Our suspect has apparently been eliminated and we're good to return as soon as we finish dinner."

Ryan was elated about the news. It immediately occurred to him to find out if he was actually required to return to Chicago with them.

When Ryan asked Agent LaMarca about it, he simply said, "Those decisions are way above my pay grade. You'll have to contact my boss about that. Here's my phone if you want to give her a call."

Like the agent had, Ryan took the phone and went outside to place the call.

"Another question?" Agent Drummond asked.

"Audrey, it's Ryan. That's really wonderful news about the case. I was wondering if I could remain in Madison instead of returning with the agents."

"Actually, that might work out well. We still need to confirm a few things on this end, and if you stay there it reduces the number of people we need to look after here. I assume you have a place to stay."

"I'll get on that right away. Thanks, and I won't let your guys go until I do," he promised.

"Say hi to Ms. Martin for me," she said, adding a chuckle as they finished the call.

Ryan was about to call Bobbie before he realized he still had Agent LaMarca's for-official-use-only phone. He went back inside to get his phone out of his briefcase and to let the agents know his plan. When he got to the table they had made great progress on the pizza. He explained he had received permission to stay and was leaving them to make arrangements. They seemed all too glad to see him go. One less person they'd have to share the pizza with.

Back outside, Ryan dialed Bobbie.

"I thought you'd forgotten about me." Bobbie's voice had a certain "Poor, poor me" tone about it.

"Never. Listen, I'm in Madison and wondered if you'd like company for the evening." Ryan hoped she didn't have other plans or he'd have to return to the restaurant and admit to needing a ride.

"Of course, but what's going on?" she asked.

"Get together with me tonight and I'll explain. By the way, I'm downtown on Mifflin Street without transportation."

"I'm still at the office. Walk over. It's only a few blocks."

"Be right there!" he replied as he headed her way.

"Can't wait. Something tells me this is will be quite an explanation."

"Knight to King four," Miles announced.

"I can clearly see the chess board. You don't have to announce your moves," Ken shot back.

Before Miles and Ken could continue their rather testy back-and-forth, Agent Drummond arrived at the safe house.

"Sorry to interrupt your game, but I have some news to share with you. We have a report that Reese has been shot and killed in an altercation with his local cartel contact," she announced.

"I can't believe it's finally over," Miles exclaimed.

"We can't be sure it's over until we have found the body. Until such time, we have to assume that Reese is still a threat," she replied.

"That could be never. I'm sure those guys are quite proficient at disposing of one in a way that ensures it will never be found," Miles pointed out.

"There is another way to be sure," said Ken.

"That is . . .?" Agent Drummond asked, even though she had a pretty good idea what he was about to suggest.

Miles answered before Ken could. "We've discussed this before. Put me out there where they can see me."

Agent Drummond paused a moment before answering. "That may have been their plan all along. Make us think Reese is dead so the threat no longer exists. Then they'd have a clear shot at you." That scenario was certainly worth considering.

"So, you're suggesting they may have staged Reese's death," said Ken.

"Doesn't matter!" Miles said adamantly. "Like I said before, this is the only way to be sure this thing comes to an end."

"If we do this, it must take place here in Chicago where we have a full complement of resources, not back in Lakeville. Any ideas on a location?" Agent Drummond asked.

"My place is the obvious choice," Ken proposed.

Agent Drummond reluctantly agreed and ordered two

agents to stay there with Ken and Miles. In case Reese or his cronies were watching Ken's condo, the agents would slip in through the back entrance at the same time Ken and Miles casually walked through the front door. In addition, there would be agents in cars randomly passing by the house to watch for any suspicious activities in the neighborhood. She also made it clear that before Miles and Ken went anywhere, she would have to approve their every movement and deploy agents to protect them.

"When you go out," she said, "you must avoid crowded places so we can keep civilians out of harm's way. I suspect if Reese is still with us, he will make his move as soon as he sees you're out in the open."

When Ryan arrived at Bobbie's office building, she was waiting at the front door. After a big hug and kiss, they walked around the corner to the lot where her car was parked. It was only a ten-minute drive to her house, but it was enough time for Ryan to give her the highlights of his day on campus and what had happened in Chicago. As soon as they walked through the front door of the house, the update ended and they raced to the bedroom.

"Can't believe it took this long to get you into my bed," Bobbie lamented.

"That's supposed to be my line," Ryan shot back.

"Quite a sexist attitude."

"Not really. Just my feeble attempt at humor. Actually, I'm quite flattered you've been so anxious for us to get together."

"Okay, now prove it was worth the wait."

Since the FBI was certain to be watching Montez Dry Cleaning, Reese and Montez agreed to rendezvous at the Airbnb Reese had rented for his stay in Chicago. It was a nicely appointed unit in the Logan Square area, not far from Montez's shop. It was a first-floor unit with both a front and a back entrance, which would come in handy if he needed to make a hasty retreat. Shortly after Montez arrived, there was a knock on the back door. It was Reese looking none the worse for wear.

"He has risen!" Montez joked.

"The plan worked perfectly," Reese replied.

"Yes, and my guy Victor told us he needed to attend to a family matter in Rockford, which is actually great news. It surely means he was the rat who was working for the FBI. It also means they've bought into our little performance. Now we just have to find Darien. First place where we'll look is his FBI-boyfriend's house. If he's still in Chicago, that's my bet."

"FBI-boyfriend?" Reese appeared genuinely shocked at Montez's revelation.

"Yep. He lives over in the Andersonville neighborhood. One of our guys drove by there a little while ago and saw the lights were on." Montez again proved himself to be more than a run-of-the-mill neighborhood gangster.

Reese smiled. "I assume you also have some inside knowledge about the boyfriend beyond where he lives."

"Let's just say two can play the informant game," Montez said.

"So, do we just wait around for him to show himself?" Reese asked.

"I have an idea on how to force him out. Let me work on it a little further and then we can discuss it." Montez got up and started for the door.

Reese paused. "Before you go, I have a question if you don't mind. How are your associates in Mexico City compensating you for all this?"

"They're not. You are. Two two-bedroom units in Ixtapa will be more than adequate."

"I'm surprised," said Reese. "Not so much by the price or method of payment but the shift in strategy by our mutual friends in Mexico City."

Montez smiled. "They must figure completing the properties makes them worth a lot more, particularly with the kickbacks from the contractors."

"Not to mention the value of adding new ones. All I have left to do now is eliminate Miles Darien, evade capture, and return to my business interests in Mexico. Seeing as though the FBI assumes I'm dead, this all sounds quite doable."

Reese pounded his right fist into his left palm for emphasis.

CHAPTER 53

J ust before Montez opened the shop for the day, three FBI agents knocked on the door.

When Montez answered, Agent Harmon handed him an envelope. "We have a warrant to search the premises."

"Not sure what you're expecting to find, but help yourself," Montez said as he let them in.

Their search lasted almost an hour after which they left empty-handed and without saying a word. Nonetheless, Montez knew the visit meant he had to take action, so as soon as he saw them drive away, he was on the phone to Reese.

"The FBI just left," Montez told him.

"I trust they didn't find anything."

"Of course not, but our missing friend Victor has put them on to us. If we're going to make a move, it had better be now," Montez insisted.

"You said you were working on a plan."

"We'll move on it tonight. They'll be watching me, so I'll have my guys pick you up at eight and fill you in on the details then. Be sure to have a weapon with you."

Miles was anxious to get things moving, not to mention how tired he was of being locked up indoors. Even though Ken's condo was far homier than the safe house, he still felt like he was in jail. When Agent Harmon arrived, Miles had his chance to let his feelings be known to someone with the authority to liberate him.

"Listen, if I'm going to be the bait, I at least have to be out and about. Don't I?" he asked.

"What do you suggest?" Agent Harmon asked.

"If they're watching the house, maybe a walk or car ride to see if they'll follow. Maybe a trip to your office. They must be watching everyone coming and going from there."

Agent Harmon laid out the plan for Miles. "Here's the deal. This morning's search has put Montez on notice that he's a suspect. We'll follow him for a couple of days. If he doesn't lead us to Reese, we'll consider your alternatives. Okay?" His proposal made perfect sense, so Miles reluctantly nodded his approval. "Glad everything here is in order. I'll see you here sometime tomorrow."

Just after Agent Harmon walked out the door, Ken walked into the room and announced, "I just got off the phone with Agent Drummond. She's bringing dinner over tonight and will relieve one of you for a couple of hours. She said you guys can arm wrestle or something to decide who gets the time off."

"Bill, you go. I'm sure your kids have been missing you," Agent Bryant offered.

"Good of you, Tom. That way you'll also save the embarrassment of losing the arm wrestling match." Agent Yarrow's reply made them all laugh.

Miles retreated to the den to check his emails. Anne had sent along write-ups on six potential new cases. There were two he could handle using his computer without needing to meet with the clients. Three of them were not urgent matters, so he would ask Anne to take the cases without promising immediate action. The last one would require him to meet with the client on Thursday, so he would ask Anne to respectfully decline the case.

After finishing his work-related emails, he composed one to Ryan to get a report on the results of his lecture and job interview. Just as he was about to click the Send button, Miles was startled by a commotion in the kitchen. The commotion turned out to be Agent Drummond shuffling the pots and pans in Ken's pantry, looking for the ones she would need to prepare dinner.

"When Ken said you were bringing dinner, I didn't expect you were the one who would be cooking it," Miles admitted. "Actually, we're both cooking it. Put on an apron, Miles!"

The two of them spent the next hour and a half preparing a dish of curry chicken and string beans. Ken pitched in by making a mixed-greens salad. Agent Bryant set the table.

"Quite a spread," Ken said, admiring the table full of food. "Too bad we're not allowed a glass of wine to go with it."

"Once we have captured Reese, the champagne is on me," Miles promised.

They all raised their water glasses as a nonalcoholic toast, and then began to eat. The scene was almost a normal dinner party among friends, though these circumstances were obviously not normal at all. After they finished their meal and cleaned up, they heard the sound of sirens rapidly approaching. Many of them. Pretty soon they saw flashing red lights brightly reflecting off the curtains in the living room. Then there was a pounding at the door.

"Fire department, open up."

The agents instinctively pulled out their weapons. Agent Drummond signaled for Ken to answer the door.

"What's happening?" Ken asked, before reaching for the doorknob.

"There's a house on fire two doors down. You need to evacuate. Now!" The fireman demanded.

After slightly pulling back one of the curtains to take a look, it was evident that there was, in fact, a fire. Even given their limited visibility it was evident the blaze was substantial. Billows of smoke and roaring flames were clearly emanating from the adjacent building. They all holstered their weapons, grabbed their coats, and left the building as instructed.

"This sure looks like something Reese might have cooked up. Stay together and stay vigilant," Agent Drummond instructed.

The fire trucks had effectively blocked all vehicular traffic on the street. As with most residential fires, this one attracted a large crowd of onlookers blocking the sidewalks. As Miles and the three agents waited for an all-clear, they scrutinized the crowd for any form of suspicious activity. Only a man running through the crowd caught their attention. When he finally caught up to his dog, they dismissed any thoughts of his being a threat.

It only took the fire department about an hour to have the blaze sufficiently in hand to allow the people who had evacuated to return their homes.

Agent Drummond called the group together. "We need to be cautious about reentering Ken's condo. Agent Bryant and I will go around back and enter the building through the rear door. Give us two minutes to get around back and another five minutes to establish that there is no danger inside. Then the two of you can enter. Does the rear door have a keypad entry system like the front door does?"

"No, it requires a key," said Ken. "It's a fail-safe I decided on in case of a power failure or keypad malfunction. Here you go." He handed her the key.

As ordered, Ken and Miles waited around front long enough

for the two agents to enter the building and search the premises. They walked to the door, and Ken punched in the keycode to unlock the door. When they entered they were startled to see a large, dark bearded intruder with his arm around Agent Drummond's neck and a hand over her mouth. He was holding a gun to her head with his other hand.

As they both reached for their weapons, a familiar voice shouted, "I wouldn't do that if I were you."

It was Reese. He and another intruder, guns drawn, had been hidden behind the front door Ken had just opened. They had no chance to draw their weapons before they would be shot, so they held up their hands in surrender.

"Smart move," said Reese. With a wave of his hand, he instructed his man to relieve Miles and Ken of their weapons while the bearded intruder kept his hold on Agent Drummond.

Reese pointed to the living room floor. "Now the two of you, on your knees over there."

Miles and Ken did as instructed.

"Where is the other agent?" Miles asked boldly.

The man who had taken their weapons menacingly waved the baseball bat in the hand that wasn't holding his gun. "He's sleeping."

Reese held up his hand, indicating he was again taking control of the proceedings. "We have some business to attend to before we adjourn our little meeting. Mr. Darien, I'm offering you a chance to save the lives of your two companions as well as the one who's 'sleeping.'"

Miles interrupted him. "There's no way you'll let them go even if I tell you what you want to know."

Reese walked over to Miles, bent over, and whispered. "I said you could save their lives. I never said I would let them go."

"Stop talking in riddles," Miles boldly demanded.

"Let's just say they'll eventually be found alive. I have no interest in giving the FBI any further incentive to hunt me down as a result of my murdering three of their agents. Instead they will be valuable assets useful for my escape. Now, let's get down to business. First, I need the name of your contact in Puerto Vallarta who provided you with my whereabouts."

"And?"

"And I need to know where Ryan Duffy is." Reese made it sound almost like a friendly request.

"What does Ryan have to do with this?" Miles did his best to keep the conversation going to buy them some time.

"Because he knows all about my operation and personnel down there. Two lives to save three. Seems like you'd be getting the better end of that deal."

"I actually don't know where he is at the moment. He went back to New York yesterday to attend to some business." Miles tried his best to make his lie sound plausible.

"I don't believe you, but nice try. You'll tell me or my friend with the baseball bat will provide you with some extra incentive." As Reese spoke, the man with the bat simply smiled. "By the way, I must say you have been a formidable foe. It's unfortunate my most recent attempt to get rid of you literally blew up before it could be implemented."

"So, it was you who sent Todd Morton to blow up my boat!" Miles's initial deduction had been correct after all.

"Good guess. Unfortunately, the idiot blew himself up instead." Reese actually sounded amused.

"I thought he was trying to exact revenge on his old buddy, Chaz, the guy who took his hand." Miles did his best to prolong the dialogue, hoping Reese would make a mistake and provide them with an opening.

"That was the beautiful part of the plan. I promised if he did my job, I'd do his. He would be somewhere far away with a solid alibi when the boat blew up and Chaz was eliminated. I was unlikely to be implicated in the boat bombing, particularly since I was nowhere to be found. It was easy to have someone get rid of Chaz. Seemed like a perfect arrangement, don't you think? Okay, enough small talk. Where's Duffy?"

Suddenly there was someone pounding on the back door. Likely it was Agent Bryant, who was no longer "sleeping." The man with the baseball bat pointed his gun at the door, intending to shoot whoever was behind it. Before he could get a shot off, Ken jumped to his feet and lunged over the coffee table in front of him, knocking the man off balance. They rolled around on the floor, furiously wrestling for control of the gun. The commotion caused the red-headed man holding a gun to Agent Drummond's head to loosen his grip just enough to allow her to elbow him in the midsection. The force of the blow caused him to release the gun and drop to the floor, gasping for air. She grabbed the gun and pointed it at Reese, who managed to fire at her first. He missed. She returned fire and did not miss. Reese fell to the floor in a heap.

Then another shot was fired. Ken and the man whom he'd been fighting over the gun stopped struggling. The shot had left the man lifeless in Ken's arms. The red-headed man who had been holding on to Agent Drummond caught his breath and rose to his feet. He held up both his hands, showing he surrendered.

Miles walked over to Reese, who lay motionless with his eyes wide open and a bullet hole in his forehead. As he stood over the body, the emotion of all that had transpired in the last few minutes, and ever since he'd first encountered this evil man, left Miles speechless and shaking. In a matter of a few seconds the carnage Reese had caused was finally over. Just as he had done so often before, Reese left multiple dead bodies in his wake. This time, however, his was one of them.

When Ken reached him, Miles wrapped his arms around him and wept.

"You could have been killed, you know," Miles scolded.

"I couldn't have died," Ken proclaimed.

"Yes, you could."

"No, because if I had died I wouldn't be able to miss you. And that would be totally unacceptable."

CHAPTER 54

A fter they were safely back in Ken's condo, Miles grabbed a beer for each of them from the refrigerator. "Ken, what do you suppose happened to Montez after all this went down?"

Before answering, Ken took a much-needed gulp of his beer. "Well, I suppose when his men didn't return after the attempt to eliminate you, he figured it went badly. Since he has so far evaded capture, he must be on the run. Audrey has made finding him a top priority."

"Not to mention his former associates in Mexico City, who certainly will do far more than simply capture him. Excuse me for a minute. There's a call I'm just dying to make," Miles added.

"Say 'hi' for me."

Miles couldn't be more excited to make the call he had been waiting to make for months. The phone rang several times before Olivia answered.

"Hi, Miles. If you're calling me while I'm on spring break it must be something important. Nothing bad, I hope." Olivia had received several unpleasant calls from Miles in the past, so her comment was more than an offhanded remark.

"Well, Ms. Sims. It definitely is not something bad. Jonathan Reese will never bother you or anyone else ever again." Olivia couldn't see it, but Miles was beaming as he spoke.

"Oh my God!" Olivia tearfully replied. "Can I tell my parents?"

"Let's do it together. I'll conference them in." Miles promptly added George and Cora to the call.

After several minutes of questions and answers, the gleeful and emotional conference call ended. Miles let out a huge sigh of both relief and satisfaction.

Before returning to Ken and his beer, Miles remembered he had one more important call to make.

It was almost midnight when Ryan heard his cell phone ring. As he checked it, he saw it was from Miles's real phone, not his FBI-issued one.

"You're up late," mumbled Ryan, half awake.

"It's over, buddy boy. It's over." Miles voice sounded downright giddy.

"Are you drunk?" Ryan had never heard Miles sound that way when sober.

"Nope, just relieved. We got Reese!"

"Captured? Dead? What?"

"Dead, thankfully. It's a long story, but it finally has an ending. Before I called you I called Olivia, and then George and Cora. They all flipped over the news. George and Cora are also relieved they can leave their cottage on Rock Lake and return home. I'm sure Molly will be too. To celebrate, they've invited you and me over for dinner tomorrow night. Now go back to sleep. I'll fill in everyone on all the details once we're all back in Lakeville tomorrow."

"About that . . ." said Ryan. "I won't actually be back there for a few days. As luck would have it, I now need to find a place to live here in Madison."

"You got the job!" Miles shouted.

"I did get the job, and well, there's more," Ryan teased.

"Bobbie too?" Miles guessed.

Ryan chuckled while holding out the phone so Bobbie could reply for him: "Definitely yes, and Miles, let's be clear. Any future collaborations between the two of you will require my approval. In *advance!*"

ACKNOWLEDGEMENTS

I am forever grateful to my wife, Jackie, and my son, David, who inspire me in my every endeavor. To my friends who have been kind enough to act as my beta readers, thank you for your guidance. As I have said before, to have found a home at BQB Publishing was my lucky break. Terri and her entire staff have ushered me through the publishing process with compassion and a steady (and often firm) hand. In addition, I would be remiss if I didn't, once again, single out my editor, Caleb, who is both my collaborator and my teacher. Finally, I must thank those of you who have read my books. Because of your generosity, I no longer have to worry if my books are trees in the empty forest that fall on deaf ears.

ABOUT THE AUTHOR

Pinkus's passion for writing was ignited at the University of Wisconsin, where he studied journalism and wrote for the campus newspaper, the *Daily Cardinal*. His career as a professional writer includes creating marketing content and materials for both digital and print media (websites, email marketing, social media posts, proposals, marketing plans, promotions, etc.). After many years as a partner in a marketing firm, Pinkus sold his interest in 2013 to focus totally on his writing. *Justified Malice* is his third novel. Pinkus and his wife live in Milwaukee, Wisconsin.

OTHER BOOKS BY HARRY PINKUS

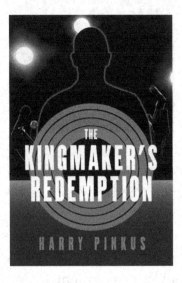

When political kingmaker Jack McKay chooses to change the arc of his life by representing a candidate he really believes in, he unleashes the full fury of his former client Liberty Party leader, Randall Davies. Davies becomes laser focused on ruining Jack's career and his life by having Jack framed for a horrible crime he didn't commit.

The heart of the story is the struggle of Jack and his team to unravel the conspiracy aimed at destroying his life. Gaining his acquittal in a suspenseful courtroom showdown would not only prove his innocence, restore his reputation and reinstate his parental rights, it would ultimately bring down the Liberty Party, their candidate, and Randall Davies in the process. If he fails, his life is ruined.

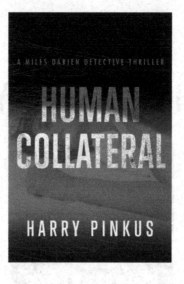

Private Detective, Miles Darien, is hired by Cora Sims to find her missing daughter Olivia, who has been living alone in Chicago.

When they eventually find Olivia, she's barely alive as a result of an infection after having a kidney surgically removed. Turns out the kidney was payment for an illegal loan given by criminals who prey on people in dire financial trouble by forcing them to use their bodies as collateral.

Olivia can't seek medical care or go to the police because the criminals have threatened to kill her if she does. Miles and Ryan must bring down the criminals to keep them from silencing Olivia.

They join forces with the FBI to look for the syndicate behind these loans. The syndicate is also hunting them down to erase any trail that would lead back to them. Who will erase who first?